THE BEST BAD BOY

BAD BOYS OF THE BAYOU

ERIN NICHOLAS

ISBN: 978-1-952280-37-5
Cover Design: Najla Qamber, Qamber Designs

AUTHOR'S NOTE

I've been published for over a decade and have written a lot of books in that time. I actually don't know how many. I've counted a few times before but there are short stories and novellas, bonus material, things that have gone out of print, or been re-worked… and I don't know how to count all of that. I usually say, "over fifty books" and figure that's safe.

But in all of that vagueness there are a few things that have become what I call my "orphans" over the years. Books and stories that don't really *belong* anywhere specific anymore. I was first published with Samhain Publishing which has since closed its doors, and all of those books came back to me, including stand-alone stories that didn't connect with anything else. I've also had some really amazing opportunities to participate in various projects and events and series for which I've written a story (or stories) and I've enjoyed them all! But projects end, and opportunities shift. So, over the years, projects, series, and publishers have come and gone. But the stories are still alive and well. They just don't really *fit* anywhere.

So I finally decided that I needed to give them a home. And a new chance to meet readers! They needed a new place to live. But I needed to put them all together and give them a connection to one another since they didn't have other connections.

And, where else would I make this new home than Louisiana?

Now I couldn't just bring these people (some of whom I've known since before I was published!) to Autre, the home of my other Louisiana books. They don't quite fit there. They have a different vibe. They came from a little different Erin Nicholas. Not totally different, of course. My voice and style have always been pretty consistent.

But these stories are a little grittier. More emotional. The people have a little more baggage than the Boys (and girls) of the Bayou or the people of Boys of the Bayou Gone Wild. They're also a little dirtier. There's always open-door sex scenes in my books, but in Bad, Louisiana, there are just more of them. These books just have a little different feel. And they needed their own home. Their own place to live and be what they are rather than trying to fit into something else.

So, I present to you Bad, Louisiana. A collection of books that have existed in Erin Nicholas world for a long time but have been rewritten and edited to fit together in a new town, with some new friends, for a second chance to meet readers and bring even more love stories to the Louisiana bayou!

I hope you enjoy them as much as I did when I first wrote them and loved them again going back for this reimagining.

If you're a long-time reader and are "afraid" that you might have read these books before, you can check out the original titles and more information here: https://bit.ly/BadBoys-ThenNow

WELCOME TO BAD, LOUISIANA!

These boys are only called "bad" because of their hometown…

Yeah, right.

I've been to Bad several times over the years and it always makes me smile. The town itself has an interesting history. It was originally, and very briefly, settled by a bunch of Germans. Did you know that Germans use "bad" in town names to denote a spa town? Yep, that's a thing.

So, I guess in this case, there was a small hot spring outside of town and the settlers claimed that made it a spa town in the new frontier. They named the town Bad Salzuflen and they'd hoped it would attract even more settlers. Particularly of the young and female persuasion.

But, unfortunately, the 'hot spring' was actually just a particularly marshy area (no one knows why it was so much warmer… or at least they're not saying) and then, before they could figure out what to do about that, the French showed up and ran the Germans out.

Well, after that no one could pronounce or spell Bad Salzuflen, but they didn't really want to go to the trouble of renaming the whole thing, so they just dropped the Salzuflen, painted over that part of the welcome sign, and the town decided to lean into the whole *Bad* thing. Especially in more modern times.

Seriously. The hair salon is called *Bad Hair Day?* (yes with a question mark so that when they answer the phone it's, "Bad hair day?" and you say, "Yes", and they say, "Come on down and let us fix it!" And there's so much more.

Here's a quick list:
Bad Habit—coffeeshop
Bad Brakes—auto mechanic shop
Bad Brews—bar and restaurant
The Bad Egg—diner/ cafe
Bad Gas—gas station and convenience store
Bad Faith Community Church—local church
Bad Hair Day?—hair salon
The Bad Place—the physical therapy clinic
Bad Medicine—the medical clinic
Bad Memories—community center

Instead of fighting it and letting everyone else mock them, the citizens decided to have some fun with it. And hey, they sell a lot of merch (like *I got Bad Gas on my roadtrip* travel mugs and *I've been to The Bad Place and survived* t-shirts) and no one ever forgets a trip to Bad!

So come on in and have some fun! It really will be a *good* time!

THE SERIES

You can read the Bad Boys of the Bayou in any order!

The Best Bad Boy: (Jase and Priscilla)
A bad boy-good girl, small town romance

Bad Medicine: (Brooke and Nick)
A hot doctor, workplace, small town romance

Bad Influence: (Marc and Sabrina)
An enemies to lovers, road trip/stuck together, small town romance

Bad Taste in Men: (Luke and Bailey)
A friends to lovers, gettin'-her-groove back, small town romance

Not Such a Bad Guy: (Regan and Christopher)
A one-night-stand, instalove, small town romance

Return of the Bad Boy: (Jackson and Annabelle)
An enemies to lovers, bad boy-good girl, pretend relationship, small town romance

Bad Behavior: (Carter and Lacey)
A hot cop, second chance, small town romance

Got It Bad: (Nolan and Randi)
A nerd hero, tomboy, opposites attract, small town romance

THE BEST BAD BOY

*The strip club owner's grandson and the preacher's granddaughter?
Yep, that sounds about right for Bad, Louisiana.*

Bad boy Jase Hawkins didn't *mean* to get naughty with ultimate good girl, Priscilla Williams. And certainly not in her grandpa's church. It just kind of happened.

But he's thought about that night for ten years.
Which is more of an annoyance than an actual problem.

Until he comes back to his tiny hometown where there's no chance in hell of avoiding the girl he can't quite get over.

Especially now that she works for the mayor and her boss has given her one very important assignment—find out what the hell Jase is doing with his grandfather's old strip club and get rid of him.

Well, that's fine with Jase. As soon as he gets the building renovated and sold, he'll head out and never look back.

But Cilla has other plans. She needs the building, and his help, to prove herself to the mayor. Her mother.

Fine. He'll give her what she wants. But he's going to get something out of this deal too.

And what he wants is *her*…in his bed for the entire time he's back to being a Bad boy.

CHAPTER
ONE

THE PORK and Peach was a terrible name for a business.

Even for a strip club.

Maybe especially for a strip club.

But if it was a strip club that was trying to convince people it was really just a bar that was famous for its ribs, pulled pork sandwiches, and peach pie, it was maybe brilliant.

Oh, not that The Pork and Peach didn't serve barbecue pork and peach pie. Branding was branding. And the sandwiches, pie, and the show during dinner were all, allegedly, the best in six parishes.

Priscilla Williams had actually believed that it was just a restaurant when she was a kid. She'd also believed that her grandfather hated barbecue ribs, and that was why her family never went there.

She had been about sixteen when someone told her that the pork referred to dicks and the peach referred to women's butts. Okay, she had been *exactly* sixteen years old. And three months. And eighteen days. She knew the exact day that she was taught what pork and peach really referred to.

And finding out the innuendo behind the "restaurant's"

name wasn't the most interesting thing that happened to her that day, as she sat at the lunch table eating a peach.

Yes, seriously.

That was what had brought the whole conversation up in the first place. Because her best friend's boyfriend at the time, Marc, had asked if she had any pork to go with her peach and *his* best friend, Luke, had graciously offered to give her some if she didn't.

Of course, she'd been clueless as to why that was funny. But they'd filled her in, delighting, as always, in embarrassing Pastor Williams's granddaughter. And Priscilla, as always, pretended to be mortified.

Honestly, the way to quickly get over being shocked about human beings and the things they thought and said and did was to eavesdrop outside of a preacher's office. Priscilla had been working after school at her grandfather's church since she was old enough to run Microsoft Word, and her grandpa's office door didn't shut tightly. The things she knew about the people in the town she'd grown up in…

The idea of men looking at and liking women's butts was hardly the most shocking thing she'd ever heard. Still, she'd had to pretend. She was the preacher's granddaughter, after all. She was a perfect, angelic princess. She sang in the choir. She led a youth Bible study. And, yes, she was the Virgin Mary in the nativity play every Christmas. Of course she was.

She wasn't supposed to know about butts and penises. For some reason. She was definitely a good girl. No question. But penises were just kind of a fact. She'd never seen a live one. Never touched one. But she knew *of* them. She also knew that men and women liked looking at each other naked. So, she didn't really understand why it was so fun for the guys in her class to tell her "shocking" things about sex.

However, she was *not* prepared for what happened next.

In a million years, she wouldn't have expected *him* to pay one bit of attention to what she and her friends were talking about.

She certainly wouldn't have expected him to stop at their table. Or *talk* to them.

Which meant it was impossible for Priscilla to hide her reaction to Jase Hawkins bracing his hand on the table next to her, leaning over, and saying, "Except peaches can also be pussies, not just asses. Which makes more sense. Nice and soft and sweet and juicy."

But where Marc and Luke could only *try* to make her face flush pink and her mind spin with new, naughty thoughts, Jase Hawkins accomplished it.

Priscilla was speechless. She was hot. She was suddenly very aware of *her* peach.

No, not the one she was holding.

Then he'd taken a hold of her wrist, lifted her hand—and peach—to his mouth, took a nice, big, juicy bite, licked his lips, gave her a grin and wink, and let her go.

Then he'd sauntered away as she gaped, literally with her mouth hanging open, after him.

And thus began her crush on Jase Hawkins.

Her stupid, unrequited, totally humiliating crush.

The bad boy of Bad, Louisiana.

The grandson of the owner of The Pork and Peach.

Jase was the boy she was supposed to pray for every Sunday, along with his grandfather.

But he was the boy who she actually prayed to be her first kiss. And the first to touch her… peach.

And the Lord was good, and, in her experience, He did answer prayers.

"I can't do this," she said into her phone, shaking her head, even though her best friend, Regan, couldn't see her.

"You have to."

Priscilla loved Regan. She really did. But Regan had this annoying habit of not always telling Priscilla what she wanted to hear.

Like that she didn't have to go into The Pork and Peach and

face the guy she'd made a fool of herself over. Three times. Okay, four if she counted the time he'd finally given in and made out with her and… she frowned, refusing to let that memory fully form.

Regan would go in there and tell Jase that he had some nerve coming back here after *ten years* and he'd better just turn his fine ass around and get the hell out of Bad.

Priscilla could only assume his ass was still fine. It always had been. *Always.*

But she did believe in God, and it was possible that He loved her enough to have given Jase a beer gut, bad breath, and a saggy ass in the past decade.

"Come on, Big Guy," she said softly, looking at the ceiling of her car.

"Cilla, you have to do it. Your mother doesn't give you any important jobs and this is your chance to prove that you can handle it," Regan reminded her.

"But she doesn't know how *big* this really is." Priscilla actually winced. She hadn't meant *big* in reference to Jase's… pork. But that was what flickered through her mind. That day in the cafeteria she hadn't yet touched a real live penis, but that wasn't true by the time Jase Hawkins left Bad.

But Regan didn't know about that. *No one* knew about that.

Except for Jase, of course.

"She knows it's big enough," Regan said. "Your mother will *freak out* if The Pork and Peach reopens. They almost have enough money to buy the place and tear it down. And now he's here and working on it? Your mom sent you to talk to him because you went to high school together, and because you claim to want more serious assignments. So get in there and handle this."

Priscilla slumped forward, thunking her head against the steering wheel. Her mom wasn't just a concerned citizen, worried about the town's reputation and disgusted by the thought of The Pork and Peach re-opening. She was the mayor.

The freaking *mayor*. Priscilla was "lucky" enough to be the granddaughter of the beloved and feared Pastor Williams *and* the daughter of the long-time, kickass, first female mayor.

Whoo-hoo.

But her mother cared about this deeply because the whole town cared about this deeply. Including *her* father-in-law. The pastor. And Priscilla was her Executive Assistant. So Priscilla had to care too.

In small towns like Bad, people didn't care about things like nepotism. It was actually expected that parents teach their kids the ins and outs of their business, whatever it was, with the expectation that those kids would stick around and help run the businesses after their parents retired. When they didn't, small rural towns died.

Priscilla's father had taken over his mother's father's company the same way. Sure, it was a multi-million-dollar company out of New Orleans, but… same idea. Kind of.

Did Priscilla want to be the mayor of Bad someday? Well, her dad had screwed up big time and almost lost everything on *that* side of the family, and since politics or preaching were the two things that Williamses did in Bad and she definitely didn't want to be a minister, she supposed running the town from City Hall would have to do.

Priscilla glared at the stupid neon sign that was in the shape of a pig. With a peach in his mouth.

Really subtle.

The neon hadn't lit up in ten years. The E in PEACH had been dark for about twelve years. But that sign was still there. Just one hundred yards past the city limits. That damned pig had been looking down and laughing at Bad for nearly thirty years.

But, at least for the past ten, the building had been empty. There had been no pork or pie—of any kind—in that place. Something Priscilla's grandfather had been incredibly pleased about.

It wasn't particularly Christian of him, in her opinion, but the night The Pork and Peach had burned, Aaron Williams had been downright giddy. No one had been hurt, but the fire had gutted the place and had been too extensive to easily clean-up and reopen. For some reason, Jarvis Hawkins, Jase's grandfather and Pastor Williams's nemesis, had simply closed up and left town after the fire.

Jase had gone with him.

"Priscilla Ruth Williams, get your butt out of that car and get in there. The sooner you tell him he's not welcome, the sooner this will all be over with."

That was easy for Regan to say from her physical therapy office six blocks away. "Sure, he's just going to say, okay, let me pack my stuff up and get out. Sorry for the inconvenience."

"No, of course he's not," Regan said. "But this is the first step."

"He's not going to care what we think. The Hawkinses never cared what anybody thought."

That was one of the things she'd been drawn to. That bad-boy-don't-give-a-shit thing Jase had going on was really attractive to a young girl who had to care what everyone thought all the time.

Being the granddaughter of the only preacher in town—there were a few Catholics in town too, but ninety percent of Bad attended her grandpa's church—came with certain expectations.

A shitload of them.

Like not saying things like "shitload". Out loud, anyway.

CHAPTER
TWO

THE CLICK-CLICK-CLICK of high heels on the hardwood floor behind him wasn't exactly a surprise. The fact that he was hearing them within two hours of being back in town was. Jase had forgotten just how fucking fast news traveled in this little town.

He grinned.

They were high heels so that meant he wasn't going to be going toe to toe with Aaron Williams. *Pastor* Williams. At least not yet.

He finished screwing the lightbulb into the socket he'd just rewired. He was going to need some light in this place as he cleaned it up and remodeled. It was a fucking mess. This was going to take forever, and it was going to be damned miserable here while he did it. He'd never expected to come back to Bad. Never wanted to. Not for a second.

Well, other than the seconds when he'd wondered what Cilla was up to and wondered what she'd do if he just suddenly showed back up in town. But he'd shoved those thoughts away quickly every time. Ideas like that were stupid. He only thought he wanted her because there was no way in hell he could have her. He knew himself well enough to realize that. Besides, it had been ten years. She'd stayed in Bad. That pretty much meant that she was married and had at least one kid by now.

He fitted a second metal plate against the holes he'd just drilled and lifted the screwdriver, twisting the screws into place.

The person behind him cleared her throat.

He grinned. And continued taking his time finishing the task. "Be with you in a minute."

He hadn't asked for any visitors or put an OPEN sign out front. He was here to work. He was going to get this place cleaned up, sign the papers that would make this somebody else's damn problem, and then get the fuck back out of town. For good this time. He didn't have time for distractions.

But he also hadn't locked the door.

"By all means, don't let someone wanting to speak with you interrupt something as important as screwing things."

Jase almost laughed, but still resisted turning. The woman was young-ish sounding. And had a bit of a sense of humor. Or maybe she'd said it without realizing how it sounded.

He was going to face whoever this was, eventually, but he wasn't interested in what anyone in Bad had to say to him. He didn't care about their opinions. Besides, he was pretty sure he already knew what those opinions were. About him, and about The Pork and Peach re-opening. So he was going to turn around in his own sweet time, on his own damned terms. And the sooner she, and the people she was reporting back to—oh yeah, he was certain she'd been sent here—got that message, the easier this was all going to be.

"Thanks for understanding that a man just can't leave a good screwing half done," he shot back.

If he wasn't mistaken, he thought he heard a little huff of laughter from her.

Jase wondered who he'd sent. Oh, he knew this messenger was sent by Pastor Aaron Williams. Someone had seen his truck and had called the retired town cop who had run the plates, figured out it was Jase, and promptly called Aaron.

Aaron ran this town. He wasn't an elected official. He was something more powerful. He was the guy who knew everyone's secrets and sins.

Jase knew this person had been sent to tell him to leave.

Well, he was all for that. As soon as he got The Pork and Peach cleaned up and the papers signed, he'd be gone. For good this time.

But he'd be fine with being left alone in the meantime.

Dammit, he'd avoided going through town on purpose. But someone must have seen him from the convenience store and gas station, which was unfortunately-but-hilariously named Bad Gas. The hard-to-forget business—that sold a hell of a lot of logo-ed merchandise—sat at the intersection of the two major highways that passed by Bad.

It wasn't the only place that had leaned into the town name either. Nearly all the businesses in town sported names that included a tongue-in-cheek nod to what they did or heard a lot inside their buildings and the word "Bad".

The diner was The Bad Egg, the hair salon was Bad Hair Day?, yes including the question mark, the medical clinic was Bad Medicine, and even Pastor Williams's church was Bad Faith Community Church.

Jase grinned. Of course, that one was an accident. All of the Faith Community Churches in the area tacked the town's name on the front. In this case, it just turned out to be hilarious and, in Jase's opinion, pretty fucking on the nose. It, of course, made Pastor Williams irate, and he insisted everyone refer to it simply as Community Church. Ninety percent of the town complied.

Jase was not in that ninety percent.

He didn't miss much about his hometown, but damn the way they leaned into their name was funny.

The last screw was finally nice and tight, and he had no more reason to be up on that ladder and not facing his visitor. Might as well get it over with.

He climbed down and turned. "So what can I—"

His boot caught on the bottom rung, and he nearly pitched face first into the floor.

Right at the feet of Priscilla Williams.

Talk about ironic.

Falling at Priscilla's feet was what most guys in Bad had been doing all her life.

Jase caught himself before he face-planted. But not before he bit out, "Goddammit!" as he jerked his boot loose and stuck his feet firmly to the ground.

He climbed up and down ladders every damned day. With these damned boots on. What the hell was his problem?

Finally, he shoved a hand through his hair and forced himself to look at her.

Priscilla.

His problem.

The girl who had shaken him up when nothing else could.

The girl who had been one of the most beautiful things he'd ever seen.

The girl who had turned into a fucking knock-out woman.

The girl who was looking at him with a mixture of emotions, including, no question about it, I-don't-want-to-be-here.

Jase wasn't sure that was an emotion, exactly, but she didn't look scared or angry. She looked… wary. But not as if she thought he was going to do something to her. More like she knew *she* was about to do something. To him.

"I'm here on behalf of the mayor," she blurted out.

It was interesting that she didn't want to do *that*. But it was clear on her face.

"Hello, Pris," Jase said, keeping his voice calm.

He really didn't care what these people thought or wanted. He *really* didn't. But he really hadn't been expecting them to send Cilla.

There was no way they could know she was his weakness. Was there? No. There was no way the sweet, perfect angel had told anyone what had happened between them. No way.

She lifted her chin and crossed her arms. "You know I don't go by Pris."

She'd never allowed anyone to call her that. Probably for obvious reasons. That was kind of a terrible nickname. It was fitting though, considering she was the preacher's granddaughter and had, absolutely, been a little priss until she was about fourteen and had finally managed to pull out the stick that had always been up her ass. Everyone knew that Regan Reynolds was mostly to thank for that.

Regan had moved to Bad in sixth grade. She'd had some trouble fitting in. She'd been—still was, he was sure—a tomboy, and she'd taken offense to the boys at school telling her she couldn't play ball with them at recess.

Priscilla had shamed them into letting Regan play. Something about *What Would Jesus Do*. They'd been friends ever since. Even if Cilla sat on the sidelines and watched the ballgames while doing her nails—seriously—as Regan got dirty and sweaty and yelled about bullshit calls.

Cilla had softened Regan's rough edges. Regan had softened Cilla's prissy ones. Regan even got to the point where she wore dresses and lip gloss once in a while. And, thanks to Regan's influence, Cilla had gotten drunk on vodka—once—and had been heard yelling, "What kind of dumbass call was that?" during the state championship softball game when Regan had been called out at home. In fact, her being called out had almost been worth hearing Priscilla Williams swearing at the top of her lungs from the stands in front of most of their hometown.

But Priscilla's *really* naughty escapade—the one and only— had been because of, and with, Jase.

He should have been the one wearing the title of grand champion because he'd taught her to French kiss, gotten her naked, and given her a very thorough and hands-on—or rather *mouth-on*— demonstration of what was really meant by *eating peaches*.

Yep, Jase had taken Cilla's oral sex and orgasm virginhood.

And he could have taken it all. She had been ready and willing to give him her actual virginity.

He'd kicked himself for being a good guy that night many, many times since then.

He let his gaze drag over her from head to toe as she stood amidst the rubble that had been the interior of The Pork and Peach. Of course, the angel would only come in here once it looked like the fires of hell had consumed it.

She had her long, blond hair up in a twisty style and pinned at the back of her head. A few tendrils were escaping, brushing sexily against her neck, softening the strict, business-like look she was clearly going for. Her eyes were made up, with thick, black lines making the deep, cobalt blue stand out even sharper against her pale skin. Her lips were a soft, pink color, just a shade darker than the flush in her cheeks and along the length of her throat. A flush Jase was pretty sure hadn't been there until she'd walked through his door.

She wasn't one to sunbathe. When she'd sat outside at Regan's ball games, she'd worn a huge-assed beach hat with a floppy brim that shaded all that gorgeous, creamy skin. There hadn't been so much as a freckle to be found when he'd undressed her that night. And he'd taken his time looking.

She was wearing a pale pink, button-down silk blouse, a black pencil skirt that hit just above her knees, and black wedge heels that were maybe an inch high. That black color was convenient, considering all the soot and ash she'd had to step through to get to the spot in the middle of what had once been the main room. He would have given twenty bucks to watch her tiptoe her way through all of that dirt and grime.

She looked professional and put together, and there wasn't even a hint of cleavage or the lacy edge of a thigh-high stocking to send his thoughts in any kind of dirty direction. But they went there anyway.

Probably *because* there wasn't a lacy edge or an inch of

shouldn't-be-seen skin. She was so fucking prim and proper and perfect. As always.

Jase wanted to mess her up. As always.

In the past, he'd stayed away from her. He'd kept her sweet and innocent and unruffled. He'd resisted those big blue eyes and those pink lips and that sweet body. And her offers. For some reason, Cilla had decided that she wanted him, and she'd come after him. He deserved sainthood for fighting it.

But even the best man stumbles once in a while. And he'd taken a pretty huge tumble one night the summer after they'd graduated.

He'd been weak *one* night. But even after he'd stripped her perfectly sweet sundress off of her body and tossed her perfectly sweet sandals over his shoulder and given her a taste of what she thought she wanted from him, he'd walked away before he'd really made her *his*. Before he went beyond the point of no return.

He'd known he wasn't good enough for her.

His halo might have gotten a little bent that night, but walking away had to have kept it at least partially intact. Because dammit, that had been the hardest thing he'd ever done. And growing up with Jarvis Hawkins as his grandfather, that was saying something.

"Well, let's see," he said, advancing on her. To her credit, she did nothing more than straighten her spine. "I can call you Pris. Or… I guess I could call you Peach. Gotta say… that's definitely what I think of when I think of you."

The pink tint to her skin got deeper and Jase felt a surge of satisfaction. He wasn't good enough for her, but she hadn't forgotten him. That was clear.

"You—" She stopped, wet her lips, cleared her throat, and continued. "You can call me Priscilla. Or Ms. Williams."

He laughed out loud at that. "No way am I calling you Ms. Williams." He shook his head, grinning. "I've known you since kindergarten." But Ms. Williams meant she wasn't married.

That shouldn't matter. But it did.

She swallowed hard. "Then I guess it's Priscilla."

"And if I don't?" He stepped around her. The last thing he needed was to stand in her personal space. That was where he could smell her and feel her body heat and, if he got especially stupid—which he'd been known to do—touch her.

"That would be pretty rude of you."

He set his tools on the bar and glanced over his shoulder. "If you don't like what I call you, maybe you shouldn't come to visit."

She should definitely *not* come to visit. Whatever she was here for now on behalf of the mayor's office—and he could guess what that was—didn't matter.

She just stood looking at him for a long moment. He looked right back at her. It wasn't a hardship. The girl he'd been crazy for had turned into a woman that was more of… everything. More curves, more soft skin, more long, silky hair. More attitude, apparently.

But then she sighed and her shoulders slumped. Jase turned more fully.

"I'm here to tell you to leave," she said, throwing her hands up as if she didn't know what else to do. "The town doesn't want The Pork and Peach re-opened, and I'm here to deliver the message in person."

Jase realized in the next second that it was tough being an asshole to the woman you could still taste on your tongue ten years later. He knew that sounded stupid, even in his own head, but he would swear to God, he could recall the taste, smell, and feel of her right now just standing there. She'd imprinted on him or something.

It wasn't a problem, generally. There was usually about six hundred miles between them, and he was damned good at pushing things away that he didn't want to think about. There had also been plenty of other women to distract him.

But right then, looking at her, he remembered it all.

"Why you?" he asked.

He would have already thrown anyone else out, so whether they knew it or not, sending Priscilla was a wise move. But no way did anyone know that. He doubted that Cilla even really knew how much she affected him. That was not the kind of knowledge that he wanted another person to have. There was way too much power in that.

"I work for the mayor's office."

"Is that right?"

"It is."

She didn't seem particularly thrilled by that. "What do you do for the mayor's office? Other than trespass on private property and try to throw people out of town... when they're not really even *in* town or doing a damned thing to bother anyone?"

The Pork and Peach, soot-covered rubble that it was, belonged to Jase's family and it sat just outside the city limits of Bad, Louisiana. There wasn't a damned thing that Bad's mayor, town council, or their sweet-good-girl-with-the-tight-ass-and-perfect-lips messenger could do about it.

Unless he let them.

Cilla took a deep breath, her spine less stiff than it had been a few minutes ago. "Everything," she finally said.

He lifted a brow. "Everything?"

She shrugged. "I do a little bit of everything for the mayor's office. I'm officially her executive assistant, but I'm pretty much the city manager. So, I do... everything."

He had to admit, he was interested in this. He wasn't sure why. Cilla had been class president, so her running the town didn't surprise him a bit. It was more her attitude about it. She seemed almost... embarrassed by it. But that couldn't be right. The Williamses were Bad royalty—yes, he found that hilarious when said out loud—and running the town was just what they did. Generation after generation. So why would Cilla be embarrassed by that?

Jase went around to the back of the bar—the second most

popular spot in The Pork and Peach after the stage, of course—and grabbed a bottle of water out of the cooler he'd stashed back there.

"Want one?" he asked, holding it up.

"Nothing stronger back there?" she asked wryly.

"Give me a few days." He didn't know why he was letting her think he was re-opening the place as a bar. Maybe because Bad didn't want him to. Eventually, they'd find out that his intentions were hardly worth clutching their pearls over, but there was just enough of his grandpa in him that Jase couldn't help but take the chance to mess with them first.

"Well, I guess if that's all you've got." She came forward and held out her hand.

He put the cold bottle in it and grabbed another before kicking the top of the cooler shut. He twisted the top and tipped the bottle back, draining half of it before setting it down and leveling her a look across the charred expanse of wood between them.

"So, this executive assistant-city manager gig," he said, leaning his forearms onto the bar. "That includes telling the first guy to put his hands down your panties to get lost, huh?"

HE PROBABLY SHOULD HAVE WAITED for her to swallow her drink of water.

Water sprayed from her mouth all over the bar. And his face.

"Holy shit, Jase!"

He lifted his hand and swiped the water from his left eye and cheek. "I see you've developed a bit of a potty mouth."

"What is wrong with you?" She was frowning at him.

"What do you mean?"

"You have to keep bringing up peaches and panties? Really?" She huffed out a breath.

He laughed. He couldn't help it. "Yeah, well, when you run into people you went to high school with, you reminisce about old times, right?" he asked, grinning at her.

Her cheeks got pink.

He went on anyway. "And, honestly, your peach and panties are absolutely up there with some of my fondest memories."

But rather than stammering or lowering her gaze or figuring out a way to get the hell out of there, she met his gaze directly and took a step closer. "Really?"

He snorted. "Well, I did prefer the half hour or so that your panties were somewhere on the floor and out of the picture. But yeah, that was definitely a good time."

That didn't fluster her either. She tipped her head. "But my peach and my panties are some of your *fondest* memories?"

And now *she* was talking about peaches and panties as if they were discussing the score of last Friday's football game.

"What are we talking here?" she asked, leaning in to also prop her forearms on the bar. "Am I number nine on the list of top ten? Or that night made it to the top twenty-five? Or are we being really serious here and I'm in the top five or so?"

And that, Jase acknowledged, was what was often referred to as having the tables turned.

Suddenly, the sweet, choir-singing, Psalm-reciting, virgin Prom Queen that he'd made lose her mind in the third grade Sunday school room in her grandpa's church had him hot and hard and sweating and on the verge of stammering very idiotic things, like "I still think about the way your lips tasted" or "Your panties had blue flowers on them". But he got his shit together before he said a thing. Because he was very afraid that "You were number-fucking-one" was right on the tip of his tongue.

"You were the best pussy I've ever eaten in a church, Peach," he told her, making sure his voice was low and deep and husky.

That made her blink at least. Her mouth also formed a sweet little O, and he actually gritted his teeth, telling himself that no, he couldn't fucking kiss her right then.

"We weren't in the church," she said after a long moment. "The Sunday school rooms are in the addition that was built on. It's not officially the church."

"Whatever makes you feel better."

"That does. Or it would," she said. Then she sighed. "I've been telling myself I should feel guilty about all of that for ten years, and I can't quite get there."

"You don't feel guilty about what we did?"

"Not really."

"What we did or where we did it?"

His mind was trying like hell to replay that particular movie reel. He had every detail still firmly engrained in his brain but he'd gotten good at shutting it down when it tried to roll through his memory. It was getting pretty tough at the moment with the star of that show reminding him of it, though.

Cilla shrugged. "It was just so… good. I feel like God shouldn't make that so good if He doesn't want us to do it."

Heat hit Jase hard and low, and his cock thickened, pressing into his zipper. Not quite to the point of pain, but he definitely noticed. He shifted behind the bar, leaning forward and dropping one hand inconspicuously to his fly, adjusting to give himself a little more room.

Her response was about as far from what he'd been expecting to hear as he could have imagined. In fact, this entire conversation was a huge fucking shock.

He liked it.

"I think that's a really good point," he finally said.

She actually laughed at that. "I'm stunned that you would agree." Her tone was thick with sarcasm.

He grinned. "I still remember that orgasm, Peach. No one should feel bad about something that spectacular."

She didn't tell him not to call her that. She didn't tell him to stop talking about all of that. She didn't tell him he was a dick for bringing it up. They just sat there looking at each other, heat zinging back and forth for several seconds.

Finally, she said, "The answer is yes."

He had a whole bunch of questions he'd love to have her say yes to. "Which answer is that?"

"One of my job duties includes telling the first guy to put his hand down my panties to get lost. Apparently."

He had to admit, he really liked how they were just going to talk about how he'd had his hand in her panties and how great that had been.

"What are your other job duties?" he asked. He wanted to know. Now that she'd relaxed a little and actually laughed and, yeah, admitted that the orgasm he'd given her had been so good she didn't even feel guilty about having it in the building attached to her grandpa's church—that was funny, he couldn't help it—she was drawing him in. But he was ten years older and wiser, and he had a life, kind of, so he wasn't worried about doing anything stupid.

Priscilla Williams was still gorgeous, even more so now, and he still wanted to do all kinds of dirty things to her and teach her all kinds of delicious, wicked things. But that was all that was here for him now. He'd given up the idea of a sweet, quiet, small-town life with history and deep roots a long time ago.

Well, about ten years ago for sure.

"I run the swimming pool in the summer," she told him.

Her tone told him everything he needed to know how she felt about that. She was not overjoyed or brimming with pride, that was for sure.

"What's that involve?" he asked, unable to completely hide the smile that was trying to escape.

"Hiring—and firing—lifeguards. Making sure the cleaning crew shows up and does their job thoroughly. Getting the three-foot, five-foot, and ten-foot markers repainted." She tapped a perfectly painted pink fingernail against her chin as if having to think hard. "Getting the lawn around the pool mowed on a regular basis. Though I use the same company that mows the park, and around City Hall, and at the baseball field and, of course, at the church, so that's handy." She actually rolled her eyes.

Jase was shocked by what a turn-on that was.

He'd never seen Priscilla be self-deprecating. That was really hot for some reason.

"Oh, and probably the most important part of that job," she said. "Deciding what we carry in the concession stand."

He stared at her.

She was also funny.

She widened her eyes. "I'm not kidding, Jase. You have no

idea what kind of mutiny I face when I run out of blue-raspberry popsicles. I mean, the sour apple and watermelon are big too, but *nothing* sells like blue raspberry." She looked at him as if she'd just imparted a significant business secret.

"I can imagine," he replied when it was clear he was supposed to say *something*.

"You like blue raspberry?" she asked.

"Who doesn't?"

"Good thing. None of the packs include peach."

He blinked at her. Wanting her so badly it hurt was *not* his fault. *She* kept bringing up the peach thing too. "Seems you want to keep my mind on peaches, Peach."

One corner of her mouth quirked. "I think I mentioned how much fun I had that night."

"You did." He wasn't going to forget that. Or let her forget it either.

"I will say though," she went on, as if they hadn't just been talking about him going down on her ten years ago. "The mermaid and pirate cakes I came up with and stock in the concession stand are a *huge* hit."

"Mermaid and pirate cakes?" He shook his head.

How was he standing in the midst of the burned out remains of his grandpa's strip club talking to his high school crush about mermaid cakes on his first day back in town? Whatever the fuck those were.

"They're mini cupcakes," she said. "The mermaid ones are teal green—of course—with pink frosting and sprinkles. The pirate ones are brown—chocolate with chocolate frosting and a gold, foil-wrapped chocolate coin on top. I thought those were appropriate for the swimming pool theme. Oh!" She smacked her hand down on the top of the bar. Dust puffed up in a cloud in front of her, but she kept going, her eyes bright. "You probably don't know about the pool theme. We redid it to be a pirate theme about two years ago. The diving board is a gang plank, and the kids climb up into the crow's nest before sliding down the slide. There's a huge plastic shark and alligator in the shallow end for the littler kids to climb on. There's a treasure chest in the middle depth that kids can dive down to—and once a week we put prizes in there for them to retrieve. And one night a month we have a pirate party. The lifeguards dress up and everything."

She was grinning, clearly thrilled with the whole thing.

"Was that all your idea?" he guessed. She'd given a lot of input when it came to Homecoming and Prom themes and decorating, as well as props and costumes for the school plays. Meaning, she'd run the whole show. Made every decision. Was always in charge.

Not that Jase had been in any of the school plays, and he'd only gone to one Homecoming dance. But he'd helped build sets and had been roped into helping construct a huge archway for prom one year by the industrial arts teacher. He didn't expect that Cilla knew that though.

"It was all my idea," she said, nodding happily. "Everyone loves it." She frowned then. "They don't really know that it was my idea though."

"Why not?"

"We raised money for it as a community and unveiled it as a city project. I mean, everyone knows that it all came from the mayor's office." She shrugged. "It's not like my name's on it."

"Who did the ribbon cutting or whatever?" But he'd known the answer before he'd asked the question.

"My mom."

Wait. That was not what he'd been expecting. "Your *mom*?" he asked. "Your parents made a big donation or something?"

She frowned, clearly confused. "No. I mean she did it as mayor, of course."

That took a second to sink in. Then it all made sense. "Your mom is the mayor?"

"You didn't know?"

"Nope."

"Do you not keep up with *any* news from here?" she asked.

He shook his head.

"Old friends? School alumni newsletter? Town website? Town social media pages?"

"Nope. Nope. Nope. Nope."

She blew out a breath. "Well, thanks for making me feel like I waste a *bunch* of my time."

"You do all of that?" he asked.

"Of course."

"The website, the Facebook page? Even the alumni newsletter?"

She shrugged. "I mean, who else is going to do it?"

He didn't have an appropriate response to that, so he wisely said nothing.

Cilla sighed and looked around. "No offense, but I'm not putting the grand re-opening of The Pork and Peach on the Facebook page."

He smirked. "How much for an ad on the website?"

She smirked right back. "Four times what I charge anyone else."

"There's probably a law against that or something."

"You going to turn me in to the district judge, my grandpa's best fishing and golfing buddy?" she asked.

She was still smiling, clearly teasing back a bit, but her words hit Jase right in the chest.

It was true. If this town wanted to keep him out, they could. It wasn't fair. It probably wasn't all on the up and up. But this was a tight-knit, small town where roots ran deep, and history mattered. The guys you fished and golfed with were expected to have your back. Even if you were a sketchy bastard at times.

Not that he cared. He wasn't sticking around. He'd known when he'd driven across the Louisiana state line that this was going to be a temporary thing. He could have a small-town life where he knew everyone sitting in the stands at the high school basketball game and where his kids could graduate with the kids they'd started kindergarten with and where he could cuss a guy out on the work site on Tuesday, play poker with him on Friday, and sit next to him in church on Sunday.

He just couldn't have that life in Bad, Louisiana.

His grandpa had seen to that.

"Well, I have a feeling all I need to do is light up that neon sign," Jase finally said, pushing aside the stupid feelings of regret. "I'm guessing the people that want to do business at The Pork and Peach will find their way here even without a post on Facebook."

Cilla actually just nodded at that. "I'm sure you're right."

He grinned, unable to keep from rubbing it in a bit. "Hope your grandpa hasn't gotten rusty on the prayin' in the past ten years when there haven't been quite as many lost souls."

"It's a lot like riding a bike. I'm sure it'll come back to him."

Jase laughed. "Just like old times."

"Ugh." She let out a groan and her shoulders slumped. "Is there somewhere else we can sit and talk?" she asked.

"We're not done?" He was half happy to think she might stick around and half dreading her sticking around.

He wouldn't mind looking at, and listening to, Priscilla Williams for however long she wanted to stay.

But the longer she stayed, the harder it was going to be not to kiss her.

And since the last time he'd kissed her she'd been a virgin, they'd been in church—yes, they had, no matter what she said— and it had ended with her coming all over his tongue, well, kissing her now that they were both adults and there wasn't one single cross or Bible anywhere near this place, it might lead to all kinds of amazingly horrible decisions.

And him making amazingly horrible decisions when a Williams was involved? Yeah, *that* was a lot like riding a bike.

CHAPTER
FOUR

HOLY HELL.

And she meant that in the most reverent, thank-you-God way she possibly could.

Jase Hawkins was *something*. Something hot and hard and big and tough and sexy and… yeah, *holy hell* summed it up pretty nicely.

"No. I don't think we're done," she told him honestly. She meant with this conversation, of course. But there was definitely a flip in her belly that said she probably meant with more than this conversation too.

She shouldn't mean that. That was asking for trouble. Jase Hawkins had grown into all kinds of hot, and, yes, she definitely had fond memories of his hand in her panties. And his mouth once her panties were long gone. But that was it. That was a long time ago. Jase Hawkins was not her type. She wasn't his type. They were not two people who should ever have anything more going on than her talking him out of whatever he thought he was doing here.

So, she really needed to quit focusing on how freaking wide his chest and shoulders were, and how tight his abs and ass were, and how great his smile and laugh were, and start focusing on what she'd come here to do.

Why had she admitted that she remembered that night in the Sunday school classroom? And that she didn't feel guilty about any of it?

It was like all of her put-togetherness and properness and professionalism just flew right out the window the second she'd laid eyes on him.

Truthfully, she'd laid eyes on his ass first. But he'd been up on that ladder facing away from her. It wasn't really her fault.

And even more truthfully, what else flew right out the window? Her good-girl side.

That had happened before.

And she'd enjoyed the hell out of it. Yes, *hell*. She was a good girl, and she didn't swear very often, but sometimes those words were the only ones that could adequately express a sentiment.

This was no time for *golly gees* and *heck yeahs*.

"Yeah, okay, we can talk," he finally said after they'd stared at each other for a very long, weird few seconds.

She was relieved. She really couldn't go back to her mom's office and give her a report that said, "Talked to him, ogled him, reminisced about the orgasm he gave me, and he's still remodeling the strip club."

"Great. Do you have an office here?"

"Well, there is an office here and I'm the owner, so I guess that makes it my office, doesn't it?"

He had a point. "Then you do own The Pork and Peach? Your grandpa gave it to you?"

"He did."

She'd assumed, but Jarvis could have still owned it and Jase could have just been running it for him. Actually, Jase being the owner was easier. That meant whatever decision she could talk him into would be fully his to make.

"How is your grandpa?" she asked. For some reason. Curiosity, she supposed. She didn't know Jase's grandpa. She could have picked him out of a line-up, probably, but that was about it. She wasn't sure she'd ever spoken a word to the man. Jarvis Hawkins hadn't liked Bad, and he'd delighted in his role of pariah.

"In a nursing home with a walker and a horrible attitude and an even worse mouth," Jase said, grimacing slightly.

Cilla winced but gave him a small smile. "I'm sorry."

He nodded. "He's declining and he hates it. He gives everyone a really hard time, as if it's their fault. He's a handful and way too much for my mom to handle." He sighed and looked around the building. "We need some money to help out with the expenses."

Oh, crap. So he was here doing this for a noble reason. Of course, some would argue that there was never a noble reason to re-open a strip club. Some of those arguing that would be related to Priscilla. But if his family needed money and still owned this place, it made sense they'd want to do something with it.

But maybe she could talk him into doing something *else* with it.

Her mind started to spin. Maybe it didn't have to be a strip club. Maybe it could just be a restaurant. Or something.

"But we should probably just go outside," he said. "The whole place is a fucking mess." Jase stopped at the end of the bar. "We can sit on the back patio."

"There's a back patio?"

He smiled. "There is. There's even still a table and chairs back there. No idea how, but there is."

She didn't know why she was surprised to learn something about this place. It wasn't as if she really knew a lot. Maybe because a back patio with tables and chairs seemed very normal. All she really knew about The Pork and Peach was that there had been ribs, and pie, and strippers. That seemed to sum it up. Oh, and she knew some of the past patrons.

That was because the men of Bad were so used to her being around, they didn't notice her when she was out and about doing her city manager thing. They talked in the post office, the café, the gas station, on the street corners. She heard about all kinds of topics. She knew the day's weather report, that the new recipe for chicken pot pies at the Bad Egg was terrible, that Levi Clark was neck-deep in debt, that Sally Gunthry needed her gallbladder out, that Dillon Thomas was going to propose to his girlfriend on her birthday. And that most of the men in town, even the ones that went to Bad Faith Community Church, missed The Pork and Peach.

Cilla followed Jase across the room toward a door on the far end that would, presumably, lead to the back patio.

She carefully picked her way across the floor. It seemed everything inside The Pork and Peach had been wood. She'd, of course, never been inside the building until today, but it seemed that every surface, from the floors to the walls to the enormous bar to the tables and chairs, was black and charred.

There was also a lot of ash and soot on the floor. It was actually crazy inside. She'd never really thought about what a building would look like after a major fire. She'd assumed that there had been *some* clean-up done to the place, but it honestly looked like the firefighters had put out the blaze, maybe scooped some of the major debris out, and then just left.

She knew that Jase and his family had just left. The next morning after the fire, in fact. They'd packed up their cars and trucks and driven out of town. That had just been it. She hadn't seen Jase again until today.

That night in the third grade Sunday school room had been the night before the fire.

She definitely needed to stop thinking about the fact that the last time she'd seen Jase Hawkins had been the night he'd kissed her like she'd always dreamed of being kissed, gotten her naked, and put his face between her legs.

Definitely.

Jase held the door open, and she stepped through, brushing

past him and telling herself not to take a deep breath. He was going to smell like charred wood and stuff, right?

He didn't. Which she knew because she took that deep breath anyway.

She kept walking, though. Even when she really wanted to turn and put her nose against his chest and breathe deep again. She wanted to put other parts of her against other parts of him too, and that was just a very bad idea on a lot of levels.

She and Jase Hawkins didn't fit. Well, they'd probably *fit*. Really well. *Really, really, really* well. But they weren't in high school anymore. They weren't kids. She couldn't just say "Oh it's just this one time and it won't hurt anything" like she had ten years ago.

They were adults now. She was trying to get her mom to take her seriously at work. She was trying to get the *whole town* to take her seriously. Coming up with things like mermaid cakes and raising money for plastic sharks in the swimming pool wasn't really the way to do that, but she had to start somewhere. Her mother had liked the idea because it made the town happy, and the sales of summer passes had increased. But Melinda hadn't cared *what* had done that, just that it had happened.

Priscilla couldn't seem to help herself though. She'd thrown herself into that project. And it had been fun. Just like she hadn't been able to help herself when she'd talked Hunter Larson into running a snow cone truck last summer. It had given the kid something to do other than hang out at the park vaping, and it had given the town something fun to look forward to in the evenings. This year they were going to expand it from snow cones into a full ice cream truck. Sure, it was kind of a pain in the ass and had, so far, lost money, but it was also going to keep Hunter and now a second kid out of trouble. And it was fun. There was no harm in that.

Her mom thought it was ridiculous.

So, yeah, getting involved with the town bad boy when he was back to rebuild the strip club was *really* not the way to show her mother that she was serious about her job. And serious about someday taking over *her* job.

The wrought iron table and three chairs were actually in decent shape considering they'd been exposed to the elements for a decade. Jase had thought to grab a towel and he wiped one of the chairs off before gesturing for her to sit while he cleaned the other one. Damn, that was almost gentlemanly.

She sat and crossed her legs, leaning back against the warm metal. The view out here was actually nice. There were no other buildings behind The Pork and Peach for miles. The Hawkins' owned the four acres around the building as well—a fact that had been brought up repeatedly in town council meetings when people suggested the town buy the building and just tear it down. At one point, about three years ago, a group of her grandpa's friends had raised what they thought was a reasonable amount. Jarvis Hawkins had laughed in their faces—well, their ears, since it had been over the phone—and hung up on them.

The back of the building looked out over a long stretch of grass that butted up against a line of trees. She knew beyond those trees the land would start getting marshy, and, another few miles further, it would give way to the bayou.

She smiled and focused on Jase. Who was lounging in the chair beside her, facing the same view. But completely focused on her bare leg.

She had to admit she liked that. She also liked the tingles it produced. If she was going to be affected by things like the smell of his laundry detergent when she passed by him too close, it was nice to know he was noticing a few things too.

This was hardly a knock-'em-dead, sexy outfit. This was one of her dress-to-impress outfits. She had a few. She loved pencil skirts and heels. But nothing too short and no heel too high. They needed to be *professional.*

Honestly, most of her "work clothes" were just jeans and shirts. She ran around a small town in Louisiana and did things like check in on if repairs had been done on the fencing around the dump. It wasn't all pencil-skirt-and-heels work, that was for sure. Which was mostly why her mother didn't want to do any of it.

But that was another topic all together.

"Would you consider doing something else with the building?" Priscilla asked.

Jase pulled his gaze from the two inches of bare skin between her knee and the bottom edge of her skirt. Slowly. His gaze tracked up her black-fabric-covered thigh, over her torso, lingered on her pink-silk-encased breasts, moved up her throat, and finally reached her eyes.

She just waited. She loved every second his eyes were on her. It made her warm and restless and made her think about his hands taking that same path. But she had a little more self-control than she had the last time he'd looked at her that way. She could enjoy it without acting on it.

It was like perusing Elyse's bakery case. She could appreciate how good everything looked and *imagine* how great it would all be on her lips and in her mouth without actually giving in.

"Something else like what?" he asked. His voice was lazy and deep, as if his thoughts were on something very different than his plans for The Pork and Peach, and he was just going through the motions of this conversation.

Damn. She might be able to resist his eyes on her, but that husky voice could be more difficult. She shifted on her chair and tugged her skirt down a little. It covered maybe an additional inch.

"Well," she said. "What if you just turned it back into a restaurant? And left the naked women out of the plans?"

He was still meeting her eyes, so she went on.

"The place is already set up to be a restaurant, obviously. You have the kitchen and everything. You were, apparently, well known for the ribs and pie too. The sign out front, the name of the place, would all still work if you just made it a barbecue place."

"You don't think that people would just assume there were strippers?" he asked. "Considering that there were for like thirty years?"

"It might bring people in initially," she agreed. "Curiosity and all that. But the news will quickly spread that it's not a strip club anymore. People will come to check it out. To see what's up. To say that they finally set foot inside the infamous Pork and Peach. Then once they try the food and… hear the live bands and realize how great the service is… they'll want to come back anyway." She was on a roll now. "And when word gets out that there aren't actually strippers, *more* people will come. Families will come in. You can pull more traffic off the highway."

"Live bands, huh?" The corner of his mouth was tipping up.

"You'll have to have live bands. Maybe karaoke. Poker night. Game day events for football and basketball."

"Game day events?" Now he was clearly amused. "Such as?"

"Like…" She trailed off. Sports weren't really her thing, but Jase had played on the Bad football team when they'd won the State Championship his senior year. "The Super Bowl is a big deal, right?"

His grin grew. "Kinda, yeah."

"So that. Stuff like that."

"What about Bad Brews? Marc's place?"

Oh, crap. Right. Marc Sterling owned the only bar and restaurant in town. Bad Brews was nicer than a typical small-town bar. He pulled patrons in from a wide radius and had amazing food. If Jase opened The Pork and Peach as a restaurant, he'd be competing with Marc.

"So do something different. Do something Marc doesn't," she said with a shrug. Marc didn't do barbecue. Or pie. But the Bad Egg had pie. Dammit.

"Right. That makes sense," Jase said, nodding. "Like, having strippers for instance."

She let out a breath. "Jase."

"You almost had me," he said, sitting forward and resting his forearm on the table. The move turned him more toward her and somehow made it seem like he was caging her in.

Her heart rate picked up. And not at all in a bad way. In a very good, I-want-this way.

"I did?" she asked. She wasn't exactly sure what it was she'd done.

"I was with you," he said. "Right up until karaoke."

She narrowed her eyes. "You're not actually going to consider doing this without the strippers at all, are you?"

He paused. His gaze flicked out to the field and then back to her. "Truth is," he finally said. "I don't really care what the building is. I'm here to sell it."

Her eyebrows rose. "Really?"

He nodded. "I'm not re-opening The Pork and Peach. I mean, if that's what someone else wants to do with it, fine, but it's not gonna be me."

Okay, that changed everything. Well, a lot of things.

Not the part about how she could hike up her skirt, climb into his lap, unzip his jeans, and ride him like... well, like she thought that would probably work.

Yeah, she wasn't sure. She was still a virgin. Not an oral sex or orgasm virgin, thanks to this guy, but a virgin in every other way. Though she'd done a bunch of reading, and some watching on her computer, and *a lot* of imagining.

Guys who wanted to date the prim and proper preacher's granddaughter, in a tiny town where they'd all been watching her light candles, sing hymns, and lead the children's worship time for years, not to mention dealing with her grandfather, were very hard to find.

Impossible to find, as it turned out.

It didn't help that when Pastor Williams's own son, Priscilla's father, had had an affair, Aaron had made a huge, public deal out of shaming both Rex and Dixie, the woman who had stupidly fallen for him.

No one wanted to be on Pastor Williams's bad side. And not messing with his granddaughter was a good first step in that.

There were guys who loved to tease her, flirt with her, make her blush, but none of them had ever been gutsy enough to actually try to make a move. Or they hadn't found her choir robes sexy. Or they'd all assumed they would have been shot right down.

They maybe would have been.

They *probably* would have been.

Getting naked, sex, all of that was the most vulnerable a person could be. Priscilla had been known all her life as Miss Perfect, Miss Straight-A, Miss Organized, Miss Know-It-All. She wasn't really the vulnerable type. She probably wouldn't have let the boys she'd known all her life see her in any situation that she wasn't totally confident in.

It was also why she had a hard time dating guys from other towns though. Regan had tried to set her up. She'd met guys through her work. Hell, she met guys at Bad Brews once in awhile.

And she just couldn't imagine ever being *vulnerable* with any of them.

That was the strange thing about Jase. There had always been something about him that made Cilla feel like she could just be herself. That she could be a little awkward and not always know what she was doing and not be perfect at everything, and he'd still think she was great. She knew that he'd kind of adored her. Not that he'd ever said that, but it had seemed clear. So she'd been more relaxed around him, more drawn to him.

That was why she'd picked him to be her first.

Not that he'd delivered. Not fully anyway. She was *very* appreciative of what he *had* delivered, but she'd been thinking about the rest of it for ten years.

But always with him. Only with him. Every fantasy had him in it.

And now, here he was. Bigger, harder, stronger, rougher, hotter than ever.

She sighed. They were such a mismatch.

Damn it all to hell.

And she meant that with every fiber of her churchgoing, believing-in-the-devil-and-hell heart.

"You're not re-opening The Pork and Peach?" she reiterated, forcing herself to focus.

"I'm cleaning up the building, fixing it up, making it look good so someone else will buy it for… whatever."

Her mind was spinning again. "So, your grandpa is willing to sell now?"

"Well…" Jase sighed and rubbed a hand over the back of his neck.

"What?"

"He has a list of people he won't sell to, and the sales contract says that whoever buys it cannot tear it down."

Ah. She had to respect Jarvis Hawkins's ability to hold a grudge and think ahead to piss off his enemies.

She nodded. "Okay." Still, her thoughts were tumbling over one another. "But the *town* could buy it, not to tear it down, but to use it for something, even if some of the town council are on that list?" she asked. She didn't know for sure who was on the list, of course, but she could guess. Best case, there were only two current council members who Jarvis hated enough.

"I guess. I mean, as long as it's not them personally." Jase lifted a shoulder.

"Great." She gave him a huge smile.

"Great?"

"I have the *best* idea." She reached out and put a hand on his forearm squeezing.

His gaze went immediately to that spot, then bounced back up to hers. She felt the muscles bunching under her touch.

"Oh yeah?"

"Yeah." She was becoming surer of it by the second.

This was how she'd felt when she'd thought up the idea for Carly's daycare kids to go eat lunch with the older people at the Senior Center . It saved Carly money and time making lunch and it got the young kids and older people interacting. It had been wonderful for both and had turned into the older people reading to the kids after lunch two days a week and a joint craft time one day a week. Now two other in-home daycares were doing it too. It was so freaking cute; Cilla almost couldn't stand it. She went there for lunch at least once a week herself, just to bask in the adorableness of it all. Sure, everyone pretty much thought the idea came from Nancy, the main cook at the Senior Center, but that didn't matter. The plan had worked and was awesome.

"Okay, lay it on me, Peach," Jase said.

His voice was definitely a little husky and his arm muscle bunched again under her hand.

She pulled back and cleared her throat. "Um, yes, well..." What had they been talking about? Oh, the use of the building. Dammit, when he called her Peach, her brain scattered a little. "The town is talking about building a new community center. In fact, the church is talking to the city council about combining efforts because the church is also finding that it needs more space for events. They're proposing joint ownership of a facility."

Jase stared at her for about three seconds, then he sat back and started laughing. Really laughing. Loudly.

She sighed and watched, waiting for him to get it out of his system.

"So you're proposing that I spend my time and money and sweat fixing this place up for your mom and grandpa?" he finally asked, lounging in his chair again, looking vastly amused.

And sexy as hell.

The guy looked sexy when he was intense and almost angry. He looked sexy when he was amused. She was in so much trouble.

She met his gaze, her chin lifting. "Yes. I guess you could

look at it that way. But it's actually for the whole town. And for you. You said you don't care what the building is used for, you just want the money from it. This is a win-win."

He studied her face, his mouth still slightly curved, but his gaze thoughtful. "There's no way they'll go for it."

"It will save them money and time over building from scratch."

"You don't know what I'm asking for the place."

"I'll negotiate with you until it's down under what they've estimated to build."

The air around them heated as his smile faded to more of a smirk than an amused grin. His eyes were still intent on hers, but she could tell he was thinking about that word, 'negotiate'.

"You think you can talk them into this?" he finally asked.

"I do." What she really thought was that if it worked, it would be huge for her standing in the community, with the city council, and with her mom. This would be a major deal. Her ability to convince them this was a good idea, and for it to actually turn out well, would be tested, but, if she passed, it would be really good.

"Why do *you* want them to use The Pork and Peach as the new community center?" he asked. "Surely you don't approve of what this building stands for?"

"I believe in second chances," she told him sincerely. "I believe things can be rebuilt and can change. And I don't think that the outside of something tells the whole story about what's inside."

He was studying her intently. She wiggled on her chair. She got the impression that Jase Hawkins saw things when he looked at her that other people didn't. A lot of people looked at her and made assumptions based on her family, the way she dressed, the roles she took on. Jase seemed to really just be looking at *her*. That was strange. And nice.

And it made her feel very vulnerable.

Dammit.

"Redeeming the bad boy sounds like a fun challenge, huh?" he finally said.

She frowned. "I was talking about the building."

"Were you?"

She took a deep breath. "Okay, fine. This could be good for both of us too. You have a chance to show people that you care about the community and are willing to work to change this building into something the town wants and needs. And yes, for me, convincing you to work with us could be great." She gave him a big smile. "We could be heroes."

He didn't argue. He didn't immediately grin and nod either. But he seemed to be thinking about it.

Finally, he said, "Seems like you'll be getting more out of it than I will."

"Money? A chance to redeem your reputation? Those are big, aren't they?" she asked, her heart rate kicking up. Now that the plan had occurred to her, she really wanted it to happen. This could be so good. And yes, she wanted him to have a chance to show the town that he wasn't his grandfather.

She frowned as that thought went through her mind. Why did she care about that? But, yeah, she wanted that. Jase wasn't Jarvis. The Pork and Peach hadn't been his. Jase had been a bit of a bad boy maybe, but how much of that had been just what people saw when they looked at him because of his family— something Priscilla knew a lot about—and how much of that was real?

"I can get the money selling to someone else." He shifted, again leaning his elbow on the table. "And I don't care about my reputation here."

Dammit. "So there's no way I could talk you into this?"

"I didn't say that."

She sat up straighter. "Really? What could convince you?"

"If I could get something I *really* wanted out of the deal."

Awareness prickled her skin. She nodded. "That's how negotiations work."

His mouth tipped up in that sexy half smile. "Ask me what I want, Peach."

Her stomach felt like she'd just gone over the top of a roller-coaster. She didn't even know what he was going to ask for, and she was already jumpy and… eager.

She wet her lips and swallowed. "Okay, what do you want?"

"You."

CHAPTER
FIVE

SHE STARED AT HIM. The little hairs on her arms stood up. The back of her neck tingled.

He just stared back at her, letting that sink in.

Finally, she sucked in air, aware that she hadn't breathed for several long seconds. "What does that mean?"

"I want you. Everything we didn't get to before."

Whoa. That was what she'd thought he meant. What she'd *hoped* he'd meant if she was being honest. But hearing him say it out loud with that heat in his eyes was… yeah, whoa.

"You might need to be more specific," she told him. Very breathlessly.

"Do I?" he asked, seeming amused.

"Well, there were lots of things we didn't get to before," she said. Her whole body was hot and tingly.

"There were," he agreed.

He hadn't moved an inch, but she felt like he was suddenly closer than he had been a second before.

"We never went to the movies before," she said. "For instance. And we never went out to dinner. We never talked about our hopes and dreams."

She knew that was not what he was talking about, but she

really needed this spelled out. Because her dirty mind was running away with her. She had all kinds of ideas of things they hadn't gotten to that she *really* wanted to try, but she would not throw herself at this man. She didn't want to come off desperate or clumsy or... *virginal*. She didn't want to make a fool of herself.

And she was baiting him. She wanted to hear him say something dirty.

So much.

There were several long beats before he did anything at all. But then he leaned in. "Okay, let me be real clear here," he said, his voice husky.

Her heart kicked against her ribs, and she pressed her lips together, anticipating his next words.

"I have no desire to see a movie with you. I've eaten exactly what I want to eat with you, but I'll absolutely take seconds. And my hope is that we can go through every dirty dream you've ever had and make them all come true."

Okay, that was pretty good. Kind of dirty. Also pretty clear. But she wanted more.

"You want sex then," she said. "And nothing more. You don't want to date or get to know each other. You just want to sleep together." She lifted a brow. "I'm just making sure we're on the same page here."

"You need it even clearer? Okay. I want to fuck you in every single position, on every single surface that we can find. I want to make you come, over and over, with my tongue, my fingers, and my cock. I want to eat you, spank you, tie you up, bend you over, and make you so sore and tired and horny that you can't walk down the Main Street of this sweet little town without thinking of me with every single step."

Her breath rushed out of her lungs. *That*. Oh, yes, *that*. That was what she'd wanted. Those words. That tone. That look in his eyes.

And those promises.

But she held back from launching herself into his lap and saying, *Start right now*. Barely.

She didn't know what she was doing. She'd never been with a guy like him. Except for him. He'd been intense. He'd turned her into someone she didn't recognize back then.

Him leaving had been devastating, on one hand. She'd just gotten a taste of all the delicious things that she wanted more of.

But it had been a relief too. He'd been too much. If he'd stuck around, she probably would have ended up doing anything and everything he asked of her. She didn't want to lose herself in a guy. She already struggled with who she really was inside her family and this town and her career…

She pulled in a deep breath. No need to panic. This was sex. And she wanted it.

"Just while you're here in town," she said.

He gave her a half-smile. "Well, I'm not going to propose and ask you to go with me."

Right. That would be crazy. He wasn't talking about falling in love. She wasn't at all the type of woman he wanted for good.

He wasn't the type of man she wanted for good either. She needed to remember that. Her feelings couldn't be hurt by already knowing that he'd have no interest in anything more from her.

Don't forget how great he was with his tongue. And that was ten years ago. He could have only gotten better. There was no way he'd been resting that tongue entirely for that long.

Cilla completely ignored that jab of jealousy because that was stupid as hell.

"And you are definitely leaving? No possibility of you deciding to stay? Settling down?" she asked.

He gave a short laugh. "I think we're safe."

That bugged her too. Which was stupid. She wanted him to like Bad? Why? Was it just the hostess inside of her? She wanted everyone to be happy here all the time? She just couldn't stop trying to sell the place to anyone who came through? It didn't matter if he liked Bad or not. He needed to fix this place up, help her fix up her status with her mom and the city council, and then him leaving would be fine. Great, even.

She blew out a breath. Could she agree to a short-term affair with Jase Hawkins while he was in town restoring The Pork and Peach into the new community center?

Absolutely.

That maybe should have been a harder decision to make.

"Okay," she finally said.

Heat and satisfaction flared in his eyes. He sat back in his chair. "Okay."

She started to rise. Her knees were a little shaky from the adrenaline. She assumed it was adrenaline. Horniness could cause adrenaline rushes, she figured.

"Come here."

She was halfway out of her chair, and she looked up so quickly that she twisted her body and pushed down on just the one arm of the chair. She didn't know exactly what happened, but it was awkward. The chair started tipping, and she was sure she was about to fall on the cement patio. At Jase's feet.

But Jase stuck his foot out, stopping the chair and securing it.

She managed to get the rest of the way straight. "What?" she asked when she was sure she wasn't going to fall.

"Come here."

He was just lounging in his chair. *Here* was his chair, she guessed.

"I, um…"

He reached out his hand and circled her wrist with his long fingers. It was a loose hold. She could have easily broken free. If she really wanted to be free.

She didn't.

"Come. Here."

He tugged and she took the step that separated them. Then he pulled her into his lap.

Oh. *Here.*

His lap was hard and hot, and she was very aware of the length of his cock—also hard and hot—against her left hip. But his hand was on her knee, her bare knee, where her skirt had pulled up as she sat, so she was kind of overstimulated in a number of places.

Her nipples beaded, she broke out in goosebumps, she felt hot and jittery, and she wanted to grind against him. She also wanted to bolt.

There was something about Jase that made her want to turn on his thighs, bury her face against his neck, and feel him wrap his arms around her. At the same time, there was an urge to run, to get as far away as she could and not look back.

They didn't need this community center. Her mother didn't have to think she was good at anything. She could live in the town where she'd grown up, where everyone gave her respect because of her last name, but where they all thought that she was really just a glorified errand girl who would be nothing without that last name.

Sure, that was fine.

Because if she sat here and let Jase touch her, she was going to be in big trouble.

She didn't know what that meant in that moment, but she could *feel* it.

Then he brushed her hair to the side, put his nose against her neck, and breathed in deeply. And it was all over.

She couldn't have left if someone suddenly offered her a million dollars and a tiara.

He turned his head slightly and ran his cheek back and forth against her neck. His stubble brushed over her skin, and she felt it all the way to her clit. She had no idea that a section of her neck was connected to her clit by nerve endings, but there it was.

She felt her eyes slide shut.

"I've missed you, Pris," he said, roughly.

No one called her Pris. At least, not without her correcting them. But she didn't correct Jase. There was something in the way he said her name that made it sexy and almost an endearment. She knew that he didn't mean he'd missed *her*, but if he'd missed anything *about* her—even if it was just sex—she was really good with that.

"So we're just going to start right now?" she asked, softly.

She was in. She was all in. It was dirty to be trading sex for him remodeling the strip club into a community center. And she loved it. She hadn't been dirty for anything or anyone ever. Except for Jase.

But this was okay. This was short-term.

It was dirty to hope that he'd bend her over inside that building a few times so that whenever she attended a community function in there, she'd think of that… of him. It was very dirty to think that it was likely that when she got married, her wedding reception would be in this building, as all wedding receptions in Bad happened at the community center…

Suddenly she shot to her feet.

Holy *shit*!

She was going to let him fuck her in the community center where she would one day share her first dance with her *husband*? Where her grandfather would make a toast? Where her friends and family would celebrate? Hell, her parents would have their anniversary party here. Her grandfather his retirement party.

"What's going on?"

She swung to face Jase. "I can't do this."

For a second, he looked hurt. Then annoyed. Then resigned. "Really figured you'd come to that conclusion about five minutes ago."

She shook her head. Crap. No. She needed this building to become the community center, and… she wanted this man.

"I mean, I can't do this *here*. Not in the building that I'll be coming…" She stopped and pressed her lips together. Everything sounded dirty now. "Not in the building where I will be *attending* any number of events over the next several years."

Jase sat back and linked his fingers, resting them on his stomach. His hard, flat stomach. That she really wanted to see without a shirt on…

"You don't want to walk in here for quilting circle and think of all the times I made you scream my name, Pris?" he asked.

"I…" She closed her eyes and pulled in a deep breath. "I'm not in a quilting circle."

He chuckled.

She opened her eyes. "Yes, okay? I'm thinking that might be hard," she cleared her throat, "*difficult* to forget, and some of the… events… might be more inappropriate than others to have that particular memory reel playing."

He studied her for a long moment, his brow furrowed. Then, it was like a light bulb turned on. "Oh, yeah, if I'm turning this place into a community center that you're rentin' for your weddin' dance, you're absolutely gonna think about me fucking you in every single corner."

How had he figured that out? She stared at him.

He chuckled again and sat forward, resting his forearms on his thighs. "What are you gonna do about the fact that I ate your sweet pussy in the very building where you're gonna be sayin' those marriage vows before you ever get to this building?"

Her cheeks were burning hot and she was breathing fast. She hadn't thought about that. "It wasn't officially in the church."

He laughed. "Okay."

She pulled in a breath. Dammit.

He reached out, running his big, hot palm up the back of her calf, past her knee and just under the hem of her skirt. Heat shot up from there, straight to her core. He tugged gently, making her take a step toward him. He tipped his head to look up at her, but he didn't move his hand any farther. It stayed right there, on the back of her thigh, burning, making an aching want rip through her body.

"Decide," he said, simple and firm.

"Between?"

"Me now. Or preserving it all for your future whoever."

Wow, why did he have to put it that way?

"I can have both," she said. Her voice sounded wobbly, even to her own ears. But she *intended* to have both. What she did with Jase Hawkins was now and temporary and sex-only and meaningless. It had nothing to do with her future whoever. "I can have a fling with you and still save special things for… him."

It felt weird to be talking about a faceless, nameless man from the future. Maybe far in the future. If he ever showed up at all.

"Well, you can save the movies and dinners for him," Jase said. "But as for this body—"

He ran his hand higher on her leg and fire licked along her nerve endings.

"And all of the amazing things that it can do and feel and want, I intend to cover all of those bases very thoroughly."

He said it as if he was just trying to be very honest about the facts.

"So you better be sure. As for *where* I'm going to do that—everywhere I can think of that will make you wet and hot and thinking of me all damned day."

And *that's* where she should have walked away. Or slapped him and walked away. That was beyond cocky. And presumptive. And bossy.

"Maybe for while you're in town," Priscilla said, instead of calling him a pig and walking away. "But once you're gone, I'll move on."

Jase nodded slowly. "Okay, Peach. If you think so."

"You're planning to break my heart?"

"Just warning you about the possibility of addiction."

She gave a little snort. "You're worried about me?"

"Just giving you one more chance to say no. Because once you say yes, you're *mine*. For as long as I'm here. For whatever I want."

Then he moved his hand. Just up and down. About three inches total. Just stroking. But her panties were history.

"I'm a big girl, Jase," she told him with far more bravado than she felt. "I know what I'm doing."

"The same big girl who jolted up off of my lap a minute ago when she realized that she'd be dancing with her grandpa at her wedding and thinking about the time she sucked me off by the DJ stage?"

Yeah, that same big girl. She was a mess.

"So, the choice is, let you do whatever you want to me while you're in town or you'll turn this back into a strip club and sell it to the first Joe Schmoe that comes along?"

"Pretty much."

She was actually relieved he said that. Because now she was going to be able to tell herself she was doing this for the community center. For the town. It was self-sacrifice. Truly.

"Fine."

"You're sure this time?" he asked, clearly amused, running his hand higher on her thigh.

She had never been more sure of anything. Which she knew should scare her. "I'm sure."

He waited three seconds. Then he squeezed her thigh and pulled her close, until she was standing between his knees. He slid his hand higher until his fingertips hit silk. Then he slid under the silk.

CHAPTER
SIX

PRISCILLA WAS SO FUCKING hot when she was battling with herself. Jase knew she wanted this. That she wanted *him*. And that she knew she shouldn't. She also wanted to walk away.

But she was standing right in front of him with his hand cupping her sweet ass. Bare. Underneath silky panties that probably cost as much as his work boots.

Hot. Soft. Smooth. Toned. He wanted his handprint there. Bright pink, just like her cheeks were at that moment.

"Spread your legs," he told her.

He had intended, initially, just to sleep with her. Have some fun sex. Yes, some very dirty sex. Yes, some of it here in this building. But just a fun, hot fling while he was in town. She wanted something from him. He wanted something from her. Seemed like the perfect deal. It would make his time in Bad a lot more pleasant, that was for sure.

And he couldn't resist her. She was fucking… everything.

But then she'd pushed him. Pushed him to say it out loud. To lay it out. And she'd seemed totally turned on by it. The idea of being bent over and fucked hard, of walking around town sore from it.

Then she'd brought that shit up about dancing at her

wedding in this building, and that was it. Jase knew he wasn't leaving this town without marking her. It would be short-term, a fling, a hot affair, but she would fucking remember it. Remember *him*. Always.

She wanted to reform the bad boy? Well, he wanted to ruin the good girl.

He couldn't wait to see who would win this battle of wills.

After a moment's hesitation, she lifted one high-heeled shoe and stepped as wide as her skirt would let her. It wasn't far, but he appreciated the effort. Very much.

He ran his palm over the curve of her butt, the callouses on his palm abrading her silky skin.

She shivered. He grinned. Yeah, maybe he'd take his time with this job and hang out in Bad a little longer than he'd originally intended.

That thought should have given him pause, but she reached out just then and put her hand on his shoulder as if needing to steady herself, and Jase couldn't do anything but slide his hand forward. As soon as he felt how hot and wet she was, he knew he wasn't going anywhere any sooner than he had to.

Trouble. She was trouble. But he was going to have a hell of a lot of fun getting into it. Literally.

He cupped her, no silk or lace between them, just bare, hot woman in his hand.

She sucked in a breath and then gave a little moan.

He watched her face as he slid his middle finger through her slick folds. So fucking wet. His cock ached. His tongue tingled. He wanted all of that in a lot of places other than his finger.

"Jase," she said on a breathy sigh.

"Seems maybe you're more amenable to our agreement than you might have let on." He ran the pad of his finger over her clit.

She moaned a little louder that time, her fingers curling into his shoulder. She nodded.

"And this is just my finger, Peach," he teased. "Imagine how agreeable I can make you when I'm balls deep."

The next shiver that went through her was stronger. "Oh, God."

Praying for strength? Or relief? Well, he was going to give her one of those. And it *wasn't* the ability to walk away from him.

He slid his finger deep.

Her pussy clenched around him, and she wobbled a little on those high heels. He grabbed her hip with his free hand, holding her steady. He pumped his finger in and out, then added a second. She took it, but she was tight. So fucking tight. His cock was screaming at him. *I want that! I want that!*

Her cheeks were pink, her eyes shut, her breathing rapid.

He let her feel it all like that for about a minute, but she wasn't going to forget what was *really* happening here. "Open your eyes, Priscilla."

He didn't know if it was the firm command or the use of her full name or what, but her pussy tightened around his fingers as her eyes flew open and locked on his. He curled his fingers into her G-spot and ran his thumb over her clit.

Her breathing hitched and she squeezed his shoulder. "Oh my God. Jase."

"That's right," he told her. "That's fucking right."

"That's… I'm…"

She was going to come. Right there, on his fingers, outside of The Pork and Peach, after ten years of him dreaming about her.

Damn, maybe miracles did come true.

"I *am* going to fuck you in every corner of this building, Priscilla. Your pleas and orgasms are going to be soaked into these walls."

Her pussy clenched, and she gasped.

"You won't be able to walk in here without thinking about me. You've sealed your fate on that one."

That pushed her over the edge. Interesting. He'd have to think about that later. Right then, though, he had a gorgeous woman, the one he'd never gotten over, squeezing his fingers with the pussy that had haunted his dreams. She cried out, coming hard, the ripples of her climax going on for nearly a minute as he continued to stroke her. He thought he could wring another one out of her, but she collapsed onto his lap as if her knees had given out. Her arms went around his neck, her body against his. His fingers had slipped out of her when she moved and he held her, practically hugging her.

Her breath was warm against his skin as she just breathed. And held him in return.

She smelled so damned good. She felt so good. Jase wanted to hold her like that for the rest of the day. He wanted her pliant and sweet and relaxed and trusting. And just here with him, alone.

He wasn't stupid or naive. Messing around with Pris in Bad meant keeping it a secret. There was no way she was going to go for dating publicly. Even if her grandfather wouldn't raise hell about it, and he would, she was going to have to live here after he left, and there would be a lot of questions about him, and them, and what had happened.

So this was going to be a secret. But Jase was okay with that. As long as he had her in his arms every fucking night while he was there.

Her phone started ringing.

She stirred. "Dammit," she muttered against his neck.

He grinned. She wasn't bolting out of his lap this time.

She sat back and took a deep breath, looking at him. Then she shifted to reach for her bag. She pulled her phone out, looked at the number, frowned, and answered.

"Hi, Mom."

Awesome. Her mom. The mayor.

"Yes, I'm just… finishing that meeting up." Her eyes found his, and she smiled a sexy, secretive smile.

He laughed quietly. She was a hell of a negotiator.

But yeah, he needed to remember that she hadn't let him finger fuck her just because she couldn't resist him. She wanted something from him. This wasn't just I-can't-keep-my-hands-off-of-you lust. It was some of that too, for sure. He didn't think she'd actually agree to sleep with someone for a business deal. The deal was a nice excuse for the Bad good girl to hike up her skirt for some hard fucking that she clearly desperately needed and wanted.

But this wasn't *just* a fling. She was expecting him to remodel this building into a community center.

A community center for Bad. Where they'd have BINGO and craft fairs and anniversary parties. Jase scrubbed a hand over his face. His grandfather would throw a fit.

Not that Jarvis would need to know. If Jase got money for the building, that was all that mattered.

"Okay, see you soon."

Priscilla disconnected the call and scooted off his lap. She smoothed her skirt, ran a hand over her hair, then pressed her lips together.

"So, um…"

She still looked disheveled. Maybe not to anyone else, but Jase could see the heat in her eyes and the way her nipples were still hard behind her bra.

Damn, he hadn't even seen her gorgeous tits.

"See you tonight," he told her. Again with that firm tone she seemed to like. And respond to.

It seemed to work.

Her eyes widened. "Tonight?"

"What did you think our deal meant?" he asked. "I'm not in town for long." He had no idea *how* long exactly and he'd already extended the non-existent timeline in his head because he wanted more of her, but reminding her of the time limit was going to get her sweet ass into his bed *tonight*. "If I'm going to get to everything I want to do to you, we've got to get started."

She gave a little shiver, which he knew was lust, and wet her lips. "Fine. I'll… see you tonight. Here?"

"You can meet me here. Before we head to my place," he confirmed. His place was the RV he'd parked on the other side of the building. He hated hotels and traveled to jobs a lot, so he'd bought the thing a few years ago. It was nice. Maybe not quite up to the Priscilla Williams overnight standards, but it had everything Jase needed.

It also had a king-sized bed. That was all *they* needed tonight. She'd be fine.

"Are you staying at your old house?" She looked confused.

His grandfather had owned a house about a mile away from The Pork and Peach. That was where Jase had grown up. But he'd managed to sell that off within a couple of months of leaving Bad. It was this place—burned out and with a pretty charred-around-the-edges reputation—that had been impossible to unload. At least when combined with the stipulations his grandfather put on any sale. It couldn't be sold to a long list of people who lived in Bad. It couldn't be demolished. It couldn't be turned into something "fucking dumb" which, to Jarvis, included an antique mall, a wine-tasting showroom, or a church.

The things it could be? A bar, a restaurant, or a restaurant with a bar. Or a bar with a restaurant, of course. He'd also mentioned that someone should make it into a brewery. Clearly, Jarvis had a narrow vision for the place.

Jase wasn't sure what his grandfather really knew about tasting showrooms, or antique malls for that matter, or why he'd thought someone would *want* to turn it into a church. He knew that Jarvis would consider a community center—that the church would partly own and would use regularly—an entry in his hell-no column if he knew about it, but Jase didn't intend to share all the details.

Jase just needed to get the building remodeled and sold. They needed the money, and Jase needed it off his plate, and Jarvis's dementia made it difficult to reason with him. And, well... this was going to get Pricilla into Jase's bed. Honestly, on his more lucid days, Jarvis would have approved of that part of the deal. There wasn't much his grandfather wouldn't do for a beautiful woman.

Jase wouldn't say he was *proud* of that fact, but he wasn't feeling too bad about it either.

"No," he answered about staying at the old house. "Sold that a long time ago."

"So where are you staying?"

He was sure she was thinking about the motel out along highway five. She definitely wouldn't want to be seen checking into a hotel with him. Especially by Betty and Wally Johnson, who had run the hotel for almost forty years.

He smiled. "Close."

She huffed out a frustrated breath. "Jase."

"No one's gonna see you comin' and goin'," he told her, knowing that was her worry. "Or hear your screams when I'm making you come so hard you forget your name."

There was that too. For sure. Hotel room walls were thin and, frankly, he didn't really want anyone but him to hear how amazing Priscilla sounded when she lost her mind.

Her eyes narrowed, but he didn't miss the little hitch in her breathing. "Where are you staying, Jase?"

"My RV. It's parked around back."

"Your... RV."

Yep, he'd known that would throw the town princess off. He nodded. "Don't worry. I had it fumigated. I think all the bugs are taken care of."

"I'll bring plenty of hand sanitizer, just in case," she said wryly.

He almost laughed. "Nice to know that the threat of a few bugs isn't enough to scare you away from this."

She looked him over. Like, really *looked him over*. Her gaze dragged from the top of his head to the toes of his boots, and she took her time on several spots in between. His cock was still pissed that he hadn't gotten out of his denim prison, and he very much appreciated her appraisal. He hadn't gone down much, and it was quite obvious that Jase was still worked up from their little bit of playing.

Yeah, she might have come nice and hard and fast, but that was just *a little bit* of playing. He had a lot more planned for this woman.

"I really want... this community center," she finally said, when her gaze had tracked back up to his.

He gave her a slow smile. "You're going to get *everything* you want, Peach."

She nodded once. "I better."

Then she turned on her high heel and sashayed her sweet ass across the patio and through the back door.

Jase let her go, listening for the sound of her car starting and pulling out of the parking lot.

Finally, he blew out a breath.

He was going to give her everything she wanted. He wasn't worried about that a bit. Priscilla Williams didn't even know all the things she wanted, and it was going to be a pleasure showing her.

But he was already worried about the things *he* was going to want.

He could already feel himself wrapping around that little finger of hers.

He might have made a huge mistake.

CHAPTER
SEVEN

HER WHOLE BODY felt hot and melty.

She was driving toward her mother's office at city hall—which was also Lady Lola's soap and perfume shop and Agatha's Tea Room. It was one of the few places in town that did not boast a name that included "Bad". Even her grandfather's church had a Bad name—accidentally, and much to Pastor Williams's chagrin. Lola and Agatha turned their noses up at all of that in general.

They were the two sisters who were now somewhere between sixty and one hundred years old. No one knew for sure. They had been widowed within a year of one another—there had been some gossip around that for a little while, but it had died down by the time Priscilla was old enough to take notice. Their childhood home, the biggest, nicest house in town, had passed on to them that same year—also part of the rumor about how they'd been sick of being tied to men who thought they could decide how the women spent their money and who wouldn't allow them to live together—and was far too big for them to simply live in. So they'd turned the first floor of the mansion into their dream businesses and offered their father's old study, library, and sitting room to the city for the Mayor's office and the city clerk's office.

The place was gorgeous. Lots of old wood and marble, high ceilings, elaborate fixtures, and huge windows.

Priscilla swore that house was about thirty percent of why her mother wanted to be mayor. The other seventy percent was, of course, the power.

But the house was definitely Melinda Williams's kind of place. The house Cilla had grown up in, which had been built to Melinda's exact specifications, was also gorgeous. But it was modern and not as "stately"—her mother's words. There was no grand staircase, or well-established, lavish flower garden out back, or a collection of stone cherubs tucked around the grounds and house.

Yes, Cilla had pointed out that Melinda could plant a flower garden and buy cherubs, but she insisted it wouldn't be the same. Lola and Agatha's had history. By that, she really meant that they'd been established by a family that had more money and influence and had been in town longer than the Williams's had. And that irked her.

Truth be told, there was *plenty* of money and influence on Priscilla's *grandmother's* side of the family. The Authements were an old New Orleans family with a manufacturing business that went back five generations. But the Williamses had moved out of New Orleans three generations ago and settled in Bad— "of all places", as her grandmother would say—so that they could be big fish in a small pond. Aaron's father, Arthur, had been pastor and had passed the pulpit down to his son. So when Aaron's son Randall had also followed in the spiritual-leader footsteps, Aaron's wife, RuthAnn Authement-Williams, had made their other son, Rex, CEO of Authement Manufacturing.

Which had thrilled his wife, Melinda. It not only meant more money, but it also kept him out of town a lot.

Then he'd taken a mistress, and she'd fallen in love with him and moved to Bad, and… well, *that* hadn't gone over so well with the Authements *or* the Williamses.

Then that mistress, Dixie Donovan, had fallen in love with Rex's COO, he'd fallen in love with her right back, they'd gotten married, and that COO had left Authement, taken a lot of business secrets with him, and started the company that was now their biggest competitor.

It had all gone very, very *bad* for Rex.

Now he slept in the guest room and he and Melinda barely spoke.

But they, by God, attended church every Sunday and sat together in the second pew on the left with the rest of the family.

Priscilla parked in the circle drive in front of the house/city hall and took a deep breath, squeezing the steering wheel. Her family was fucking exhausting. They were a bunch of drama queens and she liked to think she had nothing in common with any of them.

But she often *feared* that wasn't true. Growing up, and all through high school, she'd loved attention and the spotlight and telling other people what to do. She also loved gossip, and, when it came to being naughty with the wrong person… she was afraid maybe she was taking a little too much after her dad.

"You're fine. What you're doing with Jase is nothing like what Rex did with Dixie. Nobody is going to get hurt," she told herself as she shut the car off.

Except maybe you when you fall for him, and he breaks your heart.

Yeah *that* was not helpful self-talk, and it didn't matter if she didn't say it out loud.

"You've got this," she told the rearview mirror. "You had a successful meeting."

She could feel the hot blush even as she said the words to *herself*.

She could not do that when she said it to her mother.

But the meeting with Jase had been… wow. Just wow. That was the only word that really came to mind. She'd had no idea when she'd gotten into her car and headed toward The Pork and Peach that she'd be leaving with… wow.

She was going to walk into the meeting with her mother wearing damp panties and with plans for sex later because of the man her mom had wanted her to get rid of.

She took another deep breath. Okay, this was fine. This was more than fine. The town was going to get a community center out of the deal. She'd done something even better than getting him to leave town.

Had an orgasm on the back porch of the old strip club?

That inner voice of hers needed to shut the hell up. Yes, that was definitely better than getting him to leave town. But she couldn't be thinking of that while meeting with her mother.

Cilla needed to project confidence. She had to sell this idea to her mother. She needed her mother to see her as capable of dealing with issues. She was going to prove that she had turned this completely around. She'd pivoted this situation with The Pork and Peach—which, yes, sounded even dirtier now than it had previously—from a headache and frustration and something that needed to be dealt with to a win-win situation that everyone would benefit from.

She'd done a hell of a job.

And if she could avoid thinking of it as a *bang*-up job then that would be great.

Priscilla closed her eyes, drew a deep breath, thought about the fact that she needed to call Chad with the recycling company and ask why four blocks north of the school had been missed this past week, blew the breath out, and got out of her car.

She ran a hand over her skirt, made sure her blouse was on straight—though Jase hadn't even taken that off or so much as unbuttoned it, and she was really sorry about that—shook herself for letting her thoughts once again drift off like that and climbed the steps to the massive front door.

Because the main floor of the house was now a public office

and business, she didn't need to knock or ring the bell. Priscilla pulled the door open and stepped into the foyer.

The entryway of the big old mansion made people stop, *oooh*, and crane their necks to look around. Nearly twenty feet above there was a skylight that had stained glass pieces around the edge that threw multi-colors to the white marble floor below. There were huge potted plants on either side and a carved wooden archway in deep mahogany that led to the rest of the house. The first few steps inside the house inspired some awe, she could admit. And that was just the beginning.

She drew another deep breath. *You did a good job today. You did a good job today.*

Promises of hot, sweaty, blow-your-mind sex aside, she should be proud to tell her mother about the deal she'd made with Jase.

Besides, she didn't really think that Jase was only in it for the sex. He wanted to get some money out of that building. He would do that with this deal. Sure, he could probably sell it to someone else, but why not go with a sure thing?

Priscilla blushed again as she thought about what a sure thing she'd been for him.

She'd not only jumped at the chance to get into his bed while he was in town, she'd also dutifully spread her legs for him and not done one single thing to stop him from sliding his hand into her panties.

She put a hand to her cheeks. She *really* needed to get this under control, or she'd be blushing and sweating in front of her mother.

She didn't think she'd ever seen her mom sweat or blush. Melinda might get dewy in the deep heat of the summer if she was outside for a ribbon cutting or something. But she had this very classy, gentle way of handling everything.

Even bodily functions.

And before her traitorously horny mind could go down the path of wondering if her mom had ever even had an orgasm,

Cilla forced herself to walk down the long, main hallway to the mayor's office.

There was a large sitting room to the left of the foyer. Melinda and her receptionist and the city clerk used that as a waiting room for appointments. The city clerk's office was the next room. Linda was a nice woman who kept the books for the city and invoiced people for things like garbage pickup and renting the current community center.

And just like that, Priscilla was back to thinking about Jase and this new situation and their negotiation.

"Hi, Priscilla," Linda greeted.

Cilla lifted a hand as she passed the office. "Hi, Linda."

"Is it hot outside?" she called out. "I need to run some errands at lunchtime."

Cilla stopped and poked her head back around the edge of the door. "Not especially. It's a nice day out."

"Oh, good. You looked hot."

Yeah, well, I am hot, Linda. But that's from tropical storm Jase. Nothing for you to worry about.

Lord almighty, this meeting with her mother was going to be terrible.

"Just rushing around a little this morning," she said. What was she supposed to say? *A couple of big fingers and a knowing smile made me like this?*

"Okay, great. See you later," Linda said.

"Yep." Cilla turned and started for her mom's office again.

"Oh, hey, Priscilla," Kelsey, her mother's receptionist greeted when Cilla walked by her desk.

"Hi."

Kelsey frowned slightly. "Is it hot outside?"

Priscilla sighed. *It was hot at The Pork and Peach, okay everyone? Very, very hot.* "Not really. I'm just trying to hurry and haven't been drinking enough water."

"Oh." Kelsey seemed to think that was weird and, well, Cilla didn't care.

"Is my mom inside?" Cilla waved toward the mayor's office door.

"Oh, yes, she's waiting for you."

"Great. Thanks."

Priscilla wasn't even sure why her mother needed a receptionist. Cilla did everything for her. Except sit in front of her door and tell people she was too busy to talk to them. Which Kelsey rarely did. Melinda Williams loved the power trip that came from being Bad's mayor, but she also actually cared about doing a good job and about the town. She made time to talk to whoever needed her.

But having a receptionist made her feel more important. And Kelsey was the young daughter of one of Melinda's best friends from high school. Kelsey hadn't wanted to go off to college, so Melinda had given her a job. It was very low-paying, but, then again, it was also very low-stress and very flexible and Kelsey, apparently, made a ton of money selling some cosmetics line on the side, so everyone was happy.

Priscilla couldn't judge Kelsey. What was she doing? Running around doing the things that the town needed but that didn't fall into a neat job description like "grounds maintenance" the way Jerry's did. Jerry mowed all the grass that belonged to the city, removed all the snow in all the areas the city owned, kept fences repaired, filled in holes, that kind of thing.

Running the guy rebuilding The Pork and Peach out of town didn't really fit under any of that, so it wasn't Jerry's job.

It also wasn't Kelsey's job. Or Linda's job. Or, evidently, the mayor's job.

Which meant it was Priscilla's.

Everything that didn't fit anywhere else was Priscilla's job.

She took a deep breath, gave her mom's office door two little knocks, and then pushed the door open. "Hi, Mom."

"Priscilla," Melinda said with a warm smile. "You look… nice." But her gaze narrowed as Cilla approached her desk and then slipped into one of the armchairs in front of it. "Are you alright?"

"What do you mean?"

"You look hot."

For the love of God. Cilla gave her a big smile. "I'm completely fine. I'm… excited."

Well, that was true. Jase's RV and all of the promises he'd made on that porch this morning definitely had her excited. *She* hadn't even given herself an orgasm as fast as he'd given her one today. She absolutely had some big expectations for tonight.

And if the feel of him against her hip was any indication, *big* was not going to be a problem…

"Priscilla!"

She snapped her attention to her mother. "What?"

"I asked you how the meeting went. Twice."

Oh, shit. *Pull yourself together, for fuck's sake.*

"I'm sorry. I was lost in thought… about the meeting, actually." Very true as well. "I have some big news."

Her mother looked surprised. "Oh?"

"It went far better than expected."

"He's packing up and leaving as we speak?" Melinda asked.

Priscilla smiled. "No. Even better."

Her mother arched a brow. "How is anything better than that?"

"We discussed a situation that will be mutually beneficial."

That was also true. But Priscilla worked very hard to keep her mind on the conversation with her mother, even though her thoughts *really* wanted to wander back to that patio and replay the thing he'd said about every corner of that building…

"How so?" Melinda leaned in, lacing her fingers together on top of her desk. Her expression was one of pure skepticism.

And that, right there, was why this was important. Orgasms were sprinkles on the icing of this cake. Wonderful. Welcome. But not the most vital part.

The cake was the deal. That building turned into a community center. The deal that would take a building that had not only been a burr in Priscilla's grandfather's butt for years, but also an eyesore for the past ten years, and turn it into something wonderful. Something that looked great but that would also host important events and bring the community even closer.

The icing would be her mother acknowledging she'd done a great job. Praising her for it, even. In public, possibly. *That* would be like *pink* icing rather than just vanilla or chocolate.

Orgasms on top of all of that were just the sprinkles.

Just. The. Sprinkles.

She couldn't let them become anything more than that.

So first, the cake.

"I talked with Jase about his plans and intentions. He is here to clean up and repair the building. He wants to sell it. But he isn't planning to stay and run it and he doesn't necessarily want it to be The Pork and Peach anymore."

"What do you mean?" Melinda asked.

"He did, initially, plan to restore it exactly as it was and find a buyer interested in re-opening the business."

Her mother frowned. "Which is why I sent you out there to dissuade him."

If she'd just let me finish. Priscilla smiled. "I know. And that's what I did."

"You talked him out of it?"

"I made a deal with him."

"What kind of deal?"

Cilla locked down the dirty thoughts that tried to run through her mind and took a breath. "I asked if he would consider cleaning it up and remodeling it according to new specifications."

"Such as?"

"The community center plans."

She held her breath.

Her mother's frown deepened. "What about the community center plans, Priscilla?"

Oh, boy, her name at the end meant her mother wasn't pleased. Still, she made herself smile and sit up straight. "I asked him if he'd be willing to remodel The Pork and Peach according to our plans for the community center, and he said yes." Her smile was a lot more genuine now. Satisfaction warmed her chest. It was a *good* idea. It was. She was going to have to convince her mom. And her grandfather. But it was a good idea.

"Jase is a contractor now," she went on. "He builds and remodels for a living. I will, of course, call some references and get more information about his work." Shit, she hadn't asked him for references. Oh well, they had a meeting tonight, after all. She could get them then. After… whatever.

She had to shut that down lest her mother see her flushing pink at thoughts of Jase. "But he is agreeable to the idea of doing the remodel of The Pork and Peach as the new community center instead of restoring the bar and restaurant."

Her mother studied her. "Well, I certainly hope you didn't make him any promises," she said. "This is not something you have the authority to decide."

Cilla bristled but didn't let it show. She didn't really have the authority to do anything except charge coffee to her standing account at the coffee shop and put office supplies on the city's account. Under a certain dollar amount, of course.

"I told him about our plans and asked if he'd be willing to change *his* plans and come to an agreement that would be beneficial to everyone," she told her mother. "We didn't sign any contracts, but he took the conversation seriously."

"That wasn't really your place."

"You told me to handle the situation," she said, her tone a little cooler now. "You didn't want him to rebuild and reopen The Pork and Peach. This solves that problem."

"But now we're possibly verbally committed to using his services and making that building into our community center." Melinda leaned in. "People will be having *wedding dances* there, Priscilla."

It was so weird that her mind went to wedding dances the same way Cilla's had. There were plenty of other events that the town used the current community center for. It was where all elections were held. It was rented out for graduation parties and anniversaries and family reunions. There was a craft fair every spring. There was also a community-wide food drive twice a year. There were easily a dozen other similar events.

Priscilla knew all of this because, of course, she organized all of it. Except the family reunions and parties.

"It will save us money and time," she told her mother. "It will be much less expensive and faster to repurpose that building than it will be to build from scratch. It's already got a lot of what we need—a kitchen, bathrooms, large spaces. He can put up walls to make rooms out of some of it if we'd like, but that would still leave a big main area. It's really kind of perfect. We don't have enough money to start from the ground up, but we have enough to buy that building from Jase." She had no idea if that was true. The city had a hefty pot, but she didn't know what he wanted for the place. She had to hope that he mostly just wanted to get rid of it and make a little profit.

"It would still mean that our community center is really a strip club," her mother said.

"*Was* a strip club," Cilla insisted. She leaned in now, ready to make the point that she really hoped would drive this home. "Imagine it, Mom. What would be better than for the Williams family to *convert* a strip club into a community center? To take the place that was filthy and sinful and a shadow on our town"—okay, she was laying it on thick, but her mother had grown up listening to her father-in-law from a church pulpit; Melinda was used to preaching, that was for sure—"and *reform* it into a place where life is celebrated, where neighbors come together, where our town grows and gets stronger?"

Had she used the words *convert* and *reform* on purpose.

Damn right, she had.

She knew her family. There were buttons to be pushed, and

she wasn't above pushing them. If it was for the greater good, of course.

"And," she said, softening her tone. "Jase isn't Jarvis, Mom. I knew Jase in high school. We shouldn't assume that he doesn't care about the town and how we feel. We should give him the chance to be the one to remake the place, to do something for the town, to make up for what his grandfather did."

Cilla didn't really think it was up to Jase to make up for anything. Certainly not for the actions or attitudes of his grandfather. She didn't know that she felt Jarvis had anything to make up for either, honestly. He'd made his choices; he'd run a business. He hadn't been a nice guy, but she didn't know what all went into that. He'd hated her grandfather. She didn't know all of that history either. But, as far as she knew, none of the women who took their clothes off for money had done it under duress. They'd also made choices. If anything, her family should have been all about forgiveness and turning the other cheek.

She decided to point that out. "Shouldn't we, of all people, be ready to model giving someone a second chance? Forgiving? Seeing how something can be made new again?"

Yeah, she'd been listening to that same man preaching from the same pulpit all of *her* life. Things being made new again was a common theme.

Her mother didn't say anything for several seconds. Then she drew in a breath. "Let me think about it."

Well, that wasn't a no. In fact, it was kind of a win. Cilla smiled. "Alright. Thank you."

"I can give him a decision next week."

Cilla frowned. "Mom, he's only staying long enough to get the building put back together. He'll need to know before then what he's doing with it."

"This isn't a decision we should rush into. I'll need to talk to some people."

"So talk to them," Cilla said. "But you need to do that now. In the next day or so. He's got a lot of basic clean-up to do before he starts anything specific, but how he approaches the remodeling will depend on the final purpose of the building. It's not fair to drag this out."

Her mother seemed surprised that she was so adamant. "I suppose I could call a meeting."

"Yes. Call a meeting." Cilla didn't roll her eyes, but it was an effort.

The people Melinda wanted to talk to were people she talked to every freaking day as it was. Her father-in-law, of course. A few of her friends. The members of the city council. None of them had big business overseas that required them to be in Hong Kong for the week or anything, for God's sake. She could walk into any of their businesses within ten minutes. She could probably find a couple of them at the diner. She could definitely call them all and have dinner with them tonight.

"Fine. I'll have a few conversations."

"I'll contact his references, in the meantime," Cilla said, rising from her chair. "And I'll show him the community center plans. See if he has any concerns or questions if we go that direction." She added the last part for her mother's sake. The *if*. But they really needed to do this. And she was tempted to go find her grandfather before Melinda did.

"Fine," Melinda said as Priscilla started for the door.

Her hand had just touched the knob when her mother added, "Priscilla."

She turned back, her heart flipping. Was she going to say "Good job"?

"Be careful what you say to him when you talk. There is such a thing as a verbal contract."

Right. Not a good job. A *don't fuck this up*. Priscilla nodded. "I know. But I don't really have any authority."

Her mother nodded. "Make sure he knows that. So he's not misled."

Sure. Great. She'd be sure to let Jase Hawkins, the one guy from this town who might not think her career was a joke—

because he didn't really know any better—know that she didn't have any real authority to do anything.

"I'll handle it," she said. Then slipped out before her mother could see how hurt she was.

As Cilla headed for her car, only one thought went through her head. *I did have the authority to make one verbal contract with Jase Hawkins.*

Hot sex, all the time, for as long as he was here.

That was one agreement she was going to hold him to.

Maybe she could even get a *holy shit, you are so damned good at that* from *him* if she wasn't going to get any praise from anyone else around here.

CHAPTER
EIGHT

"I NEED to know if you can do this. Right now."

Jase looked up from the floor where he was on hands and knees trying to determine how much of the wooden flooring could be stripped down and refinished, and how much of it he would have to tear out and replace.

It wasn't looking good.

But the smooth, toned calves that were right at eye level definitely were.

He dragged his gaze up her legs, past the hem of her skirt, over her hips, waist, and breasts, and finally met the blue eyes that were watching him with a mix of exasperation and amusement.

"I can do a lot of things right now," he told her, rocking back on his heels. "You're right at the top of that list."

God, he wanted her. The few hours since she'd left him with the promise to return and to spend the night in his bed had done nothing to cool his lust. In fact, he'd almost taken his thumb off with the circular saw, and almost put a nail through his hand, because his thoughts had wandered to the most difficult question he'd had to ponder in some time—where on Priscilla did he want to put his mouth first?

Her exasperation seemed to disappear, and she gave him a little half-smile. "Good. That's very good. But I need to be number two on that list because I need to know if you can do *this* first."

She waved the cardboard tube she was holding.

He'd bet his new circular saw—that thankfully did *not* have any blood or flesh on its blade—that those were the plans for the new Bad Community Center.

And yes, it was juvenile, and he should have been long over it, having grown up here, but he wanted to laugh at that name.

Besides the funny and memorable business names, it had also been fun in high school when their rivals in Autre, the next town over, would give them shit about being "bad" to show them just how fucking bad the Bad boys could be. The football games were rough and often bloody, the Bad boys partied far harder, and when they stole the Autre girls away, those ladies absolutely went back home with stories of just how *bad* the boys down the bayou could be.

"Yes, I definitely can," Jase told Cilla, stretching to his feet.

"You don't want to look at it first?"

He shrugged. "Don't really need to."

He knew that he was a hell of a builder. That wasn't ego talking. That was experience. He was damned good, and he doubted very much that a small-town community center was going to be much of a challenge.

"You might have to adjust some things," she said. "I mean, in the building. Maybe put up some walls and…" She blew out a breath. "I actually don't know. I just know that they won't agree to changing the plans."

"The meeting with your mom didn't go well?" he guessed, holding out a hand.

She put the tube in his palm. "She's skeptical."

"That's milder than I would have expected." He took the plans over to the planks of wood he had set up on sawhorses. He'd needed a workspace that wasn't covered in soot and dust.

That meant making his own because everything in this place was covered in soot and dust.

"Oh, she's not skeptical of you," Cilla said, following him. "She's skeptical of *me*."

He glanced at her. "Why?"

"Because she thinks I'm incapable of doing anything that she and my grandpa don't specifically spell out with pictures and third-grade level instructions."

She sounded incredibly bitter, and he watched her for a long moment. He couldn't remember Cilla ever saying anything against her family.

"So, this building is about more than just saving the town some money and time?" he finally said. "And more than you just feeling good about redeeming my reputation?"

"It is," she admitted. "My mother doesn't have a lot of faith in me. That, of course, is because she and my grandfather have given me very few ways to prove myself—other than sitting in the same pew every Sunday morning, not drinking or partying, and never swearing, at least where they could hear me. They wanted to use me as proof that *they* were moral, upstanding people. But it was never really about *me* and now that I'm adult, I have to prove to *everyone*, including my own family, that I'm capable of more than leading the church choir and organizing prayer chains."

Jase straightened as he listened to her confess all of that. She sounded annoyed, but also sad, and he hated the way that tugged in his chest. He had always cared about Priscilla. More than made sense. More than he wanted to. But now… that wasn't good. He needed to not really care about anything too much while he was here.

He knew that Priscilla's grandfather had always been incredibly proud of her and her "good girl" reputation, but he'd never realized that she'd resented it. Or maybe she hadn't, until she'd grown up.

"So, you need this building to show them that you can make good decisions and negotiate deals," he summarized.

Shit, now he was definitely going to convert this building into a community center.

"Well, yes," she said, but then she sighed. "Of course, I'm not really good at negotiating deals. I promised sex for this one, and I kind of hope that's not the only way I can get people to do things for me."

His gut tightened. Well, *shit*. Ten minutes ago, he'd been feeling pretty fucking good. He was going to unload the building. He was going to get to fuck Cilla. And then he was going to leave Bad, hopefully forever.

Now he was almost reconsidering the fucking Cilla thing.

Almost.

He didn't want her to feel like that was the only way she could get him to do the project. As of right now, he was in, and he hadn't even unzipped his pants.

But he wasn't a good enough guy to say anything remotely like "you don't have to take your clothes off for me". Because he *really* wanted her to take her clothes off.

"I can do whatever they have in these plans. And I will," he said.

She lifted her chin. "For this amount?"

She passed him a slip of paper. He looked at it, knowing it didn't matter what it said.

It was a decent offer though. Maybe a little less than he could *maybe* get from someone else, but it was enough. And it was a sure thing.

And it was for Cilla.

"Yes."

She stood looking at him, not saying anything for a long moment.

"You were always nice to me in high school," she finally said.

"Was I?" He knew they'd gotten along. He'd always enjoyed being around her. But it wasn't as if she'd been bullied or left out. She'd been one of the most popular girls in school. She'd been in charge of, well, everything. From student council to prom planning. She'd had a lot of friends. Plenty of guys wanted to date her. She hadn't dated, but that wasn't because of any of them. Her grandfather had been an intimidating son of a bitch.

"You tutored me in chemistry, you knew how stupid I was about organic compounds." She gave him a little smile. "But you never told anyone that you were helping me or that I was struggling in that class."

"Why would I have told anyone that?" He ran a hand over the back of his neck. Their chemistry teacher had been one of those guys who was great at encouraging kids to embrace their talents, even if the kid was better known for his work in shop class than in upper-level science. Mr. Kent had made sure Jase knew that he was paying attention to the fact that Jase was great at science, especially chemistry and physics, and he got Jase involved in tutoring early on.

Jase had been shocked when Priscilla Williams had shown up on his list. Even more so when she'd asked if he could tutor her at her house rather than in the science room or even the library. Of course, it had been because she didn't want anyone to know she needed tutoring, but she'd acted sheepish about it only that first time. After that she'd seemed to relax and had been easy to teach.

He'd loved those days at her house after school. Away from school and all her peers, she was… softer. More comfortable. More herself.

"A lot of the guys got a kick out of trying to get the good girl to do bad things," she said with a shrug.

He scowled. "What kinds of bad things?" If someone had forced her into anything she hadn't wanted, he was going after him. There was no statute of limitations on something like that in his book.

"Swearing," she said. "Or saying something mean about someone, insulting a teacher. Even if I just did it in a small group, it would get out. I was expected to be this perfect angel all the time. They tried to embarrass me. They tried to get me to parties, and if I did show up at someone's house for movie night, they tried to sneak liquor in my drinks, or guys would try to get me to go outside on the patio or down to the basement with them." She was frowning now. "I was only that stupid once."

"What happened?" Jase was shocked at how deep and ominous his voice sounded.

Most of the guys they'd gone to school with still lived around here. It wouldn't be hard to find one and teach him a lesson, even if it was ten or eleven years later.

"Conner Vanmullen asked me to go to the basement at Randi's house to get more ice for everyone." Cilla was watching Jase carefully now. As if gauging his reaction to what she was about to say.

"And?"

"He pushed me up against the deep freeze and kissed me."

"And?" he prompted when she stopped.

"I pushed him away, told him I wasn't interested, and we went back upstairs."

"That was it? He backed off when you said no?"

"Yes."

Jase blew out a breath. "Okay. Well, I don't have to kill Conner today. That's good."

She looked surprised. "You would say something to him? Now? After all this time? Based just on what I told you?"

"I wouldn't say anything to him except 'this is for Cilla'."

"What would be for me?"

"My fist slamming into his face."

She actually smiled at that. "It's been a long time."

"Never too late to learn lessons."

"He's grown up a lot. Maybe he's learned the lesson about not touching people who don't want to be touched."

"I'd like to be sure."

She seemed a little awed by that. "And you'd just take my word for it?"

"Of course."

She shook her head. "This is what I'm talking about. You were always good to me."

He gave a sharp bark of laughter. "Helping you with chemistry and wanting to punch a guy for kissing you isn't exactly charity, Cilla."

Her eyes softened and he realized that he'd used her name, the name everyone called her, rather than Pris or Peach. He needed to be careful. He was getting soft.

"Well, he lives over on Sixth Street," she said.

Jase lifted a brow. "Is there a reason I need to know that?"

"He told everyone after that that I had been the one to kiss him and that he'd gotten my bra unhooked and had felt me up before we figured we had to come back upstairs."

The surge of possessiveness and rage that went through him was truly shocking. The rage he maybe could have chalked up to the fact that he believed all men—hell, all *people*—need to be damned fucking sure that the people they were touching wanted it. Also, that Conner had lied. That was a dickhead move that definitely needed to be addressed.

It was the possessiveness that was not good. She wasn't Jase's now and she hadn't been his back then. There was no reason for him to be unexpectedly and unnecessarily pissed that another guy had touched her. Conner *hadn't* even touched her. He'd lied about that. So Jase's feelings were absolutely asinine.

He still felt them though.

"Sixth street, huh?" he asked.

She nodded. "The blue house, second on the left."

"Okay." He pulled his truck keys from his pocket and started for the door.

"Jase!" she called after him, laughing. "I'm kidding."

"I'm not."

"Come on, wouldn't you rather spend the evening with me instead of with Conner?"

"Oh, this won't take long." But he already felt the tension draining out. She was okay. He didn't need to go find Conner. At least not tonight.

If Jase ran into him at the gas station or bar or something though, Conner was going to hear about it.

"I appreciate the gesture," she said, smiling at him.

He tucked his keys away again and crossed back to her. "If you change your mind, just say the word."

"I might have you 'ask' James Michner for an apology too while you're at it," she said. "I was almost madder at him than Conner."

"What did James do?"

"Spiked my soda one night with vodka. I couldn't really taste it. He didn't overdo it, just a little bit in each glass. But I ended up drunk and then really sick the next day. Asshole."

"Did *he* try anything?"

She shook her head. "Just wanted me to go home drunk. Thought it would be funny to see what my grandpa did."

"What did he do?"

"Lectured me and grounded me," she said.

"You really had shitty taste in friends," Jase told her.

She nodded. "True in some cases. But you know how a small town is, you're kind of stuck with who's here. Regan and Randi are the exceptions to all of that though." Cilla grinned. "Regan actually got back at both of them."

"Oh?"

"Yeah, she waited for Conner after school and made out with him, then told everyone that he has a tiny dick. Then she slipped laxatives into James's burger at lunch one day."

Jase laughed. "That's awesome."

Cilla nodded. "Pretty classic, but they both worked like a charm. After James ran out of history to go to the bathroom, she followed him. Into the boys' bathroom. And told him that if he ever did anything more than say 'good morning' to me, she'd make him even sorrier."

Jase liked Regan. "How did I not know about this?"

Cilla shrugged. "We hung out in different crowds."

He nodded. That was for sure.

"Anyway, it was always that kind of stuff," she said. "Them just trying to mess with my reputation."

"Fuckers."

She smiled and nodded. "Yeah." She tipped her head. "You never did stuff like that."

"Oh, Peach," he said. "I definitely got your bra unhooked and touched your tits."

God, one of the best moments of his life. Still.

Heat flared in her eyes. "But I wanted you to."

He nodded. "Only way that would have happened."

"I know."

That hit him hard. It meant a lot that she knew that. That she knew he never would have done anything she didn't want him to do, didn't *ask* him to do. And she had. She'd practically begged.

His body stirred with the memory. How was it that he hadn't gotten over this girl? He'd been with dozens of women. Women that were way more experienced, a lot wilder, even more beautiful in a few cases. Priscilla was gorgeous, but there were lots of gorgeous women in the world. And he'd had the luck to have a few of them say yes when he wanted to get them naked.

But no one had ever stuck with him like Cilla.

"I was never scared of you, Jase," she said quietly. "A little overwhelmed, yes. Or a lot." She gave a soft laugh. "I knew that I was not going to impress you in any way, but I knew that you would take care of me." She met his eyes. "Do you remember the first time we really talked?"

He did. He nodded.

"That's when I knew," she said. "I knew I could trust you. We didn't really know each other, you had no reason to have my back, but when I walked into school that morning, you protected me."

"You make it sound a lot more dramatic than it was," he told her.

"It would have been dramatic," she said with a smile.

She'd walked into school that day, freshman year, in white pants and a pink top. He'd been just inside the doors and when she'd walked past, he'd noticed a brown smear on the butt of her pants. He'd started walking right behind her, blocking everyone else's view, and, when she stopped at her locker, he'd turned her to face him, back to the lockers, and told her she had something on her pants.

She'd turned crimson red and confessed that she'd eaten a candy bar on the way to school and must have dropped some on the seat.

So, he'd spilled his soda on her.

Right down the front of her white pants.

Of course, he'd pretended it was an accident. Only she knew he'd done it intentionally. But then he'd slipped out of the flannel he was wearing over his t-shirt and handed it over. She'd wrapped it around her waist, and they'd gone to the office to get her excused from first period so she could go home and change.

"That was the most noble thing anyone had ever done for me," she said. "Still is." She smiled. "Well, except for when you took the rap when I ran over the curb at the Bad Egg and smashed into the flowerpot by the door."

Kids would often park their cars at the diner and then pile into one car to go to the movies in the next town or out to a party. Cilla had been coming back to drop her friends off and had misjudged the curb. It had been one in the morning, so no one else had been around to witness the accident.

Jase had been there. He'd been walking home from a buddy's house, cutting across that parking lot. He'd seen the whole thing.

"I didn't know that you knew I'd done that." He'd gone to the diner the next morning and cleaned up the mess. Then he'd apologized to John, the owner, and replaced the planter. John had agreed to keep it all quiet and not even tell people it had happened.

Cilla moved in closer to Jase, a soft smile on her face. "I didn't know for sure until right now."

His heart thumped. Shit. She was onto him. She knew he had a huge soft spot for her. She did not need to know that. No one should know that. He didn't say anything though.

"That's why I got naked with you in the Sunday school room," she said. "I knew you wouldn't tease me, you weren't setting me up for anything, and you'd never tell anyone."

Jesus. He swallowed hard. He'd known even then that she trusted him, that what they'd done, what she'd let him do, was something special. He knew her reputation as well as anyone. She was the ultimate good girl. But she'd let him close.

That was why she'd stuck with him for so long.

No one had ever trusted him the way Cilla had.

She stepped closer again and put her hand on his chest. Jase laid his hand over hers. Though he wasn't sure if he was keeping her there or if he was just worried about what was going to happen when she started moving that hand.

"The only time you ever teased me was about peaches."

Her voice was husky and his gaze dropped to her lips. "I wasn't teasing," he said. "What I told you about peaches was completely true."

She nodded. "And you told me about it so that the others couldn't keep teasing me."

"Well, knowledge is power."

She gave him a slow smile. "And then you gave me even more knowledge."

Heat ripped through him. He was so screwed here.

"Cilla—"

Her fingers curled into his chest.

"I will renovate this place into the community center

according to the plans and for the amount you proposed," he said.

Her gaze dragged up from his chest to his eyes. "Thank you."

"And you don't have to do anything else."

She frowned. "What do you mean?"

"I'm not renovating the building so I can fuck you."

She sucked in a quick breath. He knew it was the "fuck you". People didn't talk that way around her and certainly not *to* her. But she liked it.

She wet her lips. "That's nice to know."

"So… do you want to go get a pizza or something?"

Her frown deepened. "Wait, what?"

"We can go out, hang out, talk."

"No." She shook her head quickly. "I mean, that's all great. We can do that some time too, but I want to have sex. Right now. Here. Tonight."

He worked on just breathing. He gritted his teeth. He was painfully aware of the warm silkiness of the skin on the back of her hand. Had he ever really been aware of that part of a woman's body before? But it made him want to run his hands over every inch of warm silky skin she had. Every. Inch.

"I'm not going to be a gentleman, Peach," he said, his voice tight. "You have one more chance to make this something else."

"Something else like what?"

"A work relationship only. A friendship."

"But you said you wanted me," she said, looking worried suddenly. "You said that was part of what you wanted out of the deal."

He nodded. "I changed my mind. I'll do the project anyway."

"The money is more than you expected?" she asked.

"That's not…" He swallowed hard. "That's not what I mean. I realized I don't want you getting naked just to get the building done. The building and you being in my bed aren't related, okay? Tell me you get that."

"I get that."

"You know that when I make you scream, it's just about that. It's about fucking, not business. The building is separate."

She nodded.

"Say 'I know', Cilla," he said roughly. His heart was pounding, and his entire body was hot and tight. He'd never been worked up like this about fucking another woman. He enjoyed it. A lot. He definitely got hot. He anticipated it when it took a few dates to get there. But he never felt like his skin was on fire, his palms never tingled with the need to touch, his chest never ached with need.

Priscilla looked him directly in the eyes and said, "I know." Clear, confident, without even blinking.

"And you want it?"

God, he wanted to hear her say it. That she wanted it. She wanted his hands on her, his mouth on her, his body against and inside of hers.

Her hand fisted his shirt and she went up on tiptoe, her body rubbing against his as she put her mouth against his. "I want *you*."

That was it. He'd given her the chance to pull away, to end this, to walk out.

She hadn't taken it.

She was now his.

CHAPTER
NINE

JASE GAVE A LITTLE GROWL, took her face in his hands, and kissed her.

Kissed her.

His mouth was hungry and hot, and he wasted no time sweeping his tongue into her mouth. She felt everything his mouth did to hers in her pussy. She was already wet. She wanted to think it was from seeing him working, his hair rumpled, sawdust on his face and clothes, his big hands handling the tools, his back, arm, and shoulder muscles bunching under his t-shirt. Yes, she'd paused when she'd first walked in and found him working.

Or maybe it was the way he'd said, "I'm not renovating the building so I can fuck you." Specifically, the words "I can fuck you."

She loved the gritty language and the gruff tone of his voice. No one talked to her like that.

But she was pretty sure the wet panties, along with the aching need and the itchiness that seemed to be deep in her skin, had a lot more to do with remembering how nice he'd always been to her. Almost protective. And then, of course, the fact that he'd now separated the business stuff from the sex. She didn't know what had changed his mind, but she thought maybe it was the reminders of their history and that they'd been kind-of-sort-of-maybe friends long before he'd put his tongue in her pussy.

That was all nice. Really nice. Amazing even.

But she really wanted his tongue in her pussy again.

She slid her hands into his hair and just surrendered to the kiss. His hands held her still, and he was clearly in charge. She was fine with that. She didn't know what she was doing anyway, and a guy like Jase, with *a lot* of experience and testosterone rolling off of him like heat radiating off of the pavement in July, was not someone she could hope to keep up with. He would want things from her that she wouldn't understand until he showed her. Or told her.

Oh, man, she wanted to hear him *telling* her all of the dirty things he wanted.

He just kept kissing her though. It was deep and hot, dirty in its own right. His tongue stroked against hers in a rhythm that was very similar to the way his fingers had stroked her earlier on the patio.

But she wanted more. She slipped her hands under the edge of his shirt. She wanted skin, and she wanted to feel the muscles she'd been ogling.

He shuddered as she ran her hands over his abs and then up his sides. The muscles jumped under her touch, and she felt a similar shiver go through her. The power of knowing she could affect him was heady.

He pulled back then, staring down at her.

"Take your clothes off," he rasped.

"Here?" But that was a dumb question. He'd already told her about his intentions regarding her orgasms and this building. Plus, it was clear from the look in his eyes that he was about to ravish her.

She. Wanted. That.

"Here," he said firmly.

And just like that, she didn't care about the future functions that would be here, the sweet community events, or even family celebrations, that would take place here, and the fact that she would absolutely be thinking about Jase.

She stepped back and started unbuttoning her shirt.

His eyes darkened as he watched her. He didn't reach out to help, didn't say a thing. He just watched her.

As soon as she undid the bottom button, she shrugged out of her shirt. It was silk. Pale pink. But she didn't care that she was ruining it as she let it drop to the dirty floor.

She reached for the zipper on her skirt, pulling it down and pushing the expensive black fabric to the floor. It might be salvageable. But she had a dozen black skirts. She'd be fine without that one.

She stood in front of him in only her white, silk bra and panties. They weren't an exciting color. They weren't high cut or low cut for that matter. The bra wasn't even a pushup bra. She hadn't dressed for a seduction this morning.

She'd never dressed for a seduction.

But at the moment, with Jase's hot gaze on her, she felt like a goddess.

She started to step out of her shoes, but he stopped her.

"Leave them on."

His voice was gravelly, and her gaze dropped to his fly. He was clearly hard, and she felt a rush of power go through her.

"Let me see your gorgeous tits, Peach," he said.

His fists were clenched at his sides, and he was breathing a little faster. But he didn't reach out and didn't make a move to take any of *his* clothes off. That was how it had been ten years ago. She'd felt him through his clothes, but she hadn't gotten to touch any bare skin.

"Take your shirt off," she said.

He narrowed his eyes. "I told you to do something first."

Yeah, she liked his bossiness. That was probably a bad thing, considering how independent and strong and confident she wanted to be. Or she wanted to project it, anyway. But this was Jase. And it was temporary.

Still, she reached behind her and undid the tiny hooks on her bra. But she paused.

"Come on, let me see some skin, Hawkins."

He looked at her for a long moment, as if weighing how to handle this. Finally, he reached over his head, causing his shirt to climb up his abs.

God, he was ripped. Construction was a very physical job, and he probably didn't even have to go to the gym to keep in shape. But however he'd gotten that six pack, she wanted to lick every single groove and bump.

He grasped his shirt between his shoulder blades and pulled it off.

He was tanned and hard everywhere. He clearly worked without a shirt on a lot of the time. Her mouth watered.

"Take that fucking bra off," he nearly growled.

She let it fall down her arms. Her nipples immediately got harder as he drank her in.

She had never felt sexy like this. Not since that night in the Sunday school room, and, even then, it hadn't been like this. He hadn't been standing five feet away watching her. He'd been right up against her, his hands all over her. This felt different. A lot more intentional. Like she had a choice at every step to stop it all.

Not that she couldn't have stopped things back then. Jase would have never pushed her. But she'd been caught up in sensations, the feel of his touch, his kisses, the risk of it, the naughtiness of it.

No one was going to interrupt them here. No one would believe she was here in the first place. And if they did find out she'd been out here, they would assume it was about business.

What had been going on inside that classroom would have been a lot harder to lie about.

"Damn you're beautiful," he said, almost as if to himself.

She swallowed. She felt jumpy and tingly. Her skin *needed* to be touched. She ran her hands over her stomach, needing *something*. Without thinking, she moved to cup her breasts. Her nipples ached and she squeezed one. It shot heat to her clit but also helped ease the throbbing a little.

"Jesus," Jase muttered.

"Are you okay?"

He looked like he was in pain, actually.

"I can't decide if I should make you stop that or encourage you to keep going."

Oh, watching her play with her nipple was having a nice effect on him. For a second, she thought maybe she should be embarrassed about touching herself, but then she plucked and rolled her nipple, and he gave the most delicious groaning sound.

She really liked that cause and effect. She did it again.

"Panties off," he said.

"How about you take something else off?" She suddenly had the urge to see him standing there, stroking his cock.

She'd never had any urge like that before. She rarely, if ever, thought about men's cocks, honestly. And the idea of just getting to stand and take a good long look at one, especially as the guy touched himself, should have made her flush with embarrassment.

And she was flushed. But it wasn't from awkwardness. It was pure heat and desire.

"What do you want to see, Peach?" he asked.

Again, he was practically reading her mind. She must have been incredibly transparent.

"All of you," she told him honestly. "I want to see you stroking yourself, like this." She played with a nipple again.

He didn't say anything, but he unzipped. The front of his jeans parted, and she could easily see the hard ridge behind the boxers he wore.

"This what you want?" he asked. He put a hand in the front of his boxers, clearly running his palm down his shaft.

"I want to see it," she said.

On impulse, she ran her hand down her stomach and into her panties.

His jaw clenched watching her.

She was so hot and wet. Again, she should have been embarrassed, maybe, but she felt nothing except for the need to make this man crazy.

The pad of her middle finger glided over her clit, and a mixture of relief and need shot through her. "Oh," she said softly.

"Fuck." Jase had now taken his cock in his fist, and he gave it a stroke.

But his eyes were glued on the front of her panties.

"Show me," she told him. She would have liked to sound like that was a demand, rather than a plea, but that was definitely more of a begging tone.

He pushed his jeans down to rest low on his hips and pulled his cock out of the front of his boxers.

He was huge. Not that she had anything to really go by. But seriously, the idea of taking that inside of her made her eyes widen. But her inner bad girl quickly overrode any question of how that was going to work. *Oh, hell yes*, was *her* reaction. Jase would make this work and it would be amazing.

The assuredness of that thought made her push her panties to the floor and step out of them, closer to him.

"Show me how wet you are," he ordered.

She slid her finger between her legs again, over her clit, and then lower, where she was hot and achy. She definitely touched herself, so this wasn't brand new. Doing it while someone was watching her was, though. She couldn't imagine doing this with anyone else. But with Jase, it just felt hot and good.

She slipped her finger just inside, a shiver going through her, pulling her nipples tighter.

"Show me." His voice was even deeper now.

She withdrew her finger, but, before she could do anything—she wasn't even sure what she was going to do—Jase circled her wrist and lifted her hand toward his lips. His gaze was locked on hers as he drew her finger into his mouth.

She almost came right then. Her pussy clenched, and she felt a wave of pleasure wash through her.

He sucked softly on her finger, and she heard a little moan that she realized came from her. Then he lowered her hand to his cock.

Instinctively, she wrapped her fingers around him just above his own fist. He was hard as steel, huge in her hand. The skin was smooth, and so hot. She watched as he stroked up and down his shaft with one hand, moving her hand with the other.

This was so damned hot.

"Squeeze me, Peach," he said.

She did.

"Harder."

"I don't want to hurt you." She lifted her eyes to his.

His eyes were almost black, and his gaze burned as he looked at her.

"You're not going to hurt me. Squeeze my cock, Cilla," he said gruffly.

She squeezed harder and then moved her hand up and down without any guidance.

"Fuuuck," he said through gritted teeth.

Suddenly she wanted to taste him. It was the strangest urge. She didn't really think about it or if it was something he'd want—though, of course, she knew guys loved blow jobs. It was just this sudden need to have that hot length in her mouth. She wanted to feel him that way.

But he caught her as she started to sink to her knees.

"Oh, hell no."

Her gaze flew to his. "I want you in my mouth."

He gave a rough laugh. "You'll kill me. Or I'll hurt you. I'm too wound up for that."

"But—"

"Would that be your first time sucking cock, Peach?" he asked.

She loved when he talked dirty like that. She nodded.

"Then we need to take the edge off before I fuck your mouth."

Her pussy clenched. "How?"

"I need to be inside you."

"You won't hurt me that way?" She wasn't worried, at all. She loved teasing him.

He pulled her close until her belly was against his cock. "Your pussy can take me better than your mouth."

"You sure?"

"I'll *make* sure."

Then he picked her up, bent and grabbed his shirt, then hers, from the floor, and stalked toward the bar. She wrapped her arms and legs around him, hanging on, loving the way his big hands cradled her ass and the way he could carry her so easily.

He put her shirt on the bar, trying to spread it out with one hand. She reached to help him. He deposited her on top of it. That was sweet. He was keeping her bare butt from the dirty bar top. It was definitely going to ruin her shirt, but that had already happened.

He lifted his shirt to his face, wiping sawdust and dirt from his cheeks and jaw.

Then he dropped the shirt beside him, put a hand on each of her knees, and spread her legs.

Okay, so this was new. He'd had his mouth on her ten years ago, but she'd been standing, pressed against the wall, with her skirt hiked up and her panties pulled to one side.

She hadn't been *bared* like this and definitely not spread out where he could see every single inch.

"I've been craving you since I saw you standing here this morning," he said.

He looked so damned reverent as he studied her. He reached a finger out and ran it over her clit, but then pulled away just as the sensations went coursing through her.

"Jase! Don't stop," she protested.

"My hands aren't clean enough to be inside you," he said. "But I can make do with other things."

Then his mouth was on her, licking and sucking, eating at her just like the peaches he claimed to like so much.

His stubble brushed over her inner things and the crease of her hip. His tongue was magic against her clit, flicking and stroking. He sucked on her clit, and her hips lifted, trying to get closer. He moved lower, thrusting in and out of her. Then he returned to her clit and licked and sucked again.

It only took about three minutes of that to send her flying over the edge into a toe-curling orgasm.

She called out his name and felt his hands squeeze her thighs in reaction.

Before the ripples of pleasure had even started to fade, he lifted her off the bar to the floor. He kissed her deeply, stroking her tongue the way he'd just licked her.

Then he turned her to face the bar. "Hands on the edge," he said gruffly. "Brace yourself."

She heard the crinkling that indicated he was donning a condom, and she worked on just breathing.

His big palm coasted over the curve of her ass. "You are so fucking good, Peach," he said. "You taste amazing, you feel incredible, the sounds you make are driving me crazy."

She arched her back. "Good."

His hand came around and cupped one breast, his fingers teasing her nipple. The currents of pleasure built again, and she felt her inner muscles clench. He rolled her nipple as he kissed her neck and down her shoulder, and then he pinched it. Hard.

"Jase!"

She gasped, but it didn't cause pain so much as an acute stab of desire.

"Spread your legs a little and bend forward."

She did, feeling wanton. He was going to take her from behind. This felt dirtier than if he'd just put her against the wall, face to face. His hands skimmed over her ass again and then she felt the hard length of his cock against her butt.

"Tell me you're okay," he said against her neck. "Tell me you're ready."

She wiggled her ass against his cock. "I'm so ready, Jase."

His fingers dug into her hips slightly and then she felt the tip of his cock at her entrance. Jase bent his knees and then surged upward, sliding into her.

It was a very tight fit. And *oh god*, she'd never felt something so good in her life. There was a little pain, like a deep muscle stretch, and fire licked along her limbs. Goosebumps tripped up and down her body and she forgot to breathe for a second. Or ten.

"Holy hell, Pris," he said, just stopping and breathing hard against her shoulder. "Holy. Fucking. Hell."

"Are you okay?" She was nearly panting.

"So okay." He gave a gruff laugh. "Jesus, I've maybe never been better."

She was so *full*. She'd known the mechanics, of course, and she'd felt the need for this. She'd been mentally prepared, mostly, for what this would be like. But wow, she'd really had no way of knowing how it would be.

"This is…" She didn't have a word. It was pain and pleasure and made her feel weak and powerful at the same time.

"Hold on, girl," he said. "Hold on tight."

She curled her fingers into the edge of the bar, taking him at his word.

Then he moved. He pulled out and then thrust back in, making her cry out. It was so, so good.

He moved again. And again. His thrusts were deep and

seemed to light every nerve ending on fire. Her entire world was focused on her pussy. She didn't think that had ever happened before, *ever*. She would have laughed—or died of mortification—if anyone would have ever suggested that she could be reduced to caring only about that one part of her body, about having it filled and stretched. Heat and friction were the only forces she understood or cared about in that moment.

And Jase delivered.

He stroked in and out, thrusting deep, hitting every single spot that she needed him to. It was insane how perfect it all was.

She felt the glimmer of an orgasm, her inner muscles tightening just a bit, wanting more of everything.

But then he started talking.

"I've dreamed of this pussy, Peach," he said, his voice thick. "God, I've thought of you so often. You're so fucking tight. So wet. So hot. You're going to ruin me."

She was not proud of the fact that she thought *hell yeah, I will* when he said that. She didn't even know exactly what he meant by it. She certainly didn't know *how* to do it. And *ruining* someone was very out of character for her.

But yeah, she wanted him ruined. She wanted him dreaming of her, thinking about her, wanting her. She wanted him to remember this forever. She wanted him to never be able to do this with another woman, ever.

Okay, so maybe she did understand ruining him.

Who was she? What was happening?

"That's right, fucking milk me, Peach."

What was she doing? Milking him? But then she felt the way he surged into her again, harder, and the way her muscles tightened around him, clamping down as if to keep him right there, for good.

He took one of her hands from the bar, pressing it to her clit. "Come for me. I can't hold on much longer, Pris. Come for me."

The way he alternated between Cilla, Peach, and Pris got to her. There was familiarity and friendship, almost affection when he called her Cilla. Like most of her friends did. When he called her Peach, it was dirty and an immediate reminder of all the delicious things he'd ever done. Pris was something else. It was a combination of those. It was familiar, but yet a little taboo or something because she didn't let people call her that.

Only him.

It was like a reminder that she let him do a lot of things no one else did with her.

She felt her orgasm suddenly building, as if the waves were gathering energy. She circled her clit and put his mouth to her ear. "I told you your pussy could take me."

She went over the edge. She can't explain why *that* was what did it, exactly, but there was the feeling with Jase that he knew her, knew exactly what she could handle, how to handle *her*, that made her feel hot and taken care of at the same time.

She cried out, her muscles squeezing him hard, and he picked up his pace, thrusting hard and deep and fast until he was calling out her name as well.

"Cilla! Damn, *yes!*"

She slumped against the bar, resting her forehead on her hands, breathing hard. Jase ran his hands up and down her back, then eased out of her. She couldn't even lift her head to see what he was doing as she heard shuffling behind her. But then he was back, wrapping his arms around her and pulling her back against him. Her head fell back against his shoulder, and he kissed her cheek.

"Holy hell," he said again, but this time it was soft and husky.

She smiled. "You know, in retrospect, I'm glad we didn't do that six years ago. It was better I didn't know what I was missing."

He was quiet for a few beats, then he laughed against her neck. "I guess that's one way to look at it."

She pulled in a breath and turned in his arms. She kissed him. "Thanks."

He chuckled. "Ditto."

"Seriously," she told him sincerely. "That was *so* good. Imagining it and reading about it are great, and I thought I knew what to expect, but wow. That was beyond."

"Good," he said slowly.

Then she pulled back and moved toward her clothing, pulling it on one item at a time, aware of his hot gaze watching her.

When she was dressed again, she pushed her hair back over her shoulders and smiled.

"Not that I don't love watching you strip and wouldn't be happy to do the stripping myself this time, but why the hell do you have your clothes back on?"

"Because I need to go."

"Go? We're not done."

His deep, firm voice made heat slide from her belly down to settle between her legs. "I have an early morning tomorrow."

She was actually feeling a little overwhelmed. Good. Very, very good. But overwhelmed. Because something had happened that she'd realized was possible but had shoved aside as a concern. Because she'd been super ready to take her clothes off with Jase.

But, yeah, it turned out that she was the type of girl who had trouble separating sex from deeper feelings. She was the girl who immediately thought she was in love as soon as she had an orgasm with someone. She was the girl who mixed up sex and love and… Jase Hawkins was the subject of all of that.

"Pris, look at me," Jase said, his voice low and firm.

That pulled her eyes to his. She tried to look cool. Like this was no big deal. Like this was just sex and that's what she wanted.

It *was* what she wanted, for sure. But maybe she should have done it with a guy that she hadn't been thinking about for the past ten years. Who wasn't the best guy she'd ever known. Who she hadn't, apparently, fallen for way back in that Sunday school room.

Because yeah, turned out she was the type of girl to fall for the first guy she was intimate with.

"Are you okay?" he asked with a frown.

She was obviously not pulling off the cool-no-big-deal thing. She tried to smile, then she shook her head. "I'm just… a little… shook up."

His frown deepened. "Shook up? What the hell does that mean? Did I hurt you?"

Jase looked legitimately concerned and she couldn't let him think that for one second. She stepped forward and grabbed his arm, squeezing. "No. Definitely not. I'm good. I'm *so* good. It was just…" How could she say this without it sounding like she was a weirdo who thought sex and love were the same thing? "More than I expected it to be."

He was still frowning. "Now, see, typically I'd make a crack about my cock and it being *more*, but, turns out, I'm a little worried here."

Well, that wasn't making her like him any less, that was for sure. He had to be hot and willing to do the project *and* sweet enough to be concerned when she was acting a little weird?

"I'm fine." She waved her hand. "I mean, I'll *be* fine."

He moved in close and took a hold of her arms, dipping his knees to look into her eyes. "Cilla, what's going on?"

Cilla. She swallowed. "Okay, I just… that was *really* good. And I really want to do it again."

"We are very much on the same page about that."

"And I'm feeling very… fond of you. Because of it."

He frowned, then smiled, then shook his head. "You're feeling very *fond* of me because the sex was good."

She nodded. "Yes."

"And that's making you freak out."

"Freak out is a little strong, but I'm feeling a little…"

"Shook up."

"Yes."

"Okay." He squeezed her arms. He paused and took a breath. "So, Pris, I gotta ask you something."

"Okay." She didn't even bother to correct him on her name.

"Were you…" He cleared his throat. "Were you a virgin?"

She blushed hot and hard. Dammit. How had he known that? Had she messed something up? "I… have a vibrator."

Maybe not what she would have answered with if she'd been prepared for the question.

His eyebrows rose. "That's not a no."

"Well, I mean, it depends on your definition."

"Uh, no, it doesn't. There's one definition."

"Well, if you're talking—"

"I'm talking about fucking, Peach," he cut her off. "Sex. Men, live men, doing what I just did to you."

Her cheeks were burning. Which was so stupid considering what they'd just done.

"Oh, well, then yeah." She shrugged, trying to be cool and super chill about it. "That was a first then."

He stared at her. He blinked slowly. Then said, "I just fucked you from behind against my grandpa's bar, and it was your first time?"

She swallowed. That was hot. It shouldn't be. *Fucked* and *against my grandpa's bar* should not cause heat to spiral through her and her very-satisfied-just-a-minute-ago inner muscles to tighten, but it did. She smiled. "Yep. And I really liked it."

He scrubbed a hand over his face, blowing out a breath. Then he narrowed his eyes at her. "You tell a guy that you're a virgin *before* he thrusts, Pris."

She smiled, for real this time. "Well, that's not really going to be an issue now, is it?"

SHE'D BEEN A VIRGIN.

A *virgin.* Holy hell.

That was… hot. It shouldn't be. He should not feel a surge of possessive heat go through him thinking that he'd just been the first guy to sink deep into Priscilla Williams's sweet body and take her over the edge.

But he did. A *very* hot, possessive surge of caveman-like *fuck yeah.*

Still, he was a decent enough guy to realize that this was a big deal. And, her pleas and hard orgasm aside, bent over a bar was not the nicest way for a woman to lose her virginity.

Though Cilla didn't look upset.

She looked thoroughly fucked and very satisfied, as a matter of fact. Her hair was wild, her cheeks were flushed, and her nipples were still hard.

And she was feeling fond of him.

That was unexpected. It made his chest feel tight. Damn.

Jase stepped forward and reached for her hand, pulling her close. "I don't really know what to say," he told her. "Part of me thinks I should apologize but…" He looked into her eyes. "I'm not really sorry."

She gave him a smile and he wondered if she had any idea how sexy she was. "I'm not sorry either."

"Well," he said, running his hands up her arms and into her hair, holding it back as he cupped her head and lowered his mouth. "How about we take this to a soft, horizontal surface and we try it again?"

He didn't want to take her to his bed. How the hell was he supposed to ever sleep in there again without thinking of her, if he fucked her there? And how was he supposed to keep from letting on that he wasn't actually fucking her? That he was—he shuddered a little at the thought—making love to her?

He stayed away from women he thought he could fall for. He didn't ask out perky blonde bakers, or sweet, got-it-together single moms, or women he found funny and interesting.

He chose women who he found attractive but who he knew he could have one conversation with and then be done.

Because of Priscilla Williams.

He'd found out the hard way how devastatingly amazing it could be to make love to a woman he was really into. And yeah, he'd made love to Cilla that night in the Sunday school room. Maybe just with his mouth and fingers, but it had been all about how he felt about her and giving her whatever she needed. In fact, that was why he *hadn't* fucked her. Because she hadn't needed that and… he never would have left Bad. Then one day, at some point, he would have wanted to actually be *with* her, be her boyfriend, take her out, kiss her in public, claim her, *be* claimed *by* her and that would have never happened.

Her grandfather would have had a fit. *His* grandfather would have had a fit. He wouldn't have cared, but Cilla would have. For sure.

He couldn't do that to her and, hell, he couldn't do it to himself. So he'd held back, never let on how he felt about her—other than horny—and left town when his family had.

And he'd never fallen for another woman again.

He knew that, outside of Bad, no one judged him based on his grandfather. No one outside of Bad really knew his grandfather. They'd moved to Georgia, and his grandfather had bartended for a buddy. As far as he knew—and his grandpa wasn't really into hiding his shenanigans—the worst thing Jarvis had ever done there was run a high-stakes poker game. A couple of guys had been beaten up. One guy had ended up in jail. There were rumors about a stolen car and a stolen diamond bracelet. But otherwise, just a card game between friends.

It had been seedy as hell, of course, but no one got riled up like Bad had about The Pork and Peach.

Cilla pulled back out of his arms. "I can't stay," she said.

He lifted a brow. "I'm not nearly done with you yet."

Virgin or not—and they'd taken care of that hadn't they?—he was not about to pass up this opportunity to be with her for as long as he was in Bad.

He had his decent moments, but he wasn't *that* good of a guy.

"Well, I will be back tomorrow," she said. Her gaze dropped to his mouth, and she took a deep breath. "For sure." Her eyes came back to his. "But I have to get up at four a.m., and that means bed by nine and *sleeping* during the night."

Jesus. Four a.m.? She was one of those? She probably went for a run or made gourmet breakfasts. Or both. Getting up that early had to mean time for all of the above.

"Yeah, well, I can promise that if you stay you won't be sleeping," he admitted. He pulled her close and dropped a hand to her ass. "Call in sick tomorrow."

"I can't." But her voice was breathy.

"I'm about to say something I pretty much never say."

Her eyes widened. "Okay."

"Please."

He wanted her. It was a powerful, deep, twisting want in his gut. And his balls. He wanted her again, even knowing that she'd been a virgin fifteen minutes ago.

Okay, partly because she'd been a virgin fifteen minutes ago. He was aware of the not-a-good-guy-all-the-time thing. But dammit, it was the fond-of-him thing too.

"I… have to get up," she said, weakly.

"Skip your run for one morning." he pressed against her, letting her feel how hard he was.

"My run?" She laughed. "I don't run."

"Then what are you getting up at four a.m. for?"

"I… can't tell you."

He cocked an eyebrow. "You can't tell me what you're doing at four a.m.?"

"I don't *want* to tell you."

He chuckled. "At least that's honest." He moved against her, and she sucked in a little breath. "But I really want to know what I'm competing with—and losing to."

She shook her head, put her hands on his chest, and pushed. "Nope. Not telling. *But,*" she added as she stepped back. "I will be here sometime in the late morning after I get a few things done."

Well, at least it wasn't another guy. She wouldn't have been a virgin tonight if she was rolling out of some other man's bed at four a.m.

"You're coming over in the morning?"

"Yeah, I figured I could help you… paint." She frowned slightly. "Or something."

"I'm very far away from being ready to paint anything."

"Then I can help scrub or," she looked around, "sweep."

Yeah. That sounded good. He didn't have high hopes about the preacher's princess granddaughter being a lot of help with manual labor, but he had to admit that he liked the idea of having her around. As much as possible.

Damn, he was in trouble.

"Great. Bring muffins."

She was clearly surprised by his reaction, but she nodded, a little smile curling her lips. "Okay."

"And you probably don't want to wear heels if you're going to be sweeping. Unless you're thinking more about the *something*." He definitely was.

Her smile grew. "I'll be sure to wear appropriate footwear for sweeping."

"But—"

"I'll bring my heels too," she said, with a knowing smile.

Then she actually winked at him, turned on her heel—on those shoes that put her at exactly the right height to fuck against the bar—and left him standing in the middle of The Pork and Peach a little more in love with her than he had been before.

———

However, that was nothing compared to the next morning when, around ten-thirty or so, she showed up. In tennis shoes. With muffins. Wearing a toolbelt.

She also had a pair of red heels dangling from one finger by the straps.

Along with a grin that was all confident, sexy woman.

"You ready to pound some stuff?" she asked, sassy and clearly a little full of herself.

He loved thinking that perhaps last night, and her coming her brains out, had something to do with that.

"So ready." He pulled her into his arms, cupping her ass and kissing her hot and deep.

The heels slipped from her finger to *thunk* on the floor, followed by the sound of the bakery sack hitting the wood as she wound her arms around his neck and arched close, opening her mouth with a little moan.

He took advantage, deepening the kiss and backing her up against the bar. This time her shoulder blades hit the edge rather than her facing it and holding on. Her toolbelt dug into his hip, though, so he lifted his head and looked down at her.

Her cheeks were flushed, her pupils wide, her breathing fast.

"Good morning to you too," she said softly.

"Not as good as it would have been waking up next to your naked body and giving you an orgasm before your first cup of coffee," he told her.

She wet her lips. "Agreed."

"How was your four a.m. appointment?" Yeah, he was still wondering what the hell she'd been up to.

"Same as every other morning," she said.

Telling him nothing.

He nodded and squeezed her ass before letting her go. "Okay, keep your secrets. For now."

She grinned. "So, what's first? Cleaning up, muffins, or sex?"

He did like this side of her. Playful, sexy, openly admitting she wanted more of him. "You're not a little sore?" he asked, his voice dropping lower without him even trying.

He'd been thinking about fucking her all night. He'd been thinking about her being a virgin. He'd been replaying the way she'd responded to him too. The way she'd followed every command, the way she'd stripped for him, the way she'd touched him and cried out his name. She'd been all in. There had been nothing virginal about her, even thinking back. Except for her tight, sweet pussy.

And just like that he was hard.

"I'm sore in a very nice, no-regrets kind of way," she said. She lifted her hand to his face. "And I'm not *too* sore."

He wanted to take her straight to bed and not let her out for days. He pulled in a long breath. He was relieved, he'd admit it. She seemed fine. Great even. Sassy and sexy and not a bit shy or wary.

"Then we'd better eat and clean first," he told her. "Because once I start with you, I won't be done for a very long time."

She gave a little shiver. "Sounds good."

He reached for the muffins and the shoes, setting them all up on the bar. He'd cleaned that off first, scrubbing and sanding, and had been thrilled to find that it was completely salvageable. He was going to have to strip it all down and refinish it, but none of the wood needed to be replaced.

"Coffee?" he asked.

"You have coffee?"

"I absolutely have coffee," he told her, pointing to the Keurig on the counter behind the bar.

"Creamer?" she asked.

"Uh, no."

"I'll bring some tomorrow," she said. "I've had enough this morning anyway, probably."

"How about water?" He moved behind the bar to the mini fridge he'd brought along and plugged in yesterday.

"Sure."

He handed over a bottle and took one for himself.

Cilla dug into the bakery bag, pulling out four muffins. "I didn't know what kind you'd want," she said. "There's blueberry, apple-cinnamon, banana-nut, and chocolate."

He reached for the blueberry. "Any is fine, but, given the choice, I'll leave the chocolate to you."

"Oh good, I was hoping you'd say that." She reached for the chocolate muffin, peeling the paper down from around it.

"I need to get some chairs or stools in here, don't I?" he asked, leaning onto the bar opposite where she had her elbows propped.

"If we're going to make this a regular thing," she said with a nod. "But I bet I could find some. There are probably some stools over at the church."

"We're going to put church stools in here?" he asked with a smirk, in spite of really liking the idea of this being an every-morning thing.

She nodded. "This is going to be the community center. No reason why we can't raid the church storage room to make this all happen."

He would take her word for it. He wasn't so sure that her grandpa would agree, but maybe he was wrong. Maybe he'd be all in on converting The Pork and Peach to a happy, bright, innocent community building.

As Jase ate and watched her take bites by pinching off pieces of the muffin and putting them in her mouth one at a time, he tried to tell himself that he didn't care what Aaron Williams thought. Or what anyone in this town thought. As long as they went for the plan. It would make Cilla happy, and he'd get paid and rid of the building. It was a win-win, and he didn't really care if anyone else was thrilled or not.

But that wasn't entirely true, and it irked him. He shouldn't care what these people thought. He was a grown-assed man who knew who he was and what he believed, and they could fuck off if they were going to hold him up against what they thought of his grandfather.

But there was an undeniable part of him that wanted a chance to show Bad that he wasn't what they thought he was. Not even that he'd changed, but that he'd always been a mostly good guy, like all the other guys his age, and that his grandfather's actions and reputation weren't about him.

"Where'd you get that toolbelt?" he asked her, finishing off his muffin.

She grinned. "It's mine."

"Come on." He looked pointedly at her pale pink manicure.

"It is," she said. "I can't do plumbing—because gross—or electrical—because I'm scared of electrocuting myself—but I can pound and drill and screw."

She looked so proud of her pseudo-euphemisms, that he just grinned. "Yeah, you can."

Cilla looked up at him from beneath her lashes. "I don't know. I think you did most of the work last night. But I'm willing to try to make up for it."

Then she put a finger to her mouth and licked chocolate muffin crumbs from it.

Holy hell, he loved flirtatious, sexy Priscilla.

"I'll take you up on that," he told her. He wasn't going to laugh that off. He wasn't going to turn down one single thing from this woman. She wanted to play? Oh, they were going to play.

"Yeah?" Her eyes actually lit up.

He might be creating a monster here. He certainly fucking hoped so.

"Oh, yeah." He leaned in. "So, you never let another cock into your pussy." He also loved talking graphically to her because it made her lips part and her throat flush. "But you ever take one in your mouth?"

She took a little breath and then blew it out, shaking her head.

He liked that. A lot. "Never sucked anyone off?"

"Never."

"What do you let guys do, Peach?" he asked. It was none of his business, but he really wanted to know and had no qualms about asking. She could tell him to go to hell if she wanted to.

"Kiss me," she said. "Touch my breasts."

She stopped there and he waited for a few seconds. She was done talking though, it seemed. He frowned. "When was the last time someone touched your breasts?"

"A while," she admitted.

"I—" He had no idea what to say. She'd let him do so much. Everything. *Almost everything* his cock reminded him, very excited about the idea that she'd never given a blow job, but that she might want to. "Why me?" he finally had to ask.

She chewed on her bottom lip, watching him. "Because you don't treat me the way the other guys around here do," she finally said. "All I have to do is say, 'um' and they stop."

His frown deepened. "I would never push you, Pris. If you want to stop, you say it."

She nodded. "Exactly. You would stop. I know that. But you'd make me say it. You'd make me be sure I *didn't* want something as much as making sure I did. And you…" She took a breath. "I don't know. It feels like you can read me or something. I mean, I'm new to this stuff and I think there's a lot I want to explore, but, of course, I'm going to be a little unsure, and you seem to know when you can push me and what I'll like, even before I know it."

Wow. He probably should have felt a sense of pressure or trepidation at that, but he didn't. He really fucking didn't. He loved it, in fact.

"Peach, I'm going to show you everything you already think you'll like and a whole lot of stuff that you haven't even imagined."

She gave him a smile that he knew she had no idea was the sexiest one he'd ever seen.

"Thank you."

He almost laughed. "My pleasure. My absolute pleasure." He grabbed her empty muffin wrapper and tossed it in the trashcan. "Okay, let's get to work."

"I'm ready."

He was starting to realize that Cilla was pretty much up for anything. That was a huge turn-on as well. Everything about this woman turned him on.

He was definitely in trouble.

He got Cilla busy sweeping on the other side of the room from where he was tearing down drywall. Having some space seemed like a good idea. He wanted to back her up against the nearest firm surface and forget about all of the dirt and soot. But, while he could stretch his timeline in Bad, he couldn't just not work at all. He needed to do this for her. And his grandfather.

He drove his sledgehammer through the damaged portion of drywall that he needed to tear out. Honestly, this was a fantastic job for the moment. He could work off some of his tension with the wall instead of the hot blonde he wanted to press up against the wall.

He'd only gotten about three blows in when a loud voice boomed through the room.

"You bastard."

He swung toward the door.

CHAPTER
ELEVEN

IT WAS CARTER AND JACKSON. Two of his best friends. Jase felt the grin spread wide across his face as he let the hammer swing to the floor.

"Holy shit, what are you guys doing here?"

"Seriously?" Jackson asked, his boots clomping across the hardwood floor. "You've been in town for over twenty-four hours, and you haven't even texted? You're such a dick." He held out his hand.

Jase took it and they shook before Jackson pulled him in for a bro hug.

"How the hell did you know I was here?" Jase asked after Jackson had thunked him on the back in that universal sign between guys that said *I care about you but I'm not going to actually say that or anything.*

"Carter ran your plates the first day you rolled into town," Jackson said. He grinned. "You didn't really think you'd get to go incognito here, did you?"

"Carter?" Jase asked, looking at the other man. Then realized what that meant. "You're a *cop* now?"

"Yep. Old Jerry finally retired," Carter confirmed.

Jase chuckled. Carter had gotten in as much trouble as the

rest of them and the idea that he was a cop, especially in Bad, was hilarious. Jase shook his head. "I figured some of the old guys at the 4-Way saw a strange truck with out-of-state plates and had to know who it was."

Carter nodded. "Imagine our surprise to find out that our *friend* was back in town without saying a word."

Jase ran a hand over the back of his neck. "Sorry. I was gonna call."

"Uh-huh."

"I was. Things have been a little… crazy."

He cast a glance in Cilla's direction but didn't see her in the corner where she'd been working.

Had she ducked out of sight? Because of the guys? Jase frowned. What the hell? She didn't want them to know she was here? It would have been one thing if she'd been undressed, and they'd been fucking on the sawhorses. Not that he would have been apologetic, exactly, but he could have understood her not wanting them to see her like *that*. But to not want to be seen here at all?

"Uh, yeah, I'd say this is a little crazy. Holy shit, this place is a disaster," Jackson said, looking around. "We came out and fucked around a little bit a few weeks after the fire, but that was a long time ago. I forgot how bad it was."

"We got our *asses* chewed for that too," Carter said, also checking things out. "My dad almost had a stroke screaming at us for being stupid."

Jackson nodded. "I thought we were dead for sure."

"Yeah, I get it. But the building is stable," Jase told them. "I've done a full check. The damage is mostly interior and superficial, so it looks worse than it is."

"Good news. That will make fixing it up easier too," Jackson said, clapping his hands together. "So where do you want us to start?"

Jase looked at him in surprised. "Start with what?"

"With helping out," Jackson said.

"You're going to help me clean the place up?" Jase asked, just to be sure he was understanding correctly.

"Why not?"

"He's been here helping Coach out with his cattle since Coach's heart attack. Even helped put up fences and repair the barn," Carter said, clapping Jackson on the shoulder. "There were only two instances of bloodshed."

Jase knew both Jackson and Carter had headed out of Bad after graduation. He hadn't been aware either of them had come back or that Coach Karr had had a heart attack. He'd missed a lot, it seemed. It was time to catch up.

"Well, great," Jase told them. "Blood isn't even going to show up on this floor, so hey, I'm happy to have you help, and if you lose a finger or two, no one will even know."

"Oh, *some* people will know," Jackson said, wiggling his eyebrows.

Jase grinned. "Because you might actually drop a football for once in a pick-up game amongst the old-timers?"

Jackson had been the star running back on the championship football team their senior year. Until he'd been suspended. Still, Jase didn't think he'd ever seen Jackson Brady drop a ball. At least not literally.

Jackson laughed but flipped him off with one of those fingers. "I have a lot of fun with these fingers and there's a bunch of ladies who will gladly confirm that I know what to do with them."

Jase had expected exactly that response. He rolled his eyes, but he had to admit having these guys here was nice. He'd missed them, and he hadn't even realized it until they'd walked in with their cockiness, humor, and, yes, toolboxes.

"Well, some of the ladies like body parts other than just fingers," Jase said to Jackson. "So you'd better keep the power tools over on that side of the room."

He pointed toward the wall where he'd planned to rip out and replace the drywall. Now that he'd seen the building plans for the Community Center, he was going to tear the wall down and move it about eight feet out so he could wall off three smaller rooms for meetings and such.

"You might be good with hands-on stuff," Carter said. "But I'm not so sure about power saws."

"You were the one just talking about how much help I was with the barn," Jackson protested, brandishing the power saw.

"You'll remember I also mostly took advantage of your strength to make you hold things up and push and pull shit," Carter said.

Jackson definitely didn't look like he'd lost much muscle mass in the years since high school.

"Hey," Jackson said, clearly remembering exactly what Carter had just said. "You kept me *away* from the tools on purpose?"

"For footballs or bar fights, you're my guy," Carter said. "Branding irons and drills? No."

"Why the fuck not?" Jackson let the saw swing down to his side.

"Because you don't have any fucking dexterity, man," Carter said. "Fine motor skills. Precision. We always just gave you the ball and trusted you would barrel over or through anyone who got in your way."

Jackson thought about that. Then nodded. "That's fair."

Jase was loving this. He'd definitely missed these guys.

"So, I should knock down that wall that Jase is working on?" Jackson asked.

Carter grinned. "I definitely think you should knock down that wall."

Jase laughed. That would be awesome. He loved demolition sometimes. It was a great way to work off steam. But he loved putting stuff back together more. He liked making stuff look good again. Rebuilding. Refinishing. Retouching. That was his thing.

"I'm going to get to work on the floor behind the bar," he said. He looked around. God, there was so fucking much work to do. Thankfully, the only flooring that needed more than just a good scrubbing was that stretch behind the huge wooden bar.

"You refinishing the bar or taking it out?" Carter asked.

"Refinishing." He could definitely leave the bar in. The building plans included a main room where events could include meals and cocktails. Like wedding receptions.

Immediately his mind went back to the moment when Cilla had realized that she'd be here for those types of events. And that one of them might be hers someday.

He clenched his fist and forced a breath in and out. He had no business being irritated or jealous over that. It was a very safe assumption that Priscilla would get married someday. He didn't have to like something to acknowledge it was true.

And if *he* wasn't going to marry her, then why did he care who did?

But he did care. The guy better be worthy of her. He'd better see all the fire and creativity and humor and the big heart underneath her cool demeanor. She came off as in charge and put together, but there was more depth there.

She had come up with a pirate and mermaid theme for the swimming pool, including little cakes with gold coins on top. The look on her face when she'd been telling him about it had been bright and happy. Until she'd remembered that she wasn't supposed to be proud of something like that. It had been obvious that she'd thought she was getting carried away telling him about it and had shut the excitement down.

Her mom and grandfather had done a number on her. Jase didn't know her father but he'd definitely heard about Rex Williams. He'd caused a *huge* scandal when his mistress had moved to Bad. And she hadn't just moved in and kept a low profile. Oh, no, Dixie Donovan didn't understand the concept of low profile.

Which had been a problem for Rex. And his wife. And his father. And his daughter.

Not to mention Dixie's daughter, Brooke. Brooke had been in

their class in high school too. It had been quite the drama to have the daughter of one of the richest, most influential men in town and the daughter of his mistress sitting next to one another in algebra class.

Needless to say, Priscilla and Brooke hadn't been close.

And suddenly Jase was wondering about Brooke. And Jonathan, her high school boyfriend and Priscilla's cousin. And how her friends, Sabrina, Luke, and Marc, were and where everyone was now.

He hadn't cared about Bad. Or so he'd told himself. And now, within twenty-four hours, he was hoping for a damned class reunion.

Jase shook his head. And Priscilla could probably pull one together with a few hours' notice. If she could come up with mermaid cakes for the swimming pool, he'd love to see what she'd do for a class reunion.

Yeah, whoever she married better think that was awesome and encourage her to be fun and creative and enjoy her work.

"Okay, I'm on it," Carter said, pulling his focus back to the job at hand. He pulled his phone out.

"Thanks." Jase watched Carter put his phone to his ear.

"Hey, can you come over to The Pork and Peach?" He paused. "Yes, seriously." He paused again. "Yes, there's beer in it for you." Another pause. "Fine, that too. Bring your tools and truck. But definitely bring Mitch and Zeke."

Carter tucked his phone away and looked up. He met Jase's questioning gaze.

"Some other guys are coming to help."

"Who was that?"

"Zander Landry," Carter said.

Jase frowned. Zander Landry was from Autre. Autre was Bad's biggest rival. And Zander had definitely been one of the guys who was a part of that. Besides being a football player, he was also a hell-raiser. They'd partied and fought and tried to one-up the Landry boys for years. And yes, other Autre guys too, but there were a hell of a lot of Landrys.

"Seriously?"

"He's the cop over there now," Carter said with a grin.

Jase shook his head. "No way." Zander being a cop was as funny—maybe funnier—than Carter being one.

"Yep. So we've gotten to know each other better. We've all grown up. Some," he added with a grin. "And his brother, Zeke, has a construction business and his cousin, Mitch, can fix or build just about anything."

Jase definitely remembered Zeke, Zander's twin brother, and Mitch, their cousin. Again, there were a hell of a lot of Landrys, and they were all within just a few years of one another.

"And they're coming over? Just like that?"

Carter shrugged. "Yeah."

Jase didn't know how to react to that. "They don't have jobs?"

"Of course. But they'll want in on the gossip over here. They'll love having the first-hand account of what's going on with The Pork and Peach," Carter said.

"Their grandma still own the bar in Autre?"

"Ellie? Absolutely," Carter said with a grin. "She'll outlive us all."

The matriarch of the Landry family was something. She was intimidating and took no shit, but she was impossible not to like. Jase didn't know her well, but he knew his grandfather had. Ellie and her husband, Leo, and their friends and family had been on the bayou as long as Jarvis had, and Jase would guess they could all tell stories about one another that went way back.

And unlike the people in Bad, folks from Autre tended to stick around. Or come home. They didn't scatter the way the people here did. Their roots seemed deeper and stronger.

Jase felt a pang. He wanted roots like that, and he'd always wanted them in Bad. Bad was home. For better or worse. It was a little grittier, a little rougher around the edges than Autre maybe.

There were a few darker and more dramatic stories here. But it was still where his friends and memories were.

"I'm redoing this as the new community center," Jase suddenly blurted.

"No shit." Jackson looked around. "Why?"

"Cilla Williams was out yesterday." Why he didn't tell them she'd just been here, he wasn't sure. "We got to talking about what I was going to do with the place, and she suggested it."

"What *were* you going to do with it?" Carter asked.

"Fix it up and sell it." He shrugged. "Figured I might as well sell it to Bad."

Carter nodded. "Makes sense. It's a good idea. It's great that they went for it."

"You're surprised?" he asked him. Carter knew the town now better than he did.

Carter shrugged. "A little. I mean, it *is* a good idea. The building is already here and all. But, our sweet hometown isn't quite as sweet as it lets on, and I think people hold pretty big grudges here."

Jase frowned. Carter was right. He wondered how Cilla had gotten everyone on board. He'd thought maybe things had changed around here. He'd figured the men in town who had been regulars at The Pork and Peach had made a vow of silence with one another a long time ago, and getting rid of The Pork and Peach would actually help them forget about the debauchery of their younger years.

Maybe that's what had happened. But now he had a niggling doubt.

He looked around. "You think this will work?" he asked.

There was a lot of work to do and if this was going to fall through, he wasn't going to waste his time. He'd do whatever Cilla needed and wanted him to do. He understood that this was important to her because she thought she had something to prove. But maybe they were both wasting their time here.

"Let's make it work," Jackson said. "We'll all pitch in to fix it up and show the town that *we* think it's a good idea. We're the people that are going to be using the place for weddings and shit, right? Our kids will be the ones with the birthday parties here and stuff. None of us ever came to The Pork and Peach. Over time, the fact that it was a strip club once a long time ago will just be a funny story people tell."

Jase's chest felt a little tight. Jackson was right. Or he should have been right, anyway. Things could change. Old habits and past grievances should be allowed to die. Jase had driven into town telling himself that he didn't care about his reputation here, or the fact that no one would want him here or to see this building revived.

But he'd been lying to himself.

This was his home. And, until he'd been older and truly understood his grandpa's business and why people didn't like it, he'd just been a Bad boy who loved running around and raising hell and having fun with his friends, playing ball, going to school, doing normal kid things.

When he'd really started to understand that his grandfather was not just a grumpy old man but that he was actually looked down on by a lot of the town, and that the people of Bad didn't want the business, or even the family, here, it had hurt. A lot.

Jase had felt like a part of Bad. He'd felt at home here.

Until one day he hadn't.

It was about the time that the other kids his age were old enough to understand what went on at The Pork and Peach.

Their parents or their naivete, or both, had kept them from really getting what The Pork and Peach was. That had been true for him as well. He'd known it was his grandpa's restaurant, but he didn't go to The Pork and Peach. He didn't care. Just like kids didn't really care or understand what it meant that their dad was an accountant or an engineer or a banker. There was a surface-level understanding that grandpa's building served food and drinks, and Jase knew that Jarvis didn't like most of the people in Bad, especially Pastor Williams. But none of it had really sunk in any further than that.

Then, when he was about twelve, one of the boys in their class asked if Jase ever got to see the naked ladies at his grandpa's place.

Everything had changed.

He'd been embarrassed and shocked by his grandfather's business—and his absolute unapologetic attitude about it—and Jase had felt stupid for not knowing anything about it to that point.

So he'd put up a shield. He'd pretended he didn't care. He was blasé about naked women dancing in front of his grandpa every night. He was unaffected by something as normal as nakedness and sexuality.

But he'd hated every bit of it.

His friends had never treated him like an outcast. He'd still been a contributing member of the football team, still had friends, still had dates. But he'd pulled away. He knew that there were parents in town who worried about their kids hanging out with him. That the kids might sneak into The Pork and Peach or maybe they thought the strippers hung out at the house in between shows. All he knew was that people disapproved of everything his family did.

He was constantly on the edge of feeling hurt and embarrassed and resentful.

Priscilla Williams liking him, inviting him to her house for tutoring, and then wanting him to kiss her, to touch her, to get that close to her, had felt amazing.

If a girl like Cilla could like him, he figured he wasn't a totally lost cause.

Then the fire had happened, and his life had been turned upside down.

Leaving town had been a bit of a relief. There was no longer the cloud of The Pork and Peach hanging over his head. He could start fresh with no one knowing—or caring—about Jarvis Hawkins being his grandfather.

But fuck, he'd missed it.

And now, son-of-a-bitch, he couldn't help but feel the little bubble of hope in his chest. Maybe restoring the place really was his chance at a new reputation, a chance to make 'Hawkins' into something other than a word people said with their noses scrunched up. Maybe Cilla was right.

He shouldn't care about his reputation and what people here thought.

But, fuck… he shouldn't care about Cilla dancing with her future husband in this building either.

But he did.

"Okay," he finally said to Carter and Jackson. "I would love the help and I'd love a chance to make this a place people are willing to come."

"I've got tools in the truck," Carter said. "Be right back."

Jase watched them go, trying to tamp down the surge of optimism he felt. Reconnecting with old friends and doing some repairs to his reputation was nice. But this didn't change his plans. There had been a time when he'd wanted to come back to Bad. To stay. He wanted to live in a place where he had roots and history. A place where he felt like he was a part of everything. But he shouldn't have to fight for that. No matter how much he appreciated having these guys on his side, it shouldn't be this hard to feel at home in his hometown.

He wasn't sure Bad was worth the angst.

But Cilla is.

That damned voice in the back of his mind reminded him that he was in this because of Priscilla Williams. He could just be cleaning up a building and slapping a FOR SALE sign on it, but now he was all wrapped up in making it into something specific, something important, something that could cause some tension and strife in town. Hell, in his life. He didn't need that. But he was up to his neck because of that woman.

He glanced toward the corner where Cilla had been working again. The woman who had ducked out when Jackson and Carter showed up.

What the hell? No one had to know they were fucking around, but they couldn't know she was here helping? Like Carter and Jackson were? That they were old friends?

He stalked to the window and looked out over the parking lot. Carter and Jackson had both strapped on toolbelts and were pulling a big toolbox out of the back of Carter's truck.

Cilla's car was nowhere to be seen.

She'd left. Just slipped out, as if needing to escape before anyone saw her.

Okay, Peach, he thought. *You just want to make the deal and not let on that you're any more involved than that? That's fine. But you and I both know there's a lot more going on here. And there's no way in hell I'm going to let you forget about it for one second even when you're not here with me.*

He grabbed his phone and typed out a text to her. *Be back here at eight.* He thought for a second. He needed to send something that she'd be thinking about for the rest of the day. *Don't bother wearing any panties.*

Carter and Jackson came stomping back through the door just as he hit send.

"Okay, let's do this thing," Jackson said, setting the toolbox down with a *thunk.*

Jase really was grateful for their help. Cilla looked hot as hell in her toolbelt, and she definitely would have been some help. But these guys wouldn't distract him the way she would, and he would actually be able to make some progress.

Besides, these guys actually had his back.

Cilla just had him by his dick.

Jackson headed for the wall, Carter started checking out the bar, and he got busy on the floor.

"Just so you know, I had no intention of wearing panties—"

He jerked up at the sound of Priscilla's voice.

"Oh, hey, guys."

He straightened from behind the bar.

She was standing inside the back door that led to the patio. She was also blushing.

"You had no intention of wearing panties?" Jackson asked, propping the sledgehammer against his shoulder and giving her a wide grin. "Do go on."

"I didn't know you guys were here," Cilla said, her eyes darting to Jase.

"Stopped by to help Jase out," Jackson said. "We didn't know *you* were here."

"I also stopped by to help Jase," she said, gesturing to her outfit. "But I had to step out to take a call and make a couple of others."

She'd been out on the patio on the phone? Okay, so he'd jumped to conclusions. Big surprise. He'd guessed she wouldn't want people to know she was here. He had some reason for that assumption. Besides the huge chip on his shoulder.

Probably.

Jackson scrubbed a thumb along his jaw. "Huh. Not sure we're helping him out with the same stuff."

Cilla propped a hand on her hip. "I've got a hammer too."

"Yes, you sure do," Jackson nodded. "But *I've* got underwear on."

Her cheeks got red. "So do I." There was a beat, then she added. "Right now, anyway."

Jackson's eyes widened, then he let out a choked laugh. "That's good. Keeps the denim from chafing while you're... using your tools."

Jase stepped around the bar. Time to bail her out. Jackson had always delighted in teasing her. He supposed it was the sweet, preacher's-granddaughter thing. Lord knew that he loved making her blush. She was fucking pretty as hell when she was blushing. And breathing a little harder. With her gorgeous eyes wide and bright with excitement.

But fuck if he wanted Jackson to have any of those effects on her.

"Leave her alone," he said, striding across the floor.

"It's okay," Cilla said. She was actually smiling at Jackson. "I won't take that piece of advice from him too seriously. It's a pretty well-known fact that Jackson's best *tool work* happens when the denim is out of the way."

Jase was hit with a wave of surprise… and lust. He loved flirtatious Cilla. The woman who was confident and feisty. He loved her innocent and sweet and just a bit submissive too, but he liked that side only with him. She could trust him completely. He wanted her strong and sassy with everyone else. He wanted her to stand up for herself and not let people embarrass her or make her feel outmatched.

Like her mother. And grandfather.

And freaking Jackson Brady.

"That's pretty well-known, huh?" Jackson asked. He nodded. "Good."

Yes, as a matter of fact, it was. Jackson had been suspended from the football team because he'd been caught having sex with their student teacher in one of the classrooms. Jackson's reputation was *well* known. By the entire parish.

Cilla laughed and rolled her eyes, her blush gone. Her eyes met Jase's. "I thought it would be just a quick call, but it led to a couple of others, and now I need to go."

He nodded. "That's okay. Of course. You have a lot to do."

"I'm glad Jackson and Carter showed up though. They'll be a lot more help anyway."

"Well… with the stuff that requires panties anyway," Carter said, clearly not able to help himself from getting in on the teasing.

But Cilla just nodded. "Of course. I'd be sorely disappointed if he was into *you* without underwear on."

Jase's eyebrows rose. Not only was she giving the guys shit

right back, but she'd more or less admitted that there was some panty-less stuff going on between her and Jase.

He liked that.

No. He fucking loved that.

"No worry about that," Jase told her.

She gave him a sexy little smile. "I know."

Car doors slammed outside, signaling the arrival of Zander, Zeke, and Mitch Landry.

"I need to go," she said.

"Eight o'clock," Jase told her. She *was* coming back here.

She nodded. "If not before."

"Hey, barbecue at my place tonight," Carter said. "Everyone's coming."

Jase glanced at Cilla. It would be great to see everyone, but he had plans. Plans that were suddenly even more pressing.

Especially against his zipper.

It seemed that this woman turned him on when she was blushing and sweet and innocent, as well as when she was being bold. He needed her under him.

"Can't make it tonight," he said to Carter, his eyes on her.

"Oh, come on! We haven't seen you in forever. Tell him, Cilla. My barbecues are the best."

She looked at Jase. "They really are fun."

"I've got stuff to do," he told her, one eyebrow up.

She nodded, giving him a little submissiveness right then. "I know."

"Oh, knock off early tonight," Carter said. "We'll get this done. Cilla will be there." He looked at her. "Right?"

"Um…"

"Panties optional, Cil," Jackson said with a grin.

"No. They're not," Jase said without even thinking. "And don't call her Cil."

Her eyes went wide. As did Jackson's. And Carter's.

Well, shit.

Jackson nodded. "Ah. Got it."

Jase was pretty sure he did, in fact, get it. Completely. Well, he hoped Cilla didn't mind his friends thinking he had a thing for her because that was now obvious.

An interesting look crossed Cilla's face. It was a combination of heat and pleasure and, if he wasn't mistaken, cockiness.

"Oh, let's go to Carter's for a little bit," she said, stepping toward Jase.

She trailed her fingers up his arm and his entire body tightened.

"We can duck out early," she said. "No one will mind."

Something about her attitude, the look on her face, the fact that she was saying this—and very much standing in his personal space—in front of Carter and Jackson, clued him in immediately.

She wanted to tease him. Play a little at the party. Tempt him. Get him worked up.

He was so onto her. And into her.

She'd never done the flirty, teasing thing before. At least not in high school. He knew that for a fact. He hadn't partied with Cilla in high school, but that was because she hadn't partied. He, on the other hand, had done a lot of it.

The perk—or the drawback—to being Jarvis Hawkins' grandson was that people expected him to be wild. He'd embraced the stereotype for a while. What the hell? It wasn't like his grandpa, or even his mom, could really point fingers and say he was acting immorally or somehow shaming the family. His mom did the books for The Pork and Peach. It wasn't as if she hadn't known everything that went on there and just how lucrative it all was.

The wildest thing Cilla had done on the weekends had been sleepovers with her friends. He was certain Regan had talked her into trying a wine cooler or taking a drag on a cigarette. Regan was totally the type for that. They'd probably talked about boys and all of that. But they'd never snuck out and joined one of the parties he was at, that was for sure. They'd never lied and said they were at the other's house while heading to the river with the rest of them. At least, not the bad boy circle he and Jackson and Carter had run in.

If Cilla had showed up at a party, he would have noticed. And likely would have hovered all night making sure she was safe, wasn't drinking too much, and that none of the guys were getting too close. He probably would've ditched his beer and insisted on taking her home at the end of the night.

He was still pissed that Conner Vanmullen had kissed her at a movie party. Of course, he hadn't been there. He hadn't done things as tame as movie parties. The parties Jackson and Carter and Jase went to included a lot of beer, hard liquor, loud music, sometimes weed, and girls who very much wanted to be kissed.

But yeah, there was no way Cilla had teased and flirted and made out at any parties in high school.

Maybe since then, but… he had a feeling that was a no too.

She wanted that? He'd give her that. Absolutely.

He'd give Cilla anything she wanted.

He nodded. "Fine. We can go for a little while. But we're not staying. And the text from earlier stands." She was going to be there panty-less. For him. And that wasn't a "panties are optional" thing. Panties were forbidden.

Again, only for him.

She pulled her bottom lip between her teeth and nodded.

Submissive. Even while she had his balls clenched firmly in her hand.

Fuck.

She ran her hand down his arm again and then stepped around him and headed for the door.

Zeke, Zander, and Mitch came through the door as she was leaving.

"Hey, Cilla," Zander greeted.

"Hi."

"What are you doing here?"

She glanced back at Jase. "I was here with Jase."

Not "helping Jase," not "meeting with Jase." "Here with Jase." That sounded very… like it was more than business.

Like it was exactly what it had been—them together, eating muffins, flirting, talking dirty, making plans for sex later.

"Awesome. You're not staying?" Zeke asked, holding the door for her.

Yeah, if Cilla had showed up to any of those parties in high school, there was a high likelihood that Zeke Landry would have been one of the guys flirting with her.

And Zander Landry.

And Mitch Landry.

"Can't. But we'll see you at Carter's tonight."

We'll. Not *I'll* see you. We. Referring to her and him.

"Great." Zander turned to them as Cilla stepped outside. When the glass door swung back shut, he lifted a brow. "Guess I don't need to ask what brings you back to town."

Jase just smiled. He was starting to think that it was possible that Priscilla Williams was, indeed, the reason he was here after all.

"Man," Jackson said. "You've got it bad."

Jase nodded. "Yeah."

"Cilla Williams though?" Zeke asked, crossing the floor, toolbox in hand.

Again, Jase simply nodded. "Yeah."

"I did not see that one coming," Carter said.

Yeah, well, that made two—or probably six—of them.

CHAPTER
TWELVE

PRISCILLA STEPPED into the waiting room of The Bad Place, the physical therapy clinic where Regan worked. She particularly loved that name. Ninety percent of the people who went through rehab there agreed it fit.

"Hi, Syd," she greeted the receptionist.

"Hey, Cilla, how are you?" Sydney asked.

"Great. I was hoping Regan maybe had a minute?" She could have texted Regan, but she didn't check her messages when she was with patients and Priscilla really needed to plant this seed right now.

It could have waited. Priscilla knew that deep down. But there was this sense of urgency driving her. She needed to know that everything was going to work out with Jase and the community center. The sooner she had all of her plans working, the sooner she'd feel secure.

Because the way she was feeling for the guy was only getting stronger, and, if he was going to pack up and leave in another week or so, she needed to not get any more attached.

If, however, he was going to stick around for a bit and get the community center put together, she would be more comfortable getting close to him.

She hadn't expected to want to be close.

Well, at least not with their clothes on. But within five minutes of having sex with him, she'd been struck by feelings that went far beyond orgasm endorphins. That fondness she'd confessed to him was part of it. But today, having muffins with him, talking and laughing, seeing his friends show up to help him out without even being asked—and seeing how that obviously touched Jase—had made her realize that she really wanted to see him happy. She wanted to be a part of making him happy.

And when her mother had called to tell her that the city council was not on board with her plan, she'd felt a shockingly strong surge of defensiveness and protectiveness. She wanted Jase to prove them all wrong. And she wanted to help him do it.

So much that she was willing to blackmail people.

She should probably be worried about that, but she wasn't.

She was more worried about the fact that she was probably falling in love with Jase Hawkins.

"She's just finishing up with someone. She probably has five minutes then," Syd said, waving her toward Regan's office. "I'll tell her you're here."

"Thanks." Priscilla always got special treatment from Syd.

Syd was a single mom of a little boy who had some medical issues, worked full-time here, and also helped out at the bar for extra cash. So, whenever she needed treats for school or something for a potluck at church, Priscilla covered her. She baked or made Rice Krispie treats or threw together a casserole. It was no big deal and helped Syd a ton. And then Syd did things like let her sneak in to get an ultrasound on her lower back—or to ask Regan a huge favor—in the middle of the day without an appointment.

Priscilla paced the office Regan shared with her friend and fellow PT, Destiny, as she waited. Her thoughts about Jase wouldn't leave her alone.

She was falling for him.

Or was she?

It was very possible that she'd already fallen for him. Ten years ago.

She had never been that interested in any of the guys she dated here. They were nice enough, but they weren't... whatever Jase was. Exciting? Yeah, maybe that was it. Edgy? Possibly. But Jase was as sweet as he was edgy. Maybe more so. He put the tough, bad boy act on and did it very well, but he was a softy. For her, anyway. And the idea that he was different for her made her feel warm. A lot like she felt when he acted protective. Or when he kissed her. Or even looked like he wanted to kiss her.

"Hey, Cilla."

She swung around as Regan came in. "Hey."

"You okay?"

"Yeah. Well... I mean, physically, yes."

Regan Reynolds was beautiful. Curly dark hair that hung to her shoulder blades, big, warm, brown eyes, slender and toned from yoga and running, a tomboy who didn't take any shit but was kind and funny and loved taking care of her hometown.

She was also incredibly intelligent. And had a very accurate bullshit meter.

"What's going on?" She shut the door.

"I need a favor."

"Okay. Anything."

"Really?"

"Of course."

"I need you to convince the group who's throwing Coach his big party to have it at the new community center. I need you to ask Coach to ask for it, in fact."

Regan shrugged. "Okay."

Wow, it was really nice to have friends who just had your back no matter what.

"Really?"

"If you want it, I'll get it done."

"I love you."

"I love you too."

Priscilla just grinned at one of her favorite people.

Then Regan asked, "What new community center?"

Priscilla worked on just smiling as if everything was totally normal and fine. "The one that Jase Hawkins is remodeling."

Regan lifted a brow.

Regan and Randi were the only two people who knew that she'd had a crush on Jase. Regan had always insisted that it made complete sense. Good girls who had lots of rules governing their lives and lots of expectations to live up to often had a rebellious streak and it was common for them to be attracted to people who were the opposite of them. Friends like Regan—which Regan had always worn as a badge of honor—and guys like Jase.

But not even Regan knew what had happened in that Sunday school room.

"Jase is building the community center?" Regan asked. "How did that happen?"

"Actually…" Priscilla fiddled with the strap of her purse.

"What did you do?" Regan asked.

She sighed. She was evidently easier to read than she thought.

"Jase is remodeling The Pork and Peach," she said, meeting Regan's eyes. "He's fixing it up to finally sell it. I talked him into turning it into the new community center."

Regan's eyes widened. "You're kidding."

"No."

Regan gave her a huge grin. "That's awesome."

Priscilla tipped her head. "Is it? Or is it crazy? Is it hormones and endorphins giving me a false high and making me think stupid plans are amazing just because watching that man swing a hammer makes me happier and hornier than the last romance novel I read?"

So, she guessed she needed to spill her guts to someone. She pressed her lips together, watching Regan process all of that.

"So, he still looks good," Regan surmised.

That was Regan's first reaction to her confession.

Priscilla nodded. "Very."

"And he thinks this is a great idea?"

"He's… willing," Priscilla said. "He was going to fix it up and sell it anyway. This is a sure thing."

Except, it wasn't. Until she blackmailed two of their town's city council members. Two and a half actually. She was fully prepared to blackmail Luke too, but she didn't think she'd need to.

"You sure about that?" Regan asked.

"Which part?"

"Him being willing."

"Why wouldn't he be willing?" Priscilla asked.

"Because he'll have to potentially deal with your mom and grandfather. Not to mention a bunch of other people who might want input. Jase never struck me as the type of guy who wanted a lot of people up in his business." Regan moved toward one of the chairs that faced her desk. She propped her butt against the back of it and studied Priscilla. "So why do you think he's willing to put up with Bad's bullshit?"

She was dressed in khakis, tennis shoes, and a blue polo shirt with *The Bad Place* embroidered on the left breast. She looked completely composed and professional. And completely opposite of the pencil skirts and heels Priscilla wore to look the same way.

Regan was a lot more relaxed, in general, than Priscilla. Probably because her parents hadn't had four million rules and didn't say "Remember, you reflect on our whole family" to her on a regular basis. And right now, Priscilla found her friend's laid-back-it-will-all-be-okay vibe very comforting, as she felt like she was falling apart a little.

"Because of me," she admitted after a few seconds. "He's doing it because I asked him to."

Regan nodded. "And now you need Coach to insist on using the building to prove that it was a great idea."

Coach Karr was like a king in Bad. He had touched nearly every life in one way or another. He was beloved. He was so much more than a football coach. He was a mentor, a father figure, and a friend. The town was honoring him at the end of the summer by renaming the football field after him before the new season kicked off. The first without him coaching.

He'd also suffered a heart attack about a month ago, shaking everyone. Regan had been the one working with him on his cardiac rehab. Coach had loved Regan before, but having *her* coach *him* through one of the hardest, scariest things he'd done had brought them closer.

"Exactly. Coach's support will mean a lot." Priscilla was so relieved Regan was getting this.

"You can't just wait and let it *be* a great idea?" Regan asked, her tone gentler. "People will figure it out. Coach will support Jase."

Priscilla nodded. "But I have to be *sure*. And I need it now."

"Why? Because you want to prove yourself to your mom?" Regan knew a lot about her issues with her family. Not because they'd talked about them a lot, but because she was incredibly insightful. It made her a great PT.

Priscilla let out a breath. "I thought that was it," she admitted. "And it is. A little. But it's… him. I want him to feel welcome here. Even if it's not by my mom and grandpa and everyone, I want to him know that there are some who see past all of the crap with his grandpa."

"But you're *making* them see past it if you're calling in favors," Regan pointed out. "That's not the same thing."

She nodded. That was why there was a ball of lead in her stomach. "I want him to feel good here."

"Even if you're forcing it?"

"For now," she said, lifting her chin. "Eventually, they'll all see it on their own, but if I have to help it along, I will."

Regan studied her for a long moment. Then she pushed

herself to stand and nodded. "Okay, I'll tell Coach all about the new plans and tell him we should use Jase's new building."

"Thank you. Seriously." Priscilla liked Coach, and vice versa, but Regan definitely had more pull.

"Of course." Regan moved toward the door, clearly on her way back to patient care. But she paused with her hand on the knob and turned back. "You're doing a lot for him," she commented.

Priscilla shrugged. "It's for the town too."

Regan gave her a look that clearly said she wasn't letting her off the hook. "What's he doing for you?"

She blushed. She couldn't control it. She felt her cheeks heat immediately.

Regan laughed, clearly reading her reaction accurately. "Ah."

"I'm not pushing for the building because of *that*," she told her. "It's just a… perk… of him being in town."

Regan nodded, but she wasn't smiling now. "You know, you being crazy about him will make a lot of people give him a second chance too."

Priscilla straightened her spine and swallowed. "I don't know about that."

"I do. This town knows you, Cilla. They like and trust you. Of course, they'd appreciate you even more if you let them in on everything you actually do instead of letting other people take credit," she said.

It was something she'd said to Priscilla many times before. Randi had too. They didn't like that she let people believe the city council and the mayor's office came up with the ideas and did most of the behind-the-scenes work in town.

"But," Regan went on, "even so, you've lived here all your life, you've been a great neighbor and friend and mayor's assistant. If you have a personal relationship with Jase, that will matter to people. They'll probably give him more of a chance." She sighed. "I'd love to think that our little town would give a guy a second chance anyway, and maybe they will, but knowing you're Team Jase and not just in it for the community center will make a difference."

Priscilla thought about that. She would love to think that was true. Not only because it would help Jase, but because she'd like to think her town admired her, saw the things she did and who she was, and respected that. "What if my grandfather has the opposite opinion?" she asked. That was a very real possibility. Very real.

Regan shrugged. "So what? He doesn't really know Jase." She paused. "And certainly not as well as you do."

"Regan!"

Her friend laughed. "I didn't mean it like that." She winked. "Though, of course, you're the sweet, preacher's granddaughter who's always been so good… that you've fallen for this guy will make them take notice for sure. But," she went on before Priscilla could responds "what I meant was, you knew Jase in high school. You're working together on this project. You have a group of friends in common. Jackson and Carter and the guys are also well liked and respected around here. I mean, sure, Jackson had some issues he's still working on… but Carter is good."

Priscilla laughed. Yeah, Jackson had come back to town because of Coach's heart attack, to help out with Coach's farm. He definitely was working on repairing his reputation a bit too.

"But we'll get Jase together with Luke and Marc and… Nolan! Everyone loves Nolan. We'll get him back to town. If they all hang out with Jase, people will take that into account too."

Priscilla was still frowning but she felt a bubble of hope welling up in her chest. "Even despite Pastor Williams's feelings?" she asked.

"Some will still think he can do no wrong," Regan admitted. "But I think you need to give the *town* a chance. Give them a chance to prove to you that they're better than you think they are."

Priscilla winced at that. Yeah, she hadn't even approached a couple of city council members, assuming they'd be against it once her mother had spoken to them.

"Okay, so… I just need to be with Jase," she said. "I need to spend time with him and enjoy having him here and work on the project together and trust that people will see that as a character reference?"

"Yes." Regan smiled. "And I don't think that's going to be hardship for you."

Priscilla finally grinned. "No. No, it won't."

CHAPTER
THIRTEEN

CILLA CAME SASHAYING BACK into The Pork and Peach just before six.

She looked amazing. She had blue jeans on with a blousy top that was a light blue and fell partially off one shoulder and made Jase wonder about the bra situation. She also wore heels that made him want to put her up against the bar again. Immediately.

Of course, he always wanted to put her up against the bar again. Frankly, he didn't expect that urge to disappear. Ever.

But he'd sworn to himself that the next time they had sex, it would be on a bed.

As she came toward him, a sexy little smile on her lips, her hair falling down around her shoulders, her eyes twinkling, he really wished he hadn't made that promise.

He steeled himself against the urge. He could do this. He could be a good guy and take the woman to bed, for fuck's sake.

"You really want to go to this party?" he asked her, blatantly dragging his gaze down her body as she came to stand in front of him.

"I do," she said. Then she licked her lips. "For a little while."

He reached for her, bringing her up against his body. He was wearing jeans too, along with a short-sleeved button-down. He figured the dress code was pretty casual for a barbecue at Carter's but had wanted to look a little more dressed up than he did around The Pork and Peach as he worked.

Which should have been a red flag. That he wanted to dress up for Cilla as if they were going on a date.

They were going to eat burgers and drink beer in the back-yard of a guy they'd both known all their lives.

Still, they were going together, and for some damn reason that made him feel happy and like doing a little more than a t-shirt and boots.

"How long?" he asked gruffly against her neck as he let his hand slide down her side to her ass.

She gave a soft moan as he kissed her neck. "Not long."

"Tell me what time I can drag your sweet ass back here," he said, using that firm tone of voice he knew would make her nipples hard.

"Um…" She trailed off as he dragged his beard down her throat and along her collarbone.

"A time, Peach," he demanded softly. "I want an exact number on the clock."

"Ten," she said breathlessly.

He moved his mouth back up her throat and took her lips in a deep, slow kiss. He pressed her against his cock, already hard and ready to go.

When he lifted his head, he looked into her wide blue eyes. "Not ten o'one," he told her. "Ten sharp. I want you naked by ten after ten."

She simply nodded.

He slapped her ass. "Then let's get going."

She gave a startled gasp but nodded again. "Okay."

He didn't ask if they were driving together. He simply headed outside and crossed the dirt to his truck. He opened the passenger side door for her, and she didn't hesitate to climb right up.

As he turned out of the parking lot and headed west toward Carter's place, Cilla shifted on her seat. "So…"

Jase looked over, his shoulders tensing. Which was stupid. What did he think she was going to say? That they were arriving together, but they had to make it seem as if they weren't really *together*? That she was just functioning as the welcome committee? That they were just old friends?

He knew who she was leaving with and whose floor her panties were going to be on tonight. Or at least, they would be if she was wearing any. That's all that mattered.

"Luke Hamilton will probably be there tonight," she said.

That was so far from anything he'd been expecting that he just frowned at the road without replying.

"He's on the city council," she added.

"Okay."

"You got along in high school, right?"

Well, yeah. Luke had been in their class. He'd played football with them and partied with them sometimes. "Yeah."

"Good, you should talk to him tonight. Tell him about the plans for The Pork and Peach," she said.

Jase glanced over at her again. She was chewing on her bottom lip. "Thought this was a party."

She met his eyes. "It is. Of course. But it's natural that he would ask what you've been up to and why you're back. It would be the perfect time to tell him about your plans and how you're happy to be renovating The Pork and Peach into something new. How you think it's time that the town put the grudge behind it."

He frowned and turned his attention back on the road. "There is no chance that Luke doesn't already know what's going on at The Pork and Peach," he said. For one, Jackson and Carter and the other guys knew all about it. If Luke was part of the group that hung out at Carter's barbecues, then Jase was sure they'd filled him in.

But Luke was also one of the mechanics in town. He'd taken

the shop over from his dad. In fact, Luke owned it with Randi, one of Priscilla's best friends.

Luke had left for college but he'd come home and was a businessman in Bad now. As such, he was practically required to stop into Bad Habit for coffee at some point during the morning and, at least three times a week, to get his breakfast from The Bad Egg. That meant he was up on all the current gossip.

Jase had been in town for more than twenty-four hours. *He* was the current gossip.

Besides, if Luke was on the city council, he would have heard about the plans, presumably from Priscilla herself.

"Well, yes, he already knows," she confirmed in her next breath.

"Then why am I telling him?"

"It's different coming straight from you," she said. "He knows you. He knows that you're a great guy, and if you tell him that you're excited about the project, that will carry more weight than me telling him."

He gave a soft snort. "Here's what Luke knows about me, Peach. He knows that I could always drink him under the table, that I wasn't above cheating at pool, and that I never turned down a dare in Truth or Dare, even if that dare had a boyfriend."

Cilla didn't say anything, and Jase looked over. Her eyes were narrowed.

"You kissed one of Luke's girlfriends?"

"I got to third base with one of Luke's girlfriends," he confessed. With a grin.

"Jase!"

"Hey, it was a game. And she was the one who dared me. Besides, I was doin' him a favor by showing him that she was willing to cheat on him," Jase defended himself. "As I explained to him." He rubbed his jaw. "Just before he punched me in the face."

Priscilla crossed her arms. "You deserved that."

He nodded. "Yeah. But shit, I was sixteen, and, when a girl

puts her hands on your cock at sixteen, you kind of lose whatever morals you might have."

Cilla laughed softly at that. "Just at age sixteen?"

He shot her a grin. "No."

She rolled her eyes but was smiling. "I'm just saying that Luke knows you. The rest of the city council doesn't. This is a good chance to get an ally."

Jase lifted a brow as he signaled the turn onto Carter's street. "I need an ally?"

"It's never a bad idea to have an ally, is it?"

"I'm getting the impression that things with this project aren't as hunky dory as you've made them out to be, Pris," he said. He put a little *don't-lie-to-me* in his tone.

She blew out a breath. "The council hasn't met about it yet," she said. "But my mom's a little… skeptical. I think some of it is just that she likes shiny, new things and she wanted that brand-new building."

He looked over at her again. Cilla was chewing her bottom lip again.

"Some of it? What's some more of it?" he asked.

She sighed. "That it was my idea."

He scowled at the street as he pulled up along the curb in front of Carter's house. "She doesn't *want* you to have ideas?"

"She wants me to make her look good. Make *her* ideas look good. Make sure things work so that everyone is happy with things like the garbage delivery and the town festival." Cilla looked over at him. "Those are all things people just take for granted as long as they work. They don't think much about who makes sure that happens. Until there are problems. Then they know exactly who to blame. That would be my mom. My job is to make sure there's nothing for them to blame her for. She *really* wants the new building to go smoothly, so she's not so crazy about an idea that might be controversial."

That annoyed the shit out of him. Of all the people who

should want Cilla to be successful and admired and happy, shouldn't it be her mother?

His mom had raised him in a strip club, sure, but she'd always loved him. She'd always encouraged him to be happy and to do his best. She'd been stuck because of his deadbeat dad and his… well, he didn't have a perfect adjective for his grandfather. Jarvis was a complicated man. He was more than a little rough around the edges and certainly didn't like a lot of rules, but he was loyal to Jase and his mom, protective even at times, and proud. He'd shown Jase from an early age that the only people you needed to give any time or energy to were the people who knew you and loved you for who you were. In spite of the mistakes and the way things sometimes looked from the outside.

Jase glanced over at the woman beside him again. That was absolutely part of his draw to Priscilla. She wasn't scared of him or turned off by his family's reputation and history in Bad.

In fact, she was trying to help him be accepted. He didn't really need that. He didn't need any of this—the sale to the town, the building being turned into a community center, none of it.

But he kind of wanted it.

He didn't think Cilla even really knew that. But *she* wanted it. She wanted him to feel good here. He suspected it wasn't even just about the building. He thought she actually wanted *him* to be happy.

And fuck if that didn't kick him in the chest and make him want it to work out too.

"So, you believe if Luke thinks it's a great idea, your mom will feel better about it?" he asked.

Dammit. He was going to have to be charming and kiss up to Luke Hamilton. The guy who had suffered three broken ribs because Jase had missed a tackle in the playoff game their junior year. The guy who had loaned Jase and Jackson his car without question the summer after graduation… and they'd put it in the pond. Hey, he should have asked questions. The fucking guy whose girlfriend Jase had made out with because of that stupid truth or dare game in Regan's parent's basement.

Jase had never said he was sorry for any of those things.

And now he was going to have to suck up to Luke so he'd say nice things to the mayor about the Pork and Peach project.

Fuck. Fuck. Fuck.

Priscilla Williams was the only person on the planet who could make him do this.

Luke was a nice guy. Jase would even consider him a friend. Not a friend like Jackson or Carter. To those guys, he could just say "Hey, put in a good word for me with the mayor," and they would. But Luke was someone he'd known for a long time, who he liked, who he got along with—cars in ponds and semi-naked girlfriends aside.

Jase just didn't really apologize well. Or at all. Because he *wasn't* a nice guy.

"Luke is kind of a golden boy around here," Cilla said.

He rolled his eyes. That wasn't news. He'd always been a golden boy. He'd partied and played ball with them, but he'd also gotten good grades and done shit like win Homecoming King. Yeah, Jackson and Carter and Jase weren't really Home-coming King material.

"My mother really likes and respects him. A lot of people do. But he's also willing to disagree with her. He's not a peer. She doesn't intimidate him."

Something in Cilla's voice made him glace over. She was grinning.

"You like that?"

"I do," she said with a nod. "It's hilarious. My mom thinks he's great, but he also tries her patience."

Jase should be jealous maybe. It was clear Cilla liked Luke.

But Miss Cilla Williams had been a virgin until *he* got to town. If she'd wanted Luke, and vice versa, it would have happened. One thing he remembered well about Luke—well, besides the ways Jase had kind of fucked him over—was that he was a very smart guy. And did just fine with the girls. Other than Britney, the closet dare, of course. If Priscilla wanted Luke, he would have been smart enough to take her up on that. No question.

So yeah, Jase wasn't too worried.

Though, just in case, he would make sure that when Cilla begged him to fuck her later, she used his name. Loudly and repeatedly.

"Fine," he said, shutting his truck off. "I'll convince Hamilton that I'm all about this transformation." He draped his arm over the steering wheel and turned toward Cilla. "But I'm not apologizing for Britney."

She grinned. "Well, I assume you're not sorry about Britney."

"I'm not. I'm not really sorry about the broken ribs either. I missed the tackle, but he was taking too long in the pocket that whole game."

Cilla laughed. "You don't have to apologize for that either. I'm sure he's moved on."

He gave her a small grin. "But I *am* a little sorry about putting his car in the pond."

She laughed harder. "Okay, *that* he might still be irritated about."

"We did pay for the tow truck and clean up."

She nodded. "And I heard that you were a little bruised up yourself after that."

He shrugged and pointed at his forehead. "Chicks dig scars."

She scooted across the seat and leaned in, putting her lips first against the scar, then against his mouth. "Truth."

Jase cupped the back of her head, immediately deepening the kiss. He would never not take advantage of having her mouth on him. He stroked her tongue with his, deep and hot, his fingers pressing into her scalp.

He kissed her long enough that when he let her go, she was breathing harder.

Perfect.

"I'm ready to be charming as fuck," he told her. "I'll tell Luke all the reasons that this is a great idea and what a wonderful job I'm going to do and how excited I am to have a chance to fix it up. But, I'm probably going to use all my sweetness and charm up, so when I get you home, I'm going to be bossy and demanding."

"Good," she said hotly against his lips. "That's so, so good."

"The part about me winning Luke over?" He knew that was not what she was talking about.

"The part about you telling me what to do. In very graphic, dirty detail," she said huskily.

He kissed her again, then leaned back, reaching for the door. "Let's go get this charismatic shit over with."

He went around the front of the truck to open Cilla's door. Another dumb, this-is-kind-of-a-date gesture that he couldn't seem to help. She slid to the ground, then slipped her fingers between his. He fucking liked that too. This was so much more than a barbecue at an old friend's house. Dammit.

They started around the side of Carter's house toward the backyard, but Jase took a moment to appreciate the structure. He'd been distracted by Cilla and hadn't paid much attention to the house itself until now. But wow. It was definitely not like the other old houses that sat along this street.

The old house had clearly been torn down with a new one put up in its place. The house was a two-and-a-half-story warm wood and stone structure. There were tons of windows, including the floor to ceiling window on the uppermost level that was clearly a loft-like area and, Jase would guess, was the master bedroom. There was a stone chimney, the porch had been extended to wrap around two sides of the house, and the gutters and other metal accents were a cool, copper color. The house was warm and modern while still fitting in amongst the sleepy, established neighborhood with the big trees and wide front porches.

"Did Carter do this?" he asked Cilla as they rounded the corner of the house heading for the back patio.

"Some of it," she said. "But I know Zeke and Mitch Landry did a lot of it." She squeezed his hand. "It would be so great to have someone local that could do construction projects."

He tore his eyes from the stonework of the chimney to look down at her. "Oh yeah?"

That was the first time she'd said anything about him sticking around or doing any work other than The Pork and Peach.

She nodded. "Sure. I mean, the guys here are all pretty handy. Well, most of them."

It was true that a lot of the guys here grew up doing farm work or learning about cars and other manual labor jobs. Many helped with construction work in the summers or worked on area farms.

"But no one right here in Bad is building houses or putting up buildings," Cilla went on. "And I know Zeke has more work than he can handle. He'd probably love to either take on a partner or refer some of his work out."

Jase thought about that. He loved building. He wasn't sure there was enough work right here in Bad. Not a lot of people were moving into this little town, but if he did restoration and remodeling as well, it was possible he could make a living here.

He mentally shook his head. He'd been here less than a week. Less than one damned week and he was already thinking about staying. He should have known.

He looked at Cilla again.

It was her. She was making him think these things.

She gave him a huge smile, as if she knew where his thoughts were—and liked it—which made his heart kick against his ribs.

"Come on." She tugged on his hand, and he realized they'd stopped walking. "The sooner we start partying, the sooner we can leave."

Yes, leaving. That was what he was focused on. Getting out of here. With her. Taking her home, getting her naked, spending the night buried in her sweet body, and forgetting about anyone else in this town and how they felt or what they thought about him. She was the only one that needed to think he was amazing, and all she needed to be impressed by was his cock. And maybe his mouth and hands.

But as soon as they stepped around the corner of the house, he was hit directly in the face by what a huge, fucking liar he was.

"Jase! Cilla!"

Carter greeted them first but everyone else turned toward them as they approached the patio.

And holy hell, this side of the house was amazing too.

Carter had a sprawling, stone patio with a built-in grill on the end closest to the house and French doors that Jase assumed led into the kitchen for easy portability of food.

The other end hosted a huge, sunken firepit surrounded by overstuffed patio furniture. A group of women he couldn't see well enough to identify were in those chairs, their feet propped on the stone edge of the firepit. There were just a lot of flip-flops, bare feet with painted toenails, long, tanned legs, and the setting sun and the flames from the fire glinting off the wineglasses they held.

The Bad boys had always been surrounded by gorgeous girls, and most of them had been from Bad themselves. There had been some dating within the group on and off, even more just messing around, but mostly the girls and guys had just had fun, been friends, and had a good time.

Off to the side of the patio was the one thing that made this seem like a normal gathering of the people Jase had partied with in his stupid youth—a game of Cornhole was in progress. And the guys around it were as familiar as his own family. As were the red Solo cups they were holding.

He felt a little tension seep out of his shoulders.

Cilla lifted her hand to wave at everyone. "Hey, guys!"

"Get over here!" Carter called. He was brandishing a long spatula and was standing over the grill.

Jackson was with him, a beer bottle in hand. He was facing the group of women though. Of course, that view was better than the grill and Carter's backside.

Jase wondered who he was watching in particular. If there was someone specific. Maybe he'd find out later. He almost grinned. Yeah, he'd find out. These were his guys, his friends. They'd been talking about girls as long as they'd been old enough to understand why they were so worthy of attention.

"Luke is over with the group by the bar," Cilla said to him as they started forward.

He scanned the patio. There was a small cluster of men by the impressive bar a few feet from the grill. It was made of the same stone that adorned the house and patio, with a thick marble top. It would absolutely survive the elements out here.

Of course, he paid more attention to the construction of the bar than the men. He glanced at them as well. He recognized Luke Hamilton and Marc Sterling—they lifted a hand to him—but the other two men weren't immediately familiar. "This looks like a pretty regular gathering," he commented.

Everyone seemed completely at ease, not only with one another but with their surroundings.

"It is," Cilla agreed with a grin. "And Carter's got a great house for it, obviously. But we always have to talk him into it. Randi was the one assigned to that for tonight."

Jase located Randi—Miranda to her mother and grandmother—sitting around the fire. Her long, dark hair lay against her shoulder and her long, trim legs were bare beneath the hem of a flowered sundress. She'd been their head cheerleader for three years, knew more about football than most of their championship team, and could take a transmission out and replace it faster and better than any mechanic in the parish, including her partner, Luke. But damn, she looked good in a skirt.

Jase leaned in. "Those damned magical pussies. They've been messing with men since the beginning of time."

Cilla gave a surprised choke-laugh. "They're not sleeping together," she whispered.

"You sure?"

"Yes." She frowned. "Why? Do you know something I don't?"

He leaned back with a grin. "Nah. I've been gone, remember?"

"What about high school?" Cilla asked, her eyes twinkling.

"Nope. But he wanted to."

"Really?"

"Sure. But most of the guys did."

"Is that right?"

He shrugged. "She's hot. And funny. And feisty."

Cilla was grinning widely now. Then she frowned. "You think Randi is hot and funny and feisty?"

Jase nodded. "Yep."

Cilla's frown went from fake to real in a flash. "Oh."

He watched her, amused and fucking enjoying the hint of jealousy.

"I didn't know you liked her," Cilla finally said.

"Didn't everyone like Randi?" he asked, pretending not to understand.

Randi had always been a lot of fun. She wasn't afraid to get dirty and had been one of the first to show up to swim at the pond. She'd drank and cussed and laughed and partied with them. She'd also worked at The Bad Egg and had snuck them extra French fries and extra scoops of ice cream.

"Well, I suppose," Cilla said, still frowning.

Randi had been a classmate, but she'd been a tomboy where Cilla had been a... not a tomboy. Randi and Regan had been on all the sports teams together, so Randi and Cilla had become friends through Regan, but they hadn't had a lot in common.

"I didn't realize you thought she was hot," Cilla continued.

He slid his arm around Cilla's waist and pulled her against his side. He put his mouth against her ear. "I wasn't interested in her peach if that's what you're wondering, Pris," he said gruffly. "You were the only one I wanted. Then and now." He should have made that dirtier. He should have said something about her being the only one he wanted to eat or something.

But the way he said it was completely true. She was the only one he'd wanted.

A little shiver went through her, and she swallowed hard. But instead of blushing, she looked up at him. "Remember that," she said.

There was a firmness in her voice and a possessiveness in her look that made his cock immediately stir.

"Yes, ma'am," he said softly, looking into her eyes.

She wanted to claim him? He was all fucking hers. For whatever she wanted him for and for as long as she'd have him.

"OH, I'm *definitely* going to need some stories about all of this."

Suddenly there was a petite brunette in front of them, hands on her hips, big, brown eyes taking in every detail from the way he had his hand on Cilla's hip to the way she was looking up at him.

"Hey, Regan," he greeted Cilla's best friend. His smile for the other woman was completely genuine. Regan Reynolds was, and always had been, a hell of a lot of fun. Speaking of feisty.

"Hi, Jase," she said. She looked him up and down. Blatantly. "Good to see you."

"Is it?" he asked.

She nodded. "It is. The past ten years have been very good to you." She grinned up at him. "Not that you needed a lot of improvement."

That was the thing about Regan. There wasn't much of a filter there. "Uh, thanks," he said. Dammit, was *he* blushing?

"Regan," Cilla chided.

Regan laughed. "I'm commenting from a purely professional viewpoint, of course," she said. "It's my life's work to appreciate the human body and all it can do. Besides," she added, "I don't get bodies like *this* to appreciate very often."

Regan was a physical therapist. In a small town. Where a lot of her patients were older and having hip replacements.

He grinned. "Well, you—"

"Enough," Cilla broke in firmly. "No way am I going to let the two of you stand here and *appreciate* each other."

He had, actually, been about to compliment Regan right back. She was a gorgeous woman. Besides being a spitfire, she had an athlete's body. All five-foot-two of her was muscular and trim and tanned. She clearly still spent plenty of time outside. Probably playing in some adult softball or sand volleyball league. It occurred to him that this group might have teams that got together regularly. Damn, that sounded like fun.

And that thought was nearly as shocking as Priscilla Williams being possessive of him. And public about it.

Which she was.

"You're staking a claim then," Regan asked her best friend, tilting her head and regarding Cilla.

"I am," Cilla told her, squeezing closer to him.

Though that was difficult since he had her up tight against him already. But he felt the way her fingers gripped his shirt.

Regan's mouth spread into a wide grin. "Good for you, girl." She gave him a wink. "Look out, Jase. I have a feeling there's a lot of repressed… *stuff* inside this one."

He nodded solemnly. "Thanks for the warning."

"You think you can handle her?"

"I think that if I can't, I'll die a very happy man."

Regan snorted. "Good answer." She looked at Cilla. "Okay, come on. The girls are waiting for all the gossip."

Cilla shook her head. "You know I don't gossip."

"You don't gossip about other people," Regan said with a nod. "But this is about you."

Cilla sighed. "I'm not gossiping about him."

"Fine." Regan reached out and snagged Cilla's hand. "Then they'll just ask you tons of intimate questions and judge your answers by your blushing."

Cilla laughed and Jase felt a little surge of… something.

Something that felt like satisfaction. Did he want those women to know that he and Cilla were doing things that would make her blush? Fuck yes. He wanted everyone to know that. He wanted her jealous and claiming him and grinning and blushing about them being together.

But he also wasn't sure he was ready to face the crowd alone. A surge of panic suddenly gripped him. He tightened his hold on Cilla. "Uh, I need another minute with her," he told Regan.

Regan lifted a brow. "Okay. But the longer you keep her over here, the hungrier the crowd gets."

He glanced over the top of Regan's head toward the firepit. Sure enough, every pair of eyes over there was watching them. A few lifted their hands, or their drinks, in greeting. They were all grinning widely.

"I'll be quick," he promised Regan.

Regan laughed. "I really have a hard time believing that," she said, her tone, and wink, full of innuendo. Then she tucked her hands in the back pockets of her shorts and turned, heading back for the group.

"Wow, they're… a lot," he said.

Cilla laughed. "You act surprised."

He looked down at her. "I think I forgot."

"What it's like to have a big group of friends who want to know every detail of your life?"

Fuck.

Yes.

He nodded.

Her expression softened, and, for a second, he thought she was going to reach up and touch his cheek. He might have lost his composure if she had. He'd like to say he would have growled and cupped her ass and brought her in for a hot, searing kiss, audience be damned. But, honestly, he thought he would have hugged her. Just hugged her.

"Is this okay?" she asked quietly. "They really are nosy as

hell. They're used to telling each other everything. They will want to know all the details."

Instead of answering directly, he said, "I don't remember you being a part of this big crowd. You did *not* party with all these guys." But neither had he. Because this group hadn't been one big group. They'd all known one another. In a town this size, you couldn't help it. But there were too many different personalities here to be one cohesive group. In high school, that was a big deal.

Of course, everyone had grown up. Adulthood had a way of changing people. Usually. Sometimes even for the better.

"I know. It's… different now. I really like it." Cilla lifted a shoulder and looked out over the group. "Annabelle is a new addition to this group. Though she spends more time with Brooke than with us."

Jase looked down at her. There was definitely history between Priscilla and Brooke.

Priscilla winced, knowing what he was thinking. "We get along now. Or we try. But it's awkward and she doesn't feel comfortable at these gatherings. She hangs out with Annabelle mostly when she does go out. Brooke's the physician's assistant at the clinic in town," she explained.

He nodded. That made sense. Brooke had always been smart. And it fit that she and Annabelle were friends. Annabelle had been a nerdy bookworm in school who simply hadn't gone out and socialized much at all.

"She still with Jonathan?" he asked of Brooke's high school boyfriend and Priscilla's cousin. That could also make things awkward.

Priscilla's face blanched.

Jase frowned. "Cilla?"

"Um." She swallowed hard. "Jonathan was killed in a drunk driving accident seven months ago."

Jase felt shock hit him. "Jesus. Cilla, I'm so sorry." He hugged her against him. "Damn."

She nodded. "It really sucked. We all miss him. They'd only been back for about a year. He was the doctor here. It was going great. He went back to San Antonio to see some friends and…" She sniffed.

Jase kissed the top of her head. "I'm sorry," he said again.

"Thanks. Anyway, I'm trying hard with Brooke. But it will maybe always be a little awkward."

He nodded. The scandal between the Williams and Donovan families had been wild. The past was hard to totally get over, he knew that better than anyone.

"Anyway, it's nice to be included," Cilla went on, looking out over the group of people gathered. "Those of us who stayed, definitely run into each other often, and we just kind of drifted together. We end up working together in different capacities or just interacting. Marc owns the restaurant where we all eat often. Luke and Randi fix our cars. Carter keeps us safe. Annabelle teaches at the school." Cilla shrugged. "I guess I realized that these people are making their lives here, like I am. They're all staying here too. We're the town now. We're the people working here and making the town run and will eventually be having families. Our kids will be going to school here and stuff. It just seemed… time for us to all be a group in a new way."

That hit him right in the middle of the chest.

She was right. This was the future of Bad. These people were already business owners and the new city council members and the teachers and service providers in town. Someday they'd be the Little League coaches and the PTA members and the ones fundraising to repair the Senior Center and to repave Main Street. He looked down at Cilla. She was already doing a lot of that.

He wanted to be a part of it too.

He had told himself that he'd moved on from Bad, that he didn't need some tiny town in southern Louisiana, that there was a great, big world out there. But the truth was, he wanted to want something else… but he didn't.

He wanted to help re-shingle the fire station and help flip pancakes at a fundraiser for a new…whatever. The specifics weren't important. He wanted to be a part of making Bad work.

And more.

He wanted a place where he belonged. Where everyone knew—or wanted to know, anyway—his business, the details of his life, what mattered to him. He wanted to come to barbecues with this group of people that he'd known his whole life. People he could trust and laugh with, people who would show up to lend a hand and their tools when he had a big project going. People he had memories and history with. His gaze landed on Luke. Even if some of that history wasn't perfect.

"Jase? Are you okay?" Cilla asked, her hand squeezing his side.

He looked down at her. And this girl. He wanted her. For so much more than sex. Though he wanted that too. Every night. For the rest of his life.

He swallowed. "I'm good," he said. "Really good."

She searched his eyes. Then he felt her relax against him as she slowly smiled "You're happy."

"I am."

"I like seeing that."

"You're part of it," he told her honestly.

"I *really* like that."

He believed that. He believed that she wanted him to be happy. Not just because that meant he'd remodel The Pork and Peach. But because she really cared about him. He leaned in and kissed her softly.

She kissed him back. In front of everyone. Like a girlfriend would.

A bolt of desire went through him that was about so much more than physical need. He wanted *this*. Her. Clearly his. With all of their friends. Hanging out, sharing their lives, being something bigger as a group.

"Ten o'clock sharp," he said against her mouth.

"How about nine forty-five?" she asked, pulling back slightly.

He grinned. "Deal."

"Holy shit, *come on*," Carter yelled at them. "Food's gonna be ready soon."

Jase finally let Cilla go. He'd admit he felt a little naked without her. He hadn't hung out with most of these people in years. Of course, Carter and Jackson had spent the afternoon at The Pork and Peach with him. But the rest of them… it had been a while.

Luke approached.

"Welcome back, Jase." Luke extended his hand.

"Hey, Luke." Jase took his hand in a firm shake.

"Heard you've got quite the project going out on the highway," Luke said.

The guy hadn't changed much since high school. He was still almost too good-looking, with an easy smile that said *life's good*.

Jase wasn't shocked Luke was on the city council. He was, however, shocked that the guy didn't have a wife and a couple of kids by now. Then again, Luke had always had an interesting relationship with Sabrina Cassidy that had seemed to keep him from getting serious with any other girls.

He'd always insisted Sabrina was just a friend. They'd grown up next door to one another, and, as far as anyone knew, they'd never been romantically involved. They'd never gone on a date, or attended a school dance, or even held hands in public. But Luke was incredibly protective of her and, if Sabrina called, even if Luke was in the middle of a date with someone else, he would leave.

That had caused at least four break-ups that Jase knew about.

The most interesting part was that Luke's best male friend, and adopted brother, Marc, had *hated* Sabrina.

No one had ever fully gotten to the bottom of any of that.

But Luke and Marc were here tonight, and Sabrina was not.

Jase would have to ask Cilla about that. If Sabrina wasn't around, maybe Luke's love life had improved.

Cilla would be perfect for him.

Jase frowned as that thought hit him. It was true, of course. They were both pillars of the community. Both good looking, well liked, and, most importantly, well respected.

He frowned, realizing that he didn't know for certain that Cilla and Luke had never dated. They'd never slept together. That's all he knew. And that was definitely something. But, considering that he was ninety percent sure he was falling in love with her already, suddenly their dating history mattered too.

"It's not going well?" Luke asked him, reading his frown as something to do with The Pork and Peach.

Jase shook off his questions about Luke and Cilla. It didn't matter. She was his now.

That gave him pause. But it should have given him a longer one, honestly.

Still, the idea of Cilla being his, fully, in every way, to the point that their pasts didn't matter and they had their future together ahead, settled into his heart in a warm, comforting weight that felt completely right.

"It's going very well," he told Luke honestly, meaning more than The Pork and Peach, but suddenly feeling that too. "I'm really excited about the plans."

Luke nodded. "Then you've seen the building plans for the other site?"

"I have. And I think The Pork and Peach will be perfect for it." That was true. The building could be easily converted, and it made a lot of sense. "And it will save us… a lot of money." He paused as the word "us" fell out of his mouth. Easily. Without thought.

Well, it looked like he was really embracing this whole home-coming thing now. He barely kept from shaking his head ruefully.

Luke noticed his use of "us." But he simply nodded. "It will. If you think you can pull it off in a reasonable time and meet all of the requirements we need, then I think it's a great idea."

"Oh, we can pull it off," he said. He glanced at Carter and Jackson, who were listening in. "I've had a lot of help already. But once the job is confirmed, I'll hire a couple of local guys to help out."

"Great. I've got a couple of names for you, if you're open to it."

"Absolutely." Carter and Jackson and the other guys would continue to help, and they would have a great time putting the place together, but to make the job move along faster, hiring actual help made sense. They all had their own work to do. And he liked the idea of being a local employer, even if it was short-term.

Though, if things went well and there were other jobs in the area, he could hire an actual crew.

"Of course, I'd like to know that we're a go," he said to Luke, "before I get ahead of myself." Yeah, that would be good for *him* to remember too.

"Understood," Luke told him. "But I think you can confidently talk to a couple of guys, get the ball rolling. The council will meet on Monday."

"And you think everyone will go for it?" That's what he wanted—needed—to know.

"I do," Luke said. "I'm not going to bullshit you though," he added. "The mayor isn't enthusiastic. And she's got friends on the council. And friends married to council members."

Jase frowned. Even though he'd known from what Cilla said that her mom wasn't fully on board, he didn't like hearing from another source that this wouldn't necessarily be smooth sailing. "You expect a fight about it at the meeting?" he asked Luke.

The other man shook his head. "Not a fight really. Just not unanimous support. You okay with that?"

No. He wanted the town to want this. All of them. But that

was unrealistic. This wasn't just some random burned-out building. This was The Pork and Peach.

He scrubbed a hand over the back of his neck. "I'd be lying if I said I'm totally fine with it," he admitted. "I'd like to think that everyone could put their misgivings aside for the good of the town."

Luke nodded. "Sure. But," he added, "you okay enough with it to go ahead? If we have just enough support to do it, will you be on board?"

"What's just enough support?"

"There are six council members. You're going to want four votes because the mayor breaks any ties."

Jase thought about that. Would he do it even knowing that just under half of the council—and potentially the town—was not in favor? He cast a glance toward the firepit where Cilla was now sitting and laughing with the other women.

His heart thumped hard in his chest. Fuck. He was in this, for better or worse.

Was he paying for his grandfather's sins? Yeah, maybe he was. But if that's how it had to be to get what he wanted, he'd do it.

He wanted Cilla. He wanted this town. He even—dammit—wanted to erase The Pork and Peach so he could start over. Wasn't that why he hadn't called the fire department right away ten years ago? He'd been the one to discover the fire. He'd been the one to wait until he'd been sure the damage was extensive.

"Do you think you could help me get those four?" he asked Luke.

Luke gave him a smile. "You only need three more."

He appreciated that. He gave Luke a nod.

"And if I can't get you those votes, Cilla can," Luke went on. He looked over toward the firepit as well. "She's a force around here. Even if she doesn't realize it."

Jase suddenly liked Luke Hamilton a lot. He saw Cilla. Jase could only assume others did as well.

Maybe this whole, crazy thing was going to end up doing a lot more than getting The Pork and Peach made over and him a new start. Maybe it would also show Cilla that she already had influence in this town. The right kind of influence. Influence that came from respect and trust and people just freaking *liking* her rather than her family's name.

He grinned and accepted the beer that Jackson handed him, feeling more satisfied and happier than he could remember feeling in far too long.

Probably since the last time he'd been in Bad, as a matter of fact.

"Hey, Luke?"

"Yeah?"

"I'm sorry about putting your car in the pond."

Luke looked surprised for a second, then he gave a snort. "How about Britney Foster?"

"Uh…"

Luke laughed. "Yeah, that's what I thought."

Jase grinned and tipped his beer back. Hell, maybe he'd develop one of those fucking *life is good* grins himself.

CHAPTER
FIFTEEN

AT NINE FORTY, Priscilla tipped her head back and said against Jase's ear, "Take me home."

He was sitting with her on the chaise lounge by the firepit. He was reclining and She was leaning back against his big, hard body. They were mellow, having eaten and laughed and relaxed with everyone for the past few hours. But having his big body against hers, his thighs bracketing her hips, feeling his deep rumbling laugh against her back, seeing him fitting in and clearly comfortable with this group of people, made want curl through her.

It was more than physical want. She recognized that. She wanted all of *this*. Him beside her, his hand casually stroking over her hip, the other resting possessively against her stomach, while they hung out with their friends. She wanted to be a couple. She wanted to see him happy. She wanted to *make* him happy.

And having all of it, even if it was just for tonight, was also making her horny.

She felt his hand pause on her hip, then squeeze slightly.

"It's early," he said gruffly. "I was kind of hoping to hear more about this haunted camp."

She laughed. Daisy had been telling them about the camp she was trying to talk Carter into going to with her. "Not haunted. Serial killer on the loose," Priscilla corrected him.

Jase nodded against her shoulder. "Right. But scary as fuck. I got that part for sure."

"Right." Which was the point.

They were sitting on the opposite side of the firepit from where Daisy had her butt barely balanced on the edge of her chair while giving the group the run-down of the camp.

"Fuck no," Jackson said. "And I mean that with capital letters. You're cute as hell, Daisy, but if you piss off some lunatic with a chainsaw, you're on your own."

Daisy looked over at him. "Wow, how very heroic and gallant. So, note to self, never count on Jackson to save my ass." She looked at Carter, who was lounging in the chaise to her left with his "date," Lisa. "But that's okay. The big tough cop will go."

Carter just saluted her with his cup, but everyone, including Daisy, knew Carter was just playing along. He was never going to that camp with her.

Daisy was a single mom of four boys, and, when she took time off and left her kids with her mom, she *took time off*. She did all kinds of crazy shit. Skydiving, swimming with sharks, serial-killer-on-the-loose camps, apparently. She always tried to talk friends into going with her and they all came up with great reasons *not to*.

"Hey, I can be heroic and gallant," Jackson protested. "I'll save your ass if it's something like… snakes." He nodded. "Yeah, I'd save you from snakes."

Daisy rolled her eyes. "I can totally save myself from snakes."

Priscilla felt Jase snort behind her. She smiled. It was so nice just sitting here, listening to them all be… themselves. But sharing it with him. He was relaxed and had clearly had a good time tonight. After those first few minutes when he'd seemed a little nervous about seeing everyone again—which had made her melt—he'd been fine. More than fine. He'd fit right in. He'd laughed and talked and caught up with everyone as if he'd been gone for a few months rather than years.

She threaded her fingers through his where they were resting on her stomach. Who would have guessed Mr. Tough-Guy, I-Don't-Care-What-Bad-Thinks-Of-Me would have been nervous? She'd loved it. It meant it did matter. At least a little. And she wanted Bad to matter to him.

She also really wanted him to take her home. Now.

"*Or*," Jackson went on, addressing Daisy. "If some dude comes after you with a chainsaw while you're sitting around a firepit at a friend's house, I'll mess him up." He looked around the wide backyard that was now black outside of the circle of light cast by the firepit and the tiki torches set around the perimeter of the patio. "But if you go and stay at a fucking campground for the *purpose* of having a serial killer come after you… that's your own fault, and you should have to deal with that yourself."

Daisy grinned at him. "Well, that's a little better," she said. "But a *real* friend would go *with me* to that campground." She cast a glance at Carter.

"You should know, she also wants to spend the night in a haunted prison," Carter said to Jackson before tipping his beer back again.

"Jesus, Daisy," Jackson said, shaking his head. "You've got issues."

"No, I *don't* have issues. That's the thing," Daisy insisted. "I'm a badass who isn't afraid of anything."

"But you *should* be scared of serial killers," Jackson insisted. "That's *normal*. And *good*."

"What is her deal?" Jase asked in Priscilla's ear.

She grinned and looked up at him. She had to tip her head and neck, but she loved being this close to him. He felt so good. He smelled so good. And she loved that he was interested in this. "Four boys. Raising them alone. She wants to be a role model for just going out, living life, and not letting anything stop you. But she also loves getting away and the adrenaline rush. Those boys are… a lot."

Jase chuckled. "Wow. I'll bet."

"But you really will stay at the campground with her, right?" Lisa asked Carter from where she was perched beside him.

Carter wasn't actually *dating* her. She'd shown up about thirty minutes ago looking for him and inserted herself into the party. But Carter never really *dated* anyone. Women just became enamored with him, and he had a hard time getting rid of them because he couldn't be a heartbreaker.

His friends found that hilarious. He was a hardass cop and a downright grump a lot of the time. But when it came to women with hearts in their eyes, he just couldn't be mean.

The guys called him "sweet" and a teddy bear.

Priscilla thought it was because, deep down, he was hoping to fall in love.

"Uh, no," Carter told her with a chuckle.

"What if *I* was at a campground that had a serial killer running around?" Lisa asked. "You're a cop!"

"It's not a *real* serial killer," Carter told her. "It's a game. It's fake."

Lisa frowned as if confused.

"Oh, my God," Jase whispered.

Priscilla watched Lisa. Surely the woman was following this.

"But if it *was* real, you would go?"

"If there was *actually* a guy running around a campground killing people?" Carter asked, sitting up a little straighter. "Well… yeah."

"And you'd come over to my house if I thought someone was sneaking around outside in the middle of the night?" Lisa asked.

Priscilla watched the *oh shit* realization cross Carter's face. Lisa had just come up with a possible way to get Carter to her house once she was in her pjs.

Jase snorted softly, clearly realizing the same thing.

"Well, that would depend," Carter said carefully. "Walking around outside isn't illegal."

"But what if I was home at night and I heard a weird noise coming from the basement? I could call you, and you'd come over to check it out, right?" Lisa asked.

"Babe," Carter said. "The people in the movies who go into the dark basement when there are weird noises are idiots."

Priscilla laughed softly. Obviously, as a cop, Carter would investigate, but it was clear Lisa was running through scenarios to get him to her house at night, and he was going to be *sure* to shut them down.

Lisa frowned. "But you would *have* to go."

"Why?" Jackson asked her.

"Because that's what true love is."

Jackson, Carter, Luke, Marc, and Jase all snorted in unison at that.

"True love is going down the rickety basement stairs to sacrifice yourself to the demon alien monster that needs human flesh to grow and take over the world because your girl says, 'I think I heard a noise'?" Jackson asked her.

"Well… yes," Lisa told him.

"Why can't I just say, 'Holy shit. Yes, I heard it! Let's get out of here!' and make sure you get out of the house without the demon alien monster eating you? How is *that* not heroic and gallant?" Carter demanded.

"But you wouldn't know it was a demon alien monster until you went down there," Regan pointed out, her expression mischievous. "What if it's a lost little kitten? You have to go down there in case a kitten needs you, Carter." Her solemn tone was clearly fake. "I mean, that kitten could turn into your forever furbaby with Lisa."

Carter gave Regan a wide-eyed look that clearly said, *what the fuck are you doing to me?*

"Oh, she's right," Lisa told him. "What if it's the kitten we're meant to raise together forever? Oh!" she said, spinning to face the group. "I saw the *cutest* video of this guy who tied the engagement ring around the kitten's neck to propose to his girlfriend and then the kitten was the ringbearer in their wedding!"

Carter coughed as he swallowed his beer down the wrong pipe.

Regan and Daisy, however, both said, "Oh my God!" together, as if that was the cutest thing they'd ever heard.

"They're the worst," Jase said in Priscilla's ear.

She grinned and nodded. "Totally."

"And you love them," he observed.

"So much."

He laughed, the feel of it rumbling through her body and right down between her legs.

"But hey, Carter, aren't you allergic to cats?" Jackson asked.

Carter sat straight up on his chair, nearly dumping Lisa off his lap. "I am," he said, nodding adamantly. "Very."

Regan cast Jackson a look. Clearly, he was ruining her fun. "Really? I didn't know that, and I've known Carter all my life. Did you know that, Daisy?"

Daisy shook her head. "No, that's news to me."

Lisa was frowning. "I didn't know that either."

"Oh, but it's true," Carter jumped in. "I get terrible… hives. You wouldn't want me to suffer like that, would you?" he asked Lisa.

"Well…" Lisa chewed on her bottom lip.

"Brooke can give you a prescription for it," Daisy said, waving her hand. "It's obviously a mild allergy. Nothing to let get in the way of life and love."

"Silly to take medication when you don't need to though," Luke piped up. "I mean, drugs have side effects, right? That's just irresponsible."

"So, the girls are on the side of Carter saving the fictional kitten who may or may not be a demonic alien, just to fuck with Carter, not because they like Lisa and think the two of them should actually raise a cat together, right?" Jase asked.

"Yes. But I do admire the guys for trying to save him," Priscilla said with a grin.

Jase chuckled. "I fucking love this."

I fucking love you.

That thought flitted through her mind in response. That was ridiculous, of course, but that didn't stop it.

She looked over her shoulder, meeting his eyes. "Can we leave now?"

"You sure? This is really fun."

"Please, Jase," she said softly.

The please hit him hard. She knew it would.

His nostrils flared as he took a deep breath. "Yes."

She grinned.

"Oh, you like that?" he asked.

Their voices were soft so that no one else could really hear what they were saying. Especially with the demonic-alien-cat-allergy conversation going on.

"That you're so easy for me?" she asked. "Oh, yes."

He shifted behind her, and she felt the press of his cock against her butt. "Just to be clear. The opposite of easy is hard," he said, his voice gravelly. "And that's how it's gonna be when I get you home."

A hot shiver danced through her. "*Yes.*"

"You are a jerk!" Suddenly Lisa stood up and faced Carter. "I don't think you ever really loved me. I don't think you really know anything about love at all!" Then she turned and stomped toward the house.

Everyone, including Carter, just watched her go.

"Didn't you meet her last weekend?" Jackson asked after the back door slammed behind her.

"Yeah." Carter ran a hand through his hair and let out a long breath. Then he reached for another beer.

"Now *that* is scary," Daisy said. "Maybe I need to find a crazy girlfriend and try to live through *that.*"

"Well, Carter can definitely help you find one," Regan piped up. "The guy's a magnet for crazy. And that's coming from someone who's been, on occasion, described as a little crazy."

Carter didn't deny it. He just twisted the top off his beer bottle.

"Okay, time to go." Jase's hands were suddenly at her waist and he lifted Priscilla almost effortlessly out of the lounger, climbing to his feet behind her.

Everyone looked over at the sudden movement.

"I guess we're going to get out of here," she said with a little smile.

Her girlfriends all gave her knowing grins. The guys were less subtle.

"Good for you, Jase."

"Make him earn that contract, Cilla."

"The Pork and Peach isn't totally shut down I guess."

"Yep, lots of nailing to be done out there."

"You guys are so creative," she told them with an eye roll. But this was the kind of thing they gave each other crap about—juvenile crap, sure, but still—and it stupidly made her feel more included in the group.

She hadn't had a boyfriend that she'd liked enough to bring to one of these gatherings. This was mostly a group of friends getting together. There weren't really couples in this group. She assumed that, over time, as everyone did find significant others, that those people would be joining their group, but Carter was the only one to have someone here that wasn't just a friend and it hadn't gone well.

Now she and Jase were apparently the first real couple.

That felt strange.

And strangely good.

They drove back to The Pork and Peach, holding hands but not talking much. The silence was completely comfortable though.

When Jase pulled in next to the RV, he shut the truck off and turned toward her. "I want you in my bed tonight."

"Good."

"All night."

She wanted that too. She would still need to get up in the morning to do her rounds, but she wanted to spend the night in his arms. It was probably dangerous to get this attached. To find yet one more thing to miss about him after he left. But, at this point, her heart was going to be in pieces when he left anyway. She might as well have as many nights to remember as she could.

"Okay," she told Jase.

His eyes flared with emotion. Was he surprised she'd agreed? Or was he just flipping through his list of things he wanted to do to her in that bed? Wow, she really hoped it was the latter.

"Inside, Peach. Now."

She gave him a sly grin. Then she scooted to the door, pushed it open, and slid to the ground.

JASE WAS out of the truck and nearly on top of her by the time she was reaching for the door of the RV.

He reached around to the front of her jeans, popping the button and dragging the zipper down as she fumbled with the latch.

Having her up against him for the last few hours had been heavenly torture. More, sitting around that firepit with all of those people had sent another type of emotion through him. Affection. A sense of belonging. A sense of *want* that was so much more than physical lust. He wanted to be with Cilla, next to her, holding her hand, smiling at her across a crowd, cuddling with her at barbecues and birthday parties and around Christmas trees.

It was insane how fast it had happened.

Maybe.

Then again, it had started *ten years* ago. It was only now that they both really knew what they wanted and could act on it.

Tonight had cemented it for him. He wanted to move back to Bad. He wanted to be with Cilla. He wanted parties at Carter's with all of those crazy, wonderful people. He wanted to hear about Daisy's trip to the serial killer camp. He wanted to be there for Carter's next crazy-girlfriend scenario. And every other story that would come from that group. He wanted to watch them all fall in love and meet those people and add them to the group as well.

"Open the door, Peach."

She sucked in a deep breath. "I'm trying."

"I haven't even really touched you."

"I'm anticipating it."

He chuckled. "Well, you need to focus. Because I'm going to keep touching you, no matter what. I will fuck you right up against the front door of this RV if I have to. But anybody could see us from the highway. I don't care, but you might."

She laughed. "I should care more about that than I do right now."

He liked that. He shouldn't be trying to make her naughty. She was his. All of this was just for him. He didn't have to prove what she would do for him. She'd do anything. Over and over again.

But he still wanted to.

He moved in right behind her. "Do you want that, Peach? You want me to take you right here? Make you scream out? Risk that some of these nice people that we've both known all our lives will see or hear us? Because I would be *very* okay with that."

He pushed her jeans down until they hung just below the bones of her hips. He ran his palm over her flat stomach, feeling her shiver against him. "I loved claiming you tonight. Loved being there, everyone knowing we were together. Knowing they all knew where you would be spending the night." His fingers ran down over the front of her silky panties. She was hot and wet, and she moaned at his touch. "All of our friends have a pretty good idea about what we're doing right now anyway. A part of me would love very much to thrust my cock deep into your sweet, wet pussy right here and now, so you're going to have to be the one to say no."

Truthfully, the most anyone would probably see from the highway was a person standing at the door of the RV. They'd be going too fast, and the angle wouldn't be right for them to really register any details.

But he wasn't sure Priscilla realized that. And it was kind of hot to think about fucking her while people drove past even if *they* didn't know what was going on for sure.

"They might see these sweet tits bouncing," he said, running his hand up under her shirt and pulling the cups of her bra up over her breasts. He played with one nipple. It was already hard, and she whimpered softly. She shifted her ass back against his cock where it was pressing almost painfully against his zipper.

That didn't last long.

"Yes," Cilla hissed as she reached back and unbuttoned and unzipped him, immediately moving her hand inside his pants to stroke him firmly.

He shuddered at her touch. "Fuck yes, Peach. Squeeze me."

She did, right as he slipped his hand into her panties, circling her clit and causing her to groan loudly, then moving lower and into her slick heat.

"*Jase.*"

He thrust in and out a few times, spreading her wetness, relishing the feel of what he'd done to her already—what the idea of fucking by the highway had done to her—but it wasn't enough.

"Say no right now, or I'm taking you right here," he told her, withdrawing his finger and pushing his jeans and boxers to his knees. He nudged her hand out of the way. Her touch was torture and he was fighting the urge to push her to her knees and press into her mouth. He took his cock in hand, giving himself a long, hard stroke, trying to ease some of the ache.

"I shouldn't," she said, then she laughed huskily. "But I really want you to fuck me, right here, like this. With the sound of the tires on the highway and the headlights flashing by. In the parking lot of the place that was always deemed so naughty."

He jerked her jeans and panties down as well, then turned her to face him. "Next time, we'll be in my bed," he promised. Though he wasn't sure if he was making that promise to her or him.

"Don't care about that. Just need you," she said, breathlessly.

"Hang on then, Peach." He knelt to slip her jeans and panties off one foot as she kicked that shoe off. Then he hoisted her up, pressing her into the door of the RV. Her legs wrapped around him, her thighs squeezing him. Her slick heat coated the head of his cock, and he gritted his teeth. "Dammit, condom."

"I'm on the pill," she said, reaching between them, trying to line his cock up with her entrance.

"Peach," he said roughly. Her hand on him, her wetness against him was almost too much. "*Pris*," he said firmly, squeezing her ass.

Her eyes found his. "What?"

"Are you sure? I'm clean, but—"

"Jase, fuck me," she said. "*Please.*"

He wasn't a guy who would argue with a lady… okay, he was completely a guy who would argue with a lady, if needed, but not the lady he wanted more than he wanted his next breath, and especially not when she was half naked and wrapped around him with her sweet pussy lined up perfectly.

He thrust with a groan. Her fingers tightened against his neck, and she moaned.

"Yes. Oh, yes, Jase."

He pulled back and surged forward again. The friction and heat were so sweet, so perfect, he felt it in every damned nerve ending. She was wrapped around him like he was all that was keeping her grounded, as if everything in her world centered on where they were connected.

Or maybe that was just him.

Of course, they were connected by her lips against his neck, their chests pressed together, his hands on her ass, her thighs squeezing his sides, her ankles linked at his lower back, and, of course, he was buried balls deep inside of her.

A place he never wanted to leave.

He thrust in and out

"Cilla, you're everything," he said in her ear.

"Jase. *Jase!*"

He felt her pussy squeezing him and he picked up the pace. Her back was pressed against the side of the RV, but she didn't seem to care. She gripped him tighter, gasping and moaning his name.

"God, you feel amazing." His voice was gravelly.

The flicker of headlights bounced off the side of the RV, and the sounds of tires whirring on the highway hit his ears as her moans grew louder. There was the screech of an owl. Crickets and frogs serenaded them.

And then her moans got louder, and all he could hear was her.

"Jase! Oh my God, *yes!*"

He felt her inner muscles clenching, holding him, milking him, and he knew he wouldn't last much longer. "Cilla, come for me, honey."

"I'm so close. I'm so…" And then she went over the edge, calling his name, her body squeezing him hard, pulling everything out of him.

He felt his balls tightening, the tingling beginning at the base of his spine and then erupting. He pumped into her, her name falling from his lips as he emptied himself into her.

The waves of pleasure rushed over him, and he clasped her tightly to his body, locking his knees to keep them both upright. He let go of her ass with one hand, bracing it against the RV, just dragging air in and letting it out.

She clung to him, her breaths sawing in and out raggedly as well for several long moments.

Finally, he pulled back and looked down at her.

She grinned up at him, looking very pleased.

"I really like this sex thing," she said. "Really glad to be finally doing it."

He growled softly. He was damned grateful she'd waited for him.

That was usually the kind of thing he bit back. But fuck it. It was time to start saying this.

"Thank you for waiting for me, Pris," he said, his tone full of affection.

Her expression softened. "I can't imagine it being anyone but you, Jase."

And, just like that, she grabbed his heart and squeezed it.

"I want to stay." See, that was another of those things he would have typically tried to swallow. But it was time to say it.

Her eyes widened. "You do?"

"Yes."

"Like stay here? In Bad? Really?"

"Yes. I… this… all of this is everything I've ever wanted."

Her lips parted. Then she pressed them together and swallowed.

"Say it, Cilla. Say whatever it is."

"Me?" she asked. "Am I a part of it? If you stay?"

He gave a choked, disbelieving laugh. How could she not know?

"You're *the* reason, Cilla. You're the whole reason."

"The *whole* reason?"

"The life here. The friends. The… everything. I love it all. *With you.* Without you, it doesn't matter. All of this with you is what I want."

"Oh my God." Suddenly she squeezed him tight, putting her face into his neck and hugging him with her arms and legs.

He chuckled, squeezing her back. "Are you okay?"

"I'm so happy!" She pulled back to look at him. "Oh, Jase. I'm…" She paused and her voice softened. "I'm in love with you. I want you to stay. So much."

He felt a little dizzy. Maybe he'd been holding his breath.

Maybe the adrenaline rush was just that powerful. Whatever it was, he crushed her against him and dragged in oxygen. She let him just hold her, hugging him back.

Finally, he managed, "I love you too."

"Thank God."

He gave a short chuckle. Then loosened his grip and lifted his head, looking at her. "Time for bed."

She nodded.

He was already getting hard again. Who knew that telling someone you loved them, and hearing it back, could make lust surge like this? But damn. Yeah, he'd never wanted anyone more. Okay, that had already been true. He'd never wanted to be buried so deeply inside someone, pressed up so tightly against someone, so connected to someone that it was impossible to tell where she started and he ended.

With one hand, he tugged his pants up just enough that he wouldn't trip and break either of their necks. Then he somehow managed to get them both inside without even shifting her off his cock. That was pretty impressive, he had to admit.

Her one shoe was still in the gravel outside, but somehow that seemed appropriate at the moment. A little dirtier twist on the glass-slipper-Cinderella thing. Where the shoe was a hell of a lot stronger than glass, the steps were steps into an RV that had brought him back to his hometown—reluctantly—rather than a palace, and the girl was running *toward* the guy, who was no fucking prince at all.

He took her into the bedroom and lowered her onto the king-sized mattress, following her down immediately. Her legs were still wrapped around him, and she shifted just enough to settle him fully between her thighs and deep inside her. He was fully hard again now, and he began moving in long, slow, deep thrusts that made her moan and gasp. Her fingers dug into his ass, then ran up his back. She kissed him deeply. She said his name with a soft, breathy, affectionate tone that he wanted to hear forever. It was the kind of sweet almost-whisper that he could imagine hearing when she tiptoed into a nursery and found him rocking their baby. Or when she opened a particularly meaningful gift from him on their twenty-fifth wedding anniversary. Or when he asked her to marry him in the first place.

His pace picked up instinctively. He thrust into her deeper, faster, wanting to take her to that peak again. He knew exactly the angle, exactly where to put his hand on her hip to tip her pelvis, exactly where to put his mouth against her neck, and exactly what to say to get her there.

"I love you, Peach. I fucking love you so damned much."

She gasped, arched into him, and came with a cry. He thrust again, harder, faster, deeper, and was soon following her into that bliss.

As he lay panting, half on top of her and half to the side to avoid crushing her, he realized that he'd never known sex could be like that.

Because he'd never made love before.

He brushed her hair back from her cheek with one full palm and pressed a kiss to her shoulder. "Holy hell, that was so good."

She let out a long sigh and then turned toward him. As much as she could with him still mostly on top of her, his one leg pinning hers down. She gave him the most beautiful smile ever, and, for a second, he could breathe. She literally took his breath away.

"I'm so glad you told me you were staying before you did that to me," she said. "Because I would be devastated to think I would have to give that up. Ever."

His heart seized at *ever*.

He fucking wanted to propose to her. Right then, right there. Just like that. He'd been back in Bad for a handful of days. But here he was, not only planning to stay, but he now wanted to get married. Have babies. Start a business. Be a true part of this community.

"I think *you* did that to *me*," he finally said. His voice sounded rough and gritty.

"Oh, no," she said. She shifted, pulling herself out from under him. Then she pushed his shoulder, urging him to his back.

She kicked her remaining shoe off, pushed her jeans and panties down her leg, and dumped everything over the side of the bed. Then she swung a leg over his hips, straddling him. "But I'm *very* happy to do something to you this time." She stripped her shirt and bra off, tossing them to the floor.

"This time?" His hands were already resting on her hips. He was blatantly ogling the view too. She was perched on top of him, her naked body fully exposed, looking like a damned goddess. And not just the hair and lips and breasts and pussy and thighs and everything else he physically craved about her, but her expression and her attitude too. She was feeling sexy and strong and confident and… in love.

She was in love with him, and she knew he loved her too, and that was putting that cocky, sexy, I've-got-you-right-where-I-want-you look on her face.

He fucking loved everything about it.

"Yeah, this time." She circled her hips and lifted her hands to her breasts, teasing her nipples.

"You're insatiable."

"Yeah, I am. Thanks to you."

God, she looked hot. She was everything he could possibly want. Smart, funny, generous, and so damned beautiful.

He squeezed her hips. "I might need a minute."

"Okay. I'm good for a little bit." She gave him a wicked smile as she plucked and rolled a nipple with one hand. The other hand slid down to her clit where she pressed and circled, rocking her hips gently on him.

He felt his cock stirring. "Okay, I might not need as long as I thought."

She grinned. "Want me to stop?"

"Fuck no." He lifted his gaze to hers. Somehow. If someone would have asked if he *wanted* to see Priscilla playing with herself, he would have given a firm *hell, yeah*, but he'd had no idea it was something he *needed* to see.

He knew she loved the dirty talk, so, even though he was feeling softer and more emotional than he *ever* had during sex, he said, "If you stop before you come, I will flip you onto your back, tie you to this bed, and tease you with a vibrator until you've come four times before giving you my cock again."

Her eyes widened and her fingers stilled.

"Peach," he said warningly. "Don't stop."

"I don't know… that punishment sounds kind of amazing."

He chuckled and swatted her ass. "I'll add it to the list. How about you just make yourself come like this for me because you love me?"

Her smile softened from teasing to sweet. "You want this?"

He nodded. "So much."

"I'll do anything for you."

"Even have an orgasm? Gee, thanks." But he winked. He also put his hand on top of hers and pressed her finger against her clit. "Keep going. Please."

She was true to her word. She did do it for him. And a few other things that night.

And if he hadn't been fully addicted and ready to change his entire life for her already, he would have been by the time she rolled over and tried to leave his bed at four a.m.

PRISCILLA ROLLED OVER CAREFULLY SO she wouldn't wake Jase. She was amazed by how big the bed in the RV was, actually. She'd had no idea that RVs could hold king-sized beds. But the whole thing was enormous. She could see being very comfortable here. Maybe they could take it out camping. Not that she was the camping type. At all. Her idea of a campfire was the firepit at Carter's house. But in this thing? Where she could have Jase all to herself, out somewhere quiet and isolated, where they could make love all weekend long without anyone calling or stopping in or needing them for anything?

Yeah, that was going to happen.

And yes, she was using the term *make love*. Because last night —okay, earlier this morning if she was being technical—had been so far beyond sex that she didn't even have words for it.

The pleasure had been the same. Intense, bone-deep, toe-curling. His body, the things he did to hers with it, his hands, his mouth, all of it had been the same as the first time. But this had been… everything. This had *felt* like they'd expressed something in a way that was impossible to express any other way. Something she couldn't imagine expressing to anyone else, ever.

She shivered with giddiness as she grinned and slipped out from under his body and the sheet. She had never not wanted to get up at four a.m. more than she didn't want to get up now, but she had to.

She had a town to take care of.

And Jase would be here when she got back.

She had to suppress an actual squeal of delight at that thought.

He was staying. Because of her. *With* her. They were going to make this work. She wasn't going to have to give him up.

As she slipped into her bra and shirt, she realized that one shoe was still outside. Her grin only grew at that. It was far too early for anyone to be stopping by The Pork and Peach, so no one would have seen it out there. But she realized that she wouldn't have minded if they did. Last night it had felt so right for them to be together, and she would absolutely love to walk into The Bad Egg or Bad Habit holding Jase's hand, greeting people and smiling. She'd stand in line for her sugar free cinnamon vanilla latte from Elyse with her arm around Jase, making it clear they were together.

Jase was such a good guy. A very, very good guy. He always had been. He'd just had the wrong last name. She knew something about that herself. Yes, he'd been a bad boy. All of the Bad boys had been. But they had been *good guys*. Good guys who liked to have fun and ruffle feathers, sure, but they'd been loyal and hard-working and knew right from wrong when it really came down to it. Had they all made mistakes? Of course. They'd been kids. Jase had been a kid. Saddled with a family reputation that wasn't his fault.

But they had all grown into great men. And Jase was, by far, one of the best.

He was absolutely, in her opinion anyway, the best of the Bad boys.

She grinned as she stepped outside with one shoe in hand and used her phone's flashlight to locate the other one.

She shook the dirt from it and slipped her foot inside. These heels were not the ideal footwear for her morning errands, but they would have to do today. She hadn't spared any time to stop by her place to change.

She had taken three steps toward her car when the RV door opened and she heard, "You don't really think you're going off alone this morning do you?"

She gasped and spun to find Jase coming down the steps, pulling a t-shirt on. She got a very nice look at his abs before the green cotton covered them. He ran a hand through his tousled hair as he came to stand in front of her.

"I can't miss these things," she told him. She knew she was smiling up at him like a lovesick fool. Because she couldn't look at him without her stomach flipping and her heart swelling and feeling like she wanted to hug him and gush about all of her feelings and then strip him down and ride him hard like she had last night. All of those urges hit her at once as she looked up at him.

"Then I'm coming too," he said. He started toward her car.

"You are? It's four a.m.!"

"Yeah. Which is fucking ridiculous," he agreed. "But I'm not ready to let you go, and I get the feeling that you're not going to be willing to negotiate about this."

"I'm not." Though this man had a way of getting her to do things that just might make her miss her morning rounds for the first time in almost a year.

He stopped by her car and opened the driver's door, looking back at her. "So, let's go. You can tell me what the fuck happens in this sleepy little town at four a.m. that's so damned important on the way."

She grinned and crossed the dirt. She went up on tiptoe, gripping the front of his shirt, and pulling him down for a kiss. "I love you," she told him.

His eyes flared with emotion, and he moved her until her back was against the back door of the car and he was pressing into her. "Say it again," he demanded gruffly.

"I love you."

"I love you, too."

"Now get your hot ass in my car and maybe I'll have time to give you a blowjob in the shower when we're done with this."

He pressed his hips into hers. She could feel the bulge there and wanted, badly, to go back inside right now. She hadn't had her mouth on him like that yet and she *really* wanted to.

"I'm going to hold you to that, Peach."

"Good."

He kissed her hot and hard and then rounded the car and got in.

Grinning like an idiot, she slid in behind the steering wheel.

"So?" he asked as we pulled out onto the highway. "What the hell is all this?"

"My paper route," she told him, looking over with a smile.

"Your what now?" he asked.

"My newspaper route."

"You have a… what does that mean?"

She pulled into the parking lot of Bad Gas and drove to the east side of the building. She pointed. "They drop the Times-Picayune off here. And I deliver it to everyone who subscribes."

"You have a paper route," Jase said, shaking his head.

"I've only been doing it for about a year, but I got tired of having to replace the carriers when they quit or didn't do the job well, so I decided it was easier to just do it myself." She shifted her car into park. "Wait here."

She got out and started to grab the stack of papers.

"Like hell," Jase said, joining her and hefting the stacks of papers, then throwing them into the backseat for her.

"Thanks." She gave him a grin.

"You really deliver the Times-Pic every morning at four a.m.?" Jase asked as she got back behind the wheel.

"Well, three times a week. Once a week I deliver the Bad News."

He just shook his head disbelievingly.

"If you want something done right, do it yourself," she told him with a shrug. She turned the car out of the parking lot and headed for her first stop.

Of course, the paper route wasn't the only thing she did while she was out and about the town while it was quiet and no one was around. It was nice that a lot of people in Bad got the New Orleans newspaper. The Bad News was mostly local things—the town fish fry, basketball team practice notices, rummage sales, obituaries. The things that really mattered directly to the town. But the Times-Pic covered more state and national issues and news. There was entertainment and politics and a great living section.

But the best thing about a lot of people in Bad subscribing to the larger paper was that it helped Priscilla out too. It was a great reason to drive around and check on people.

Jase was clearly still dealing with the fact that this was not even in the top ten things he'd thought she was doing at four a.m. every morning. But he was also amused, it seemed.

After her first ten stops, where she just pulled up, got out, tossed the paper onto the front step, and got back into the car again, she parked at the end of Rosewood Lane. This area was an older part of town. Big houses with wide front porches, sidewalks that weren't quite straight anymore, tall, solid trees that had seen a lot of life, and a lower price point than the "other" side of town. The side where she'd grown up.

There were a lot of older people who had lived in the Rosewood area for fifty-plus years, but there were also some young families and even some singles who couldn't afford the newer homes or who were renting over here.

It was not a "bad" part of town. But it was just a little worn around the edges. Like a well-loved blanket that had been cuddled a lot or a favorite pair of jeans that had been washed over and over again.

Priscilla got out and opened the back door again, this time grabbing her huge bag. She filled it with papers, three books, the four small boxes of cereal, bananas, and the dog leash she always brought along. She shut the door quietly—most of the neighborhood was asleep after all—and then motioned to Jase.

He got out of the car with a puzzled look.

"We're walking for a little bit here," she told him.

"'Kay." He shut his door softly too and joined her on the sidewalk.

They started toward the two-story blue house on the corner. It needed a coat of paint and some new shingles. The lawn was covered with toys, there were three shoes on the walk to the front door—none of them matched—and two bikes behind the minivan parked in the driveway.

She moved the bikes first. Lydia never looked—her hands full of bags and kids and her mind on a million other things—before she backed out and she'd ruined two bikes already. They'd gotten them replaced with donations, of course, but one of these times it was going to do major damage to her van.

Priscilla tidied up the yard, gathered up the shoes and set them just inside the door of the front porch—where the kids were supposed to put them—and tucked the plastic grocery bag that held the cereal and bananas in with them.

Then she headed back down the walkway.

"You didn't leave a paper," Jase said.

"Oh, they don't get a paper," she told him. "But a few of the neighbors do." Only about six people on this whole street did. But this street needed some other things. Like TLC.

"You stop by that house on your paper route, but they don't get a paper?" he asked.

"Right."

They were talking in hushed tones. No one inside the house would have likely heard them even at normal volume, but there was something about the dark and the early morning and the secretive tasks at hand that seemed to call for whispering.

"Because they need other things," Jase said. It wasn't a question.

She nodded. "I know Lydia, of course." Most everyone in Bad knew everyone else, but being Pastor Williams's granddaughter and the mayor's daughter and assistant meant that she truly did know almost everyone. Or knew of them, at least.

"But I noticed a few things the first couple of times I passed by," Priscilla went on as they crossed the street. "Then I asked some questions. She's a mom of three and a nurse. She works twelve-hour shifts and she's always really tired when she gets home. She just doesn't have enough time or energy or help. Mrs. Conner," she pointed across the street, "has complained to city hall a few times about what a mess Lydia's yard always is, and Annabelle told me that the kids don't always get there in time for breakfast at school. So…" Priscilla shrugged. "I help out."

Annabelle taught high school, but, in such a small town, it was easy enough to keep tabs on all of the kids and families at the school. And Annabelle was the type to pay attention. Priscilla had asked Annabelle to let her know if any families or individual kids needed anything.

She didn't know if it came from the sense of altruism she'd been raised with in the church or her belief as a city employee that the town should be supporting their families or if she was just nosey. She liked to think it was one of the first two. But the last one was possible. She never talked about the people she helped with anyone, though. Not until Jase. But she knew he'd keep the information between them.

"You clean up her yard and bring them breakfast."

"Not because she can't afford it, but I know she tries to get them to school for breakfast because it's easier and saves her time. She already has to get all the kids ready for school and get herself ready for work. She just doesn't always get them there on time. So I just bring little stuff. Basics."

"Stuff they can eat in the van on the way to school," Jase said.

She nodded. "Exactly."

"That's pretty great, Cilla."

She smiled. "Thanks. I just hope it starts their day off a little better."

"I'm sure it does."

She tossed a paper up on Mrs. Conner's front step. Margaret Conner needed to be more tolerant and less judgmental. So Priscilla also, anonymously, left a couple of typed-up Bible verses about those topics in her mailbox. But she didn't mention *that* to Jase. She told herself that she was trying to be helpful by doing that. But that was also a little judgy on *her* part, and she knew it.

They walked past a couple more houses until they got to Andrew Thompson's house. "This one is really fun," she told Jase with a smile.

They headed around the side of the house. There was a doghouse out back, and she called softly, "Hey, Wiggle."

A moment later a tiny white, gray, and black puppy came barreling out of the house. He woofed and she dropped to her knees, gathering him close, quieting him. Since she visited so early in the morning, it was important he didn't bark with her.

"Hi, baby. Hi, sweetie." He licked her face and chin, his body wriggling, his tail wagging madly.

He was clearly part shepherd of some kind, but Andrew had found him by the road, and they had no idea what mix he was exactly or where he'd come from. The vet in Autre had checked him over and said he was healthy and had given Andrew and Priscilla a crash course on puppy care.

"Who is this?" Jase asked, grinning as she got to her feet.

He put his hand on the puppy's head, stroking and accepting kisses to his fingers and palm.

"This is Wiggle," she said. "Andrew adopted him about a month ago."

"And you can't resist saying hi to him every morning?" Jase asked.

"Andrew's mom didn't want to keep him. She thought he'd be too much work. Andrew is ten and autistic. His teacher and another mom with an autistic son think that a dog could be really good for him, but his mom doesn't have time to take care of a dog. So I help."

"Of course you do."

She looked up to find Jase watching her with an affectionate expression.

That made her feel warm, and she grinned. "It's not like it's a hardship," she said. "Look at him." She held the puppy up, and Wiggle licked Jase's chin.

He laughed. "He's cute as hell."

She nodded. "He is. And I assured Andrew's mom that I'd take him if need be but that I thought we should give Andrew a chance. So, when I come by in the morning, I take Wiggle with me, so he gets his walk. We also work on commands, and I give him his breakfast and clean up the yard. Then, when Andrew gets home from school, he does another walk and plays with him, feeds him again, cleans up. But that way he's got a grown-up helping him out."

Jase nodded. "That's pretty cool. I think every kid should have a pet. It teaches you a lot."

"It does. And Andrew has a hard time at school. He needs someone to love him unconditionally."

"We all need that," Jase said, a little gruffly.

She smiled. "Yeah, we really do."

They put Wiggle on the leash, something he was getting more used to and better about, and they started up the block to finish the route, the puppy trotting along happily beside them.

Priscilla tossed three papers onto steps without stopping, but then they got to Jeremy Franklin's house.

"We have to go around to the side. He never hears me knock on the front door."

"You're knocking?" Jase asked. "Won't that wake him up?"

"Exactly." She grinned as they stopped by Jeremy's bedroom window, and she rapped on the glass three times. "Jeremy is new in town," she explained as she waited for a sign that he was awake and out of bed. "He served some time in jail and had a hard time finding work because of it. Coach hired him to do some farm work part-time, and Luke and Randi have him doing some work at the shop." She knocked on the window again, harder. This time a light came on inside. "But he has a hard time waking up and getting to work on time, so I get him up each morning."

"Wow," Jase said.

She looked over. "What?"

"I shouldn't be surprised that Coach and Luke and Randi—and you—gave the guy a chance, but that's awesome."

She nodded. "People make mistakes. If we never give them a chance to make up for it then we're saying that we don't deserve a second chance either, and that would make *me*, personally, very nervous."

She knocked once more and finally heard the knock in return. She smiled, turned away from the window, and started back around the house.

"He has to knock back?"

"He can turn the light on from his bed and then go back to sleep." She stepped off the lawn and onto the sidewalk. "To knock on the window, he has to get out of bed. Once he's up, he won't go back to sleep."

"And you know about the layout of his bedroom, how?" Jase asked, his voice dropping lower.

She grinned. She liked him possessive. She shouldn't, but she did. She liked him wanting her to be *his*. "He told me. The day he stopped me at the coffee shop and begged me to *make* him knock back before I left him alone because he'd gone back to sleep and missed his shift with Luke."

Jase nodded. "Okay. I don't see any reason for you to know exactly where his bed is in relation to his window."

She laughed. "I don't either."

They were quiet as they walked toward Karen Woodstrom's house, but, when they stopped in front of her gate,

Jase asked, "And Luke let him come back after he missed that shift?"

"Yeah."

"Good guy."

"Very. There are a lot of them here."

Jase nodded.

"You'll fit right in."

Without warning, he reached out, snagged the front of her jeans, and pulled her close. He gave her a deep, sweet kiss. "Thanks for being one of those people that believes in giving second chances," he said against her mouth.

She felt the prickle of tears at the back of her eyes. "Thanks for confirming, very clearly, that it's the right thing to do."

They kissed again, but Wiggle reminded them that they had more work to do. He jumped up on his hind legs, front paws on Priscilla's jeans. He was fine with frequent stops, but they couldn't last too long.

She laughed and patted him. "Yes, we'll keep moving. You're being such a good boy." She looked around. "Hey, Darwin. Hey kitty, kitty, kitty," she called softly.

She turned in a circle. The cat liked the porch next door, the tree in the side yard, and the bushes by the front fence.

"Come on kitty, time to go in."

"There's a cat this time?" Jase asked.

"Darwin," she confirmed. "Karen's back screen door doesn't latch tightly, and he gets out every night. She panics in the morning—full-blown anxiety attack—when she can't find him. But she never remembers to latch the door. So it helps everyone when I find Darwin during my route and put him back inside."

"And Wiggle is okay with Darwin?"

"Oh, sure," she told him. "Though Darwin is less enchanted with Wiggle."

"And does Karen get a paper?" Jase asked. He sounded amused. He was also clearly searching the area for the cat.

Priscilla smiled. "She does."

"Well, at least it's not a stop just for the cat."

She put a hand on her hip. "No, it's a stop to help Karen with her anxiety."

Jase faced her. He nodded. "I know. I was teasing. I'm sorry. I think this is… really nice."

She nodded, accepting his apology. "Okay. Good."

He didn't think this was silly. He couldn't. She loved doing this. She loved helping these people out, and if he thought it was a waste of time… how would that make her feel about *him*?

"*Meow*." The cat came sauntering out from under the neighbor's porch.

"Good morning, Darwin," Priscilla said with a smile.

"He comes for you?"

"He does." She bent and scooped up the orange tabby with one hand, nuzzling him a little. "The first time I had to be more… insistent. And it definitely took longer. But the second time it was raining, and he was freezing cold and was so happy that I was able to let him back in that we came to an agreement. He gets to go out and do his cat business, but when I come by, it's time to go back inside before Karen even knows he's gone." She spoke as she carried him around to Karen's back door. She pulled it open, set Darwin down, and told him "See you tomorrow," to which he gave her a flick of his tail and headed into the house. She shut the door firmly, making sure the latch caught.

"I could fix that. Easily," Jase said, eyeing the door. "I could bring my tools along tomorrow."

She smiled. "That's sweet. But I don't think it needs to be fixed. Karen has a little dementia—not bad enough that she can't live alone, but enough that she's forgetful and anxious at times. Darwin is her best friend. She loves him so much that she never lets him out. If the door was fixed and he couldn't get out by himself, he'd never get to go out. But he always comes to me, and I'm able to get him back inside before she wakes up. It's really a win-win for them both this way."

Jase shook his head with a slight smile.

"What?"

"You even care about the cat's feelings in this?"

She gave a little gasp. "Well, of course! Darwin should get to live his best life too."

Jase chuckled. He looked at her bag. It was still pretty full. "Okay, where to next?"

"A paper next door, and then Lauren's house."

"Let's go."

As they headed up the sidewalk, he slipped his hand in hers, lacing their fingers. Her heart stuttered. She looked up at him.

"You're pretty amazing, you know that?" he asked.

"Because I find cats and bring cold breakfast to some kids and make sure a guy gets up in time for work?"

"Yes." He said it simply. He didn't try to make it more than it was but…

It didn't need to be more than it was, did it? What she was doing made a difference for those people and it made her feel good. It was all-around just a good thing. Simple. And good.

She smiled as she tossed the paper onto Arthur Bekins's porch.

Then they crossed the street to Lauren's house. But instead of approaching the house, Priscilla went to the little beat-up red Honda sitting at the curb. She opened the back door and pulled the three books out of her bag, putting them on the back seat under the pink sweater that was always there for this exact purpose.

"What's this about?" Jase asked.

"Lauren is a junior at the high school. She's incredibly bright. In fact, she struggles a little because she's not really being challenged enough. Her mom is a religious freak and closely monitors—and censors—what she reads."

"A religious freak?"

"She goes to my grandpa's church," Priscilla confirmed the unspoken question. "And I've overheard the things she comes in wanting counsel on. She even bothers my grandpa a little, honestly."

"So you sneak Lauren books?"

"Yes." She lifted her chin. She knew that some people, including her grandfather, would find that terrible. She was going against a mother's wishes for her own daughter.

But that daughter had come to Annabelle begging for help. Annabelle had wanted so badly to help but wasn't sure what she should do. She didn't want to cause an issue that the school might have to address if she was the one to supply the books. So Priscilla had assured Annabelle that she would do it. Annabelle gave Priscilla the books she thought Lauren would enjoy and would challenge her. Then Priscilla brought them to Lauren, giving Annabelle plausible deniability. Priscilla had zero guilt about giving Lauren classic books that generations of people had read and loved and learned from.

"Good for you," Jase said.

"Really?"

"Yeah." He gave her a grin. "You know I like the bad-girl, rebellious streak in you."

She smiled, but then frowned. "Do you think it's bad I'm doing this?"

Jase took her upper arms in his hands and made her look at him. "No. I really don't. You're helping people, Cilla. You're giving them little things. But little things can make such a huge difference. Maybe one of these books will teach her something that will make her want to be a scientist or an astronaut or a teacher or doctor. Maybe one of them will make her want to be a writer. Or maybe they'll just entertain her when it's hard to sleep or give her an escape when her mom is being crazy. You can't control what people do with what you give them, but giving it to them, for the right reasons, matters."

She stared at him for a long moment. Then she threw her arms around his neck and hugged him. It was a full body hug and he returned it, wrapping her up and pulling her close.

They held each other for a long moment, and she felt her heart hammering and her eyes stinging. "God, I *really, really* like you, Jase Hawkins."

He squeezed her. "Ditto, Priscilla Williams. Fucking ditto."

She pulled back and gave him a big smile. There was nothing sexual about the moment and that made her almost as happy and warm as anything they'd done naked.

"Thank you for letting me come with you this morning," he said, his voice gruff.

And she knew he was feeling some of it too.

"I'm so glad you did."

They smiled at each other goofily for another long moment, but Wiggle gave a little woof and ran around them, winding his leash around their ankles, anxious to get moving again.

She stepped back, carefully. "I have a couple more papers to deliver but those are all the extra stops. We have to take Wiggle home and give him breakfast on the way back to the car though."

He smiled. "I really liked all of this."

"Now you know why I don't hate getting up at four a.m.."

He nodded. "And now it won't be quite so hard letting you get out of my bed. I'll probably even come along again once in a while."

"You don't have to."

"I want to."

And that was exactly what she'd wanted him to say. "You're always welcome. Wherever I go."

"Good. Because I really want to be wherever you are."

She tilted her head and gave him a grin. "We're getting a little mushy."

"Yeah."

"You okay with that? Is your bad boy reputation going to survive?"

He sighed dramatically. "Well, I'm going to have to bend you over a sawhorse and talk dirty to you when we get back, just to be sure to balance out the sweetness from the puppies and old ladies and little kids."

Priscilla nodded. "You *really* should do that."

He took Wiggle's leash from her. "How about a nice morning jog, pup?" he asked the dog, starting to run toward Wiggle's house.

She laughed. "I still have papers to deliver."

"You do that. I'll clean up his yard and give him fresh water."

He was going to clean up dog poop in order to get her home faster? Yeah, that was love. "The dog food is in a bin by the back door. Give him breakfast too."

Jase gave her a thumbs up, and he and Wiggle took off down the block.

By the time she caught up with them, her papers all delivered, the dog had been played with, fed, and watered, and was already snoozing in his house again.

Jase, on the other hand, didn't seem a bit tired. He threw her over his shoulder and carried her to the car.

And then made good on his promise about the sawhorse.

Very good.

IT WAS SHOCKINGLY easy to fall into a routine over the next four weeks.

Jase would wake up to an empty bed, but when Cilla returned from her "morning rounds", as she referred to her paper route and other stops, she had stopped by her house, showered and dressed for the day, and then come back with muffins and coffee that they ate at the bar—using stools that she had, in fact, "borrowed" from the church storage closet.

The first three days, Cilla stuck around and helped clean up a little before the guys showed up to help with the big stuff, but he'd hired a crew of four quickly, including Jeremy, the guy Cilla woke each morning. Coach and Luke had been trying to get the guy enough hours to equal full-time but they were relieved that Jase could also offer him work, and, between the three of them, he was very busy. And happy.

The other three guys were young guys who Zeke Landry had recommended, and they all knew their way around a construction site and worked hard.

They were making amazing headway within just a few days, and Carter and Jackson were able to go back to *their* regular jobs.

Jase saw them though, almost every day. They all got

together for lunch at least four out of five weekdays, and Jase now joined them. Sometimes it was at the café, sometimes it was at Marc's bar, Bad Brews, and once in a while, it was just sitting around with sandwiches on the tailgates of their trucks in The Pork and Peach's parking lot or even down on Main Street, between Luke's garage and the police station where Carter was. Jackson didn't have an office yet, but he made a point of coming through town around noon each day. It was nice.

No, it was really fucking great.

Jase loved it. He loved talking with the guys, catching up, and bullshitting. Within a week he'd felt like he never left. The guys had all matured, had new responsibilities and perspectives since he'd last been in Bad, but, for the most part, his friends were the same guys deep down. Where it mattered.

They were sitting on the back of Carter's truck at the curb outside Bad Brakes, and Luke had just sauntered out to join them when Cilla pulled up and honked.

Jase waved at her, grinning like a fool, he was sure, and jumped off the tailgate.

"A girl pulls up and honks and you jump?" Carter asked.

"That girl?" he asked. "Definitely."

They all laughed. He made a beeline straight for Cilla's driver's side window. "Hey, Peach."

"Hey." She gave him a grin that shot straight to his cock. "I want to take you to lunch today."

"Is that code for you want a quickie in the backseat of your car?" he asked, brushing a strand of hair back from her cheek and tucking it behind her ear.

Her eyes flared with heat, but she shook her head. "Actual food. Sorry."

He laughed. "Well, I like food too. Maybe not as much as quickies, but it's still good."

"How about a raincheck on the quickie?" she asked.

"Deal."

"So, get in. They only serve until one."

"They?"

She smiled. "Just get in."

He turned back to the guys. "I'll see you guys later."

"Lucky fucker," Jackson said.

"Yeah, just rub it in," Carter added.

But they all waved to Cilla, who waved back sweetly. Jase got in, and she pulled away.

"They'll be even more jealous when they find out that you not only get lunch, but also a show today," she said.

"Lunch and a show?" He settled back in the seat. "My interest is definitely piqued. I would assume you were talking about a private strip show on the newly completed stage at the community center, but you already said no quickie and I would *absolutely* be getting that if you were stripping for me."

"You're right." Cilla shot him a flirty, mischievous look that he loved.

The new community center was definitely coming along. A lot of the basic interior repairs had been finished, including the new stage. It was on the opposite end of the main room from where the stripper stage had been and was much bigger. It needed to be because of the fashion shows, little kid Christmas programs, and the other things that they planned to do with it. He loved seeing the place coming together. He was actually surprised by how much he liked seeing it made over into something new.

The dark wood walls were now fully drywalled and just needed to be painted. The scarred wood flooring was now mostly white and gray tile. The wooden beams overhead had been painted, and the windows had been widened. They still needed to put in new doors, put up some interior walls, and replace appliances... there was a long way to go. But the progress was significant. Anyone could see they were serious about the work.

They'd taken down the Pork and Peach sign too.

That had been an interesting day, actually. He hadn't

expected to be emotional about it in any way, and yet it had been nostalgic watching the thing come down.

They'd stored the stupid thing in one of Coach's barns. He said someday it would be worth money. Jase sincerely doubted it, but it didn't feel right to haul it to the dump either, and he appreciated Coach storing it.

They hadn't replaced it with anything yet. They needed to see what the city wanted to call it—if it would just be The Bad Community Center or if someone would come up with something more fun, like Let the Bad Times Roll, which Jackson had suggested and thought was hilarious.

The exterior also needed more work. That was something else the city council needed to meet about again and decide on. Since they hadn't built the building from the ground up, some of the exterior plans weren't exactly as drawn up. Jase could put almost any exterior over the existing, but, before he went through that hassle, Cilla was going to talk to the council about the idea of just repainting or residing what was already there.

Cilla turned into a parking lot at the end of Main Street.

"The Senior Citizen Center?" he asked her.

"Yep." She smiled. "I come to lunch here at least once a week, and I wanted you to see another program I put in place."

She was so… cute. He'd used a lot of adjectives to describe this woman in the past, but cute had never been one of them. But she was. She loved this shit. These little "programs" of hers were going on all over town.

Like the "program" where the two retired engineers, who had sat at the coffee shop and bitched about how kids these days didn't know basic math and couldn't even count back change, now had tutoring hours twice a week at their table in Bad Habit.

Or the "program" where the three young moms, who complained that teenagers left the park littered with trash, now took their kids on a daily walk that included park clean-up. It was a great way to keep the park looking great and teach the little kids about civic duty and how to respect public places. At least, that's how Cilla had sold it to those moms. And it had worked. They even got their names on a little plaque at the park's entrance near the flower garden she'd also "let" them plant and care for.

Heaven forbid someone complain about something in town, because they would end up in charge of helping fix that something.

He thought it was awesome. She was awesome. And it was clear everyone thought so.

They headed inside and were greeted with the aroma of spaghetti sauce and garlic bread along with the sounds of music and little kid laughter.

They stepped into the large, main room to find the tables had been pushed to the sides, creating a big open space in the center. There were couples filling that space, and it looked like they were dancing. But the couples were a little odd.

Each was comprised of a senior and a child. The kids couldn't have been more than about four or five. Some of the seniors stood, some sat, some were in wheelchairs, but each was paired with a child. They were facing one another, and, yes, they were definitely dancing.

"What is this?" he asked, feeling a smile in spite of not knowing exactly what he was really looking at.

Cilla's grin was huge when she looked up at me. "A couple of the local daycares come up here for lunch twice a week. In addition to sharing the meal, they also do various activities together. It's amazing. The older people get a new kind of stimulation, and the kids learn to interact with older people naturally."

"Are they dancing?" he asked.

"Kind of. Once a week they do a quiet activity like reading or coloring or a craft. And once a week the activity is more… active. They toss balls or play corn hole or bat balloons back and forth. They call this the mirror game. One of them does something and their partner has to do the same thing as if they're looking in a mirror."

There was a lot more giggling going on than anything else, and he found himself laughing along with them.

"It's contagious, isn't it?" Cilla asked, looking up at him.

"It is. This is great."

"I love coming and just observing. It's so sweet and so good for everyone."

"And no one has any idea that you're behind this, right?" he asked her.

She flapped her hand, waving that away. "Not really. The daycare providers bring the kids. The Senior Center staff makes this all work. They come up with the games and things. I just got it started."

"But no one knows that, do they?" he pressed.

She shook her head. "Not many."

He turned and watched her instead of the kids and their playmates. She was enchanted by the whole thing, clearly. And he was madly in love with her. In part because this enchanted her.

"You could be mayor, you know."

Cilla looked up at him quickly. "What?"

"You could be mayor. Right now. If you wanted to."

She laughed. "No way."

"Well, you'd have to come out about all of this stuff you've been doing," he conceded. "But if everyone knew what all you've done, you'd win hands down. And," he added, "I think you'd probably win anyway. Plenty of people know you. Have known you for a long time. They know how you get stuff done. And the people at the pool would talk. And the people here would talk. Daisy would talk. Luke and Randi. Carter. Annabelle. Regan. Those are local businesspeople and life-long residents. Their parents and siblings live here. You have the support and respect and trust of a whole town full of people who also have support and respect and trust." He nodded. "If you wanted it, you could have it."

She swallowed and wet her lips.

He watched her for a moment before he asked, "But you don't want it, do you?"

She frowned. "I don't know what you mean. I've been groomed to be in charge all my life."

"Yep. You have. Which means that if you wanted it, *really* wanted it, you would have been putting all that feistiness and fire into it, and you'd be running this town by now." He paused. Then said, "Which you've done. You *do* run this town. In all the important ways. In the ways that matter, not just to this town, but to you."

Her expression softened. "Do you think so? You think it matters to them?"

He looked out at the room full of people of all ages, smiling and laughing, having one of the best moments of their day. Maybe their week. Because of Cilla. "Are you kidding?" He looked back at her. "It absolutely does. You make this town better. Every day. In a thousand ways."

She looked sincerely touched by that and his heart squeezed. Didn't she know this?

"And I think you like it this way," he went on. "You like being behind the scenes. You know that people need stuff done, not just words and platitudes and being told what they should do to make their lives better or how they should live differently. Because you've seen *that* your whole life. You've seen your family out front telling people how to live and how to treat one another. But you've also seen that there are still gaps. There are still things… *people*… that are getting missed. In spite of all the words. So, you're actually *doing* something about it."

Some of this he hadn't put into actual words before now. It had occurred to him, even when she'd first come to convince him to leave town, that Cilla was a do-er. In a family of talkers. Preachers, literally. But now that Jase was saying it all out loud, it made even more sense.

"And," he added, "you don't need to be in front of committees trying to motivate other people to do things, or making speeches about the things that should be done, or in a pulpit—literal or figurative—talking about the way things *should* be. You just get out there and make it happen. You *need* to actually help and serve. That's what makes you happy too."

There was a beat of silence while she just stared at him. Then he heard someone clear their throat behind him. Jase glanced over his shoulder.

And froze.

It was Aaron Williams. Cilla's grandfather.

One of those people who did a whole lot of talking.

Well… fuck.

Jase winced and turned. "Hello, Pastor Williams." He extended his hand.

Aaron took it, giving it a firm, but friendly, shake. "Jase. Nice to see you."

Was it? Well, at least that was the polite thing to say.

"I'm sorry. I didn't mean to insult you with what I said," Jase said, tucking his hands into his pockets, assuming the pastor had overheard.

Aaron shook his head. "You didn't mean for me to *overhear* what you said."

"Well… yes."

"So that's not exactly insulting. You weren't directing it *to* me."

"I can honestly say I would not have said that if I'd known you would hear," Jase told him dryly.

The other man chuckled. "Well, I hope you would have still said the lovely, and true, things about my granddaughter." He gave Cilla a smile. "Hello, sweetheart."

"Hi, Grandpa," she said. Her smile was weak, though.

"I would have said those things," Jase agreed. "They're all true. She does a lot of wonderful things for this town."

"Indeed, she does," Pastor Williams said. Then he took a breath and met Jase's eyes. "And you're also right that people need more than words and platitudes. Though, I would argue that words can be very helpful at times. And I try very hard not to be too cliché."

Jase winced again. "Of course."

"But we can talk all about what you think of my sermons sometime after you've heard a few," he said with a smile that actually seemed genuine. "I'm sure Priscilla can make room in the pew for you."

Aaron Williams looked every bit the nice old man, and he had a calm, comforting, small-town preacher's voice and demeanor. But he didn't beat around the bush.

Jase nodded. "I think I can find my way to the church." Because what was he going to say?

"I'll ring the bell extra loud this Sunday just for you," Pastor Williams said. Then he gave Jase a wink.

An actual fucking wink. Like a friendly, this-will-be-great wink.

What was going on?

Aaron looked at Cilla. "He knows you well."

She nodded. "He does."

"I like that. You deserve to be seen."

Jase felt his eyes widen. That was very… supportive of him. He'd always had the impression that Aaron Williams had a certain idea about how things should go in this town, and that absolutely included with his family.

Of course, there was a reason that Cilla hid her light and Aaron was a part of that.

Yeah, Jase knew that hiding-your-light thing had to do with a Bible story or something. There was some verse about not hiding your light under a basket but letting it shine so everyone could see it. And he knew that particular verse, or whatever it was, because it had been on a poster in that Sunday school classroom where he had first debased Priscilla Williams.

Ironic.

"I'm seen enough." She reached out and took Jase's hand.

He laced their fingers together and gave her hand a squeeze.

"Are you?" Aaron asked her, frowning slightly.

"I am." She lifted her chin.

"I guess I'm glad you feel that way." Aaron looked almost sad.

Jase looked down at Cilla. What was going on?

"But you have to know that *we* would really like to be a part of the things you're doing. The things that make you happy," Aaron went on.

Cilla took a deep breath and then let it out. "It looks like you know what's going on with me anyway. As usual."

"If you mean that I found out you're seeing Jase, then yes," Aaron agreed. "But I would have loved to hear about it from you."

She shook her head. "It's really just so much easier to do my thing and not go over everything with you and Mom."

Aaron nodded. "I understand that."

"Do you?" she asked. "I've been in the spotlight all my life as a Williams. People have always watched what I do and have judged the way I act and react. I've been told for as long as I can remember that what I do and say and *how* I do it and say it reflects on you and your ministry and on Mom and her leadership roles. But I've finally been included in a group of people that don't care about all of that. Who are fine with me no matter what. And," she looked up at Jase and took a breath, "like Jase said, I'm good behind the scenes. I'm okay without people knowing everything I'm doing. Not just because it's easier, but because I do know it's important, and feeling good about it myself matters more than if you and Mom approve."

"You don't think we would approve of you helping Lydia and Jeremy and Andrew and the rest? You don't think we would be proud of the work you've done with the recycling program and with the pet adoption and here?" Aaron gestured with his hand to include the room where the mirror game was, apparently, wrapping up.

"You know about all of that?" Cilla asked.

"Of course I do," Aaron said gently.

She sighed. "Of course you do."

"And I think it's wonderful. But not sharing it with us doesn't give us the chance to support you and *tell* you that it's wonderful. It doesn't allow us to tap into our resources to get them even more help—"

"It's okay for you and Mom to not be involved in every single thing that happens in this town!" Cilla interrupted. "See? That's part of it too. I didn't want you to take it over. I *like* helping. I like being creative. But every time there's something that involves you or Mom, that all gets overridden. You two always have to be the stars. Helping our neighbors doesn't need to have a star. Bringing senior citizens together with little kids for playtime and helping a single mom have less hectic mornings and getting a lonely new widower involved with fostering kittens… none of that has to have a star, Grandpa. It just needs to be done. Without worrying about praise and kudos." She took a shaky breath. "I know it's hard to believe, but I don't need your support and praise. I'm doing okay on my own."

Aaron seemed taken aback by all of that. Jase sure as hell was.

The Priscilla he had known had been very aware of her place in town as a Williams and had let that guide her. Not just her good girl side, but even her bad girl side. If it hadn't been downright scandalous, he wasn't sure he would have gotten her into that Sunday school classroom on the night that changed his life.

But now, this woman was strong and clearly sure of herself and had figured out, somewhere along the way, how to be who she wanted to be *and* be a Williams in Bad, Louisiana at the same time.

He was proud of her.

Slowly, Aaron seemed to process all of that. He finally nodded. "I can see that you're doing okay on your own," he said. He looked at me, then back to his granddaughter. "I'm very sorry that you don't want us involved, but I can see that that's on us too. But I'm mostly sorry that it carries over to not wanting to involve us in your relationship."

Cilla frowned. "What are you doing here, anyway? You don't come up here for lunch."

"No, but I know that you do. I saw you pick Jase up on Main Street and head in this direction. I thought maybe I'd have a chance to talk to you both together. Since you haven't brought him to the house or to church."

Cilla sighed. "Why would I bring the grandson of your arch nemesis to your house, Grandpa?"

Aaron nodded. "I suppose that's a fair question. And I probably should have started by telling you that my feelings for Jarvis do not extend to Jase."

Cilla's eyebrows rose, but not as high as Jase's did. "They don't?" Jase asked.

"Of course not. He's your grandfather," Aaron said. "Just like my granddaughter is her own person, I know you are too. My beef with Jarvis isn't about you."

"Because he's not reopening The Pork and Peach," Cilla said. "If he were, you'd feel differently."

Aaron frowned. "I did not like or approve of Jarvis's business, no. But my feelings for him were about more than that."

"What were they about?" Jase had to ask.

Aaron blew out a breath and hitched a shoulder. "Mostly two young, stupid, arrogant, stubborn men who were enough alike to drive the other crazy and different enough to not see eye to eye on almost anything." He shook his head. "Our rivalry went *way* back. Long before I ever dreamed of being a preacher. I'm sure before he would have ever thought of owning a strip club." Aaron gave a short laugh. "Though that might not be true. He might have been thinking about that at age fifteen."

"Your conflict started with him when you were fifteen?" he asked. Damn, these guys really could hold a grudge.

"It did," Aaron nodded.

"Over what?" he asked.

Aaron gave him a wry grin. "A girl, of course."

Jase's eyes widened. "You fought over a girl?"

He nodded. "Literally. I broke his nose. And she still chose him." He paused. "It was your grandmother by the way."

Jase felt his mouth drop open. "No."

"Yes." Aaron nodded. "I was madly in love with her." He shrugged. "And I, of course, then had to hate the man who won her heart."

"*That* was the reason you and Jarvis never got along?" Cilla demanded. "Really?"

"Of course not. That's just how it started. And neither of us could ever swallow our pride and let it go," Aaron said. "But it evolved over the years. We were very different people. We saw the world very differently. He didn't respect the path I took. He found me condescending and pompous. I didn't respect the path he took. I found him crude and felt that he was leading people astray." Aaron shrugged again as if there just wasn't much more to say about it. "Your grandfather could be a real ass."

Jase gave a soft snort and nodded. "No arguments from me."

Aaron pinned Cilla with an unwavering gaze. "But none of that has to do with Jase. Which I would have been happy to tell you if you'd come to me and told me you were involved with him."

"I…" She swallowed. "I just didn't want to deal with it. I wanted to just do my thing." She moved in a little closer to him. "Like the stuff with Jeremy and Lydia and everyone. I just wanted to do what I knew in my heart was right. I've been trying to get out of the Williams' shadow for so long, and when Jase came to town and Mom told me to find out what he was doing here and talk him out of it… and I went out to The Pork and Peach to do that… I realized that I'm really under her thumb. I first proposed the idea of the community center to Jase because I wanted to show Mom that I could do a great job with negotiations and projects. But it quickly became about it being a good thing for *him*. And for the town. When I found out she went and talked to the city council members, I just got mad. I knew the project was the right thing and that she was against it was really the last straw. I just decided that while she obviously had a say in the community center, she wasn't going to have a say in anything that was just about me and that I knew was good and right." Cilla looked up at Jase again and smiled. "Like Jase and me. This is good and right, and I don't care what she thinks."

His heart kicked against his ribs. But it was an almost painful thump. He loved that she was so sure of them and that she was willing to stand up to her mom. But he hated the idea that she felt like she had to choose.

He was willing to prove himself to her mom. He didn't have to change to do that. He just had to let Melinda Williams get to know him. He was a good guy. Mostly. He was a great contractor. And he loved her daughter. He could win Melinda over. Probably.

He hated that Cilla was hiding all her good deeds from the people of the town. He understood why, but her light needed to shine. And he hated that she was hiding *them* from her family. Again, he understood it. But he didn't want her going around, following her heart but afraid of people finding out what was *in* her heart.

"You need to give your mother more credit," Aaron said with a frown. "Hell, you need to give a lot of people more credit, Priscilla."

Hearing the pastor say "hell" was interesting. His tone had also gotten harder. He was clearly upset.

"More credit for what?" Cilla asked. "She told me not to make Jase any big promises about the building and then went to have 'conversations' with the city council members. I know what that means."

"It means that she went and talked to them about your idea," Aaron said. "You don't know what she told them."

"I can imagine. She really wants that new building."

"Your mother likes new, shiny things," Aaron said. "But that doesn't mean she's completely unreasonable. And you definitely don't know what the council members said in return." He frowned. "You didn't give any of *them* credit. You didn't let them ask you any questions or talk to Jase or even meet about it. You didn't give *yourself* any credit for pitching them a great idea. Or Jase any credit for being able to present impeccable credentials and references or to talk through their questions and concerns. You just jumped straight to blackmail. *Blackmail*, Priscilla. Imagine how I felt when I found that out."

Confusion rocked through Jase. Then surprise. He looked at Cilla, but she was staring at her grandfather. Her grip on Jase's hand was almost painfully tight.

"You… I don't…"

Her grandfather's frown deepened. "You surely don't want to add lying to the list." He sighed. "Chuck told me. He was stunned that you would do that. But he was also hurt because he said he would have definitely listened to you about why you thought they should look at The Pork and Peach for the project. You didn't even give him a chance."

Jase wasn't following this entirely, but he watched Cilla's throat work as she tried to swallow. Her eyes were wide and her cheeks pink. She pressed her lips together.

He focused on Aaron. "I don't understand. What's going on?"

"She didn't tell you how she convinced half the city council to vote in favor of you redoing The Pork and Peach as the new community center?" Aaron asked. He actually seemed surprised.

Jase shook his head. "I assumed she just told them about all of the pros to doing the project that way."

Aaron nodded. "She should have." He glanced at his granddaughter. "Instead, she used secrets she knew against at least two of the three who voted in favor. I assume Luke voted on your behalf because you're friends."

He was still trying to grapple with what Aaron was telling

him, but his spine stiffened. "We are friends. But Luke cares a lot about this town. I trust that he voted for what he thought was best."

Aaron nodded. "And because Luke knows you and knows what your plans were for the building, that your intentions were good, that you wanted to do this because you care about the town too, this *is* what he thought was best." He focused on Cilla again. "All things that would have been good—and *convincing*—for Chuck and Marie to know."

"Who are Chuck and Marie?" Jase asked, directing the question to Cilla.

"Chuck is a farmer. Marie works at the library. They're both on the city council," she said, her voice a little hoarse. Like maybe she was trying not to cry. She didn't quite meet his eyes, focusing on his chin instead.

"And you *blackmailed* them into agreeing to vote for The Pork and Peach project?" he asked. He swallowed hard. "Into voting for *me*?"

"It sounds worse..." She didn't finish the sentence though.

"Does it?" he asked. He dropped his hold on her hand and shoved his hand through his hair. His heart was pounding, and he felt a little light-headed. He was reeling.

She swallowed. "Okay. No. It is what it sounds like."

His girlfriend had forced two people to give him a job.

He hadn't gotten the project because he was great at what he did. Or because he was a Bad boy who'd come home and was welcome and accepted.

It was because Cilla was a Williams, which meant she knew secrets and had dirt on people, and she'd used it to get him work. And to get her way.

"Jase." Her voice was thick and pleading.

He stared at her. "I can't believe you did that."

"I shouldn't have," she said. "I know. My grandpa's right. I didn't even give them... or *you*... a real chance. I just assumed they'd fight me." She shrugged. "I'm so used to my ideas not mattering or not being acknowledged, and I wanted this to happen so badly that I just… panicked, I guess. I did what I felt would make it a sure thing."

"Your ideas don't matter and aren't acknowledged because you don't let people know about them," he said, exasperated. "Including this one. Jesus, Cilla." He glanced at Aaron and grimaced. "Sorry."

Aaron just shook his head. He looked sad.

"You keep hiding who you really are from everyone," Aaron told his granddaughter. "So, no, you can't expect them to just assume that you're right and know what's best and are dedicated. And *still* Chuck said he wished you'd told him the plan. When are you going to let your light shine, Cilla? If you *really* don't care what people think and you really want to just follow your heart because you know what's good and right, then *do that*. But do it out loud. Let people see it. Let them… trust you. Or not. But they don't know what to think because they don't really *know* you."

A tear tracked down her cheek and Jase had to resist the urge to reach up and swipe it away. He loved her. He wanted her to be happy. And he knew that she was mostly happy with how things were, doing her little jobs in the quiet, dark, early morning. He knew that she found satisfaction in talking people into pet adoption and park clean-up. But he really thought, while she didn't want to be out in front, leading the way, she'd be happier if she let people really know her. Let them see that she might not be a preacher or a leader, but she was someone worth listening to and who set a pretty fucking great example.

And then it hit him like a brick to the forehead.

He had to do that too.

He'd been gone ten years. When he had been here, he'd been a rebellious shit. For a few years, he'd lived up to everything anyone would have expected from a strip-club-bar-owning-town-black-sheep's grandson. It had been fun at the time. Stupid teenage boys could get away with some of that shit.

But he was a man now. He wanted to make a life here. He wanted what he'd had at Carter's house with everyone. What he had eating lunch with the guys. What he had leading a construction crew here in Bad. What he had sleeping with Cilla in his arms.

He could fight. He could dig in and insist that people just needed to deal with him and get over the past.

Or he could *show* them that he wasn't that smart-mouthed, stupid kid anymore and that he was ready to be a real part of this town.

And that he didn't need his girlfriend calling in favors, throwing her name around, and fucking *blackmailing* people to make him a place here.

He couldn't believe she'd done that.

"I'm sorry, Jase," she said again, softy. She reached out and squeezed his arm. "I… don't know how to fix it. I know you won't believe this, but I think Chuck and Marie will still be behind the idea. I know this taints it. And I'm very sorry, but—"

"Who else is on the council?" he asked.

She blinked at him. "What?"

"Who else? You talked to Chuck and Marie and Luke. But there are six members. Who else?"

She swallowed. "David Callaway, Sheila Green, and Ben Davis."

He knew them all. Not personally. Not well. David was a good friend of Aaron's. Sheila was married to one of the bankers, who was also a good friend of David's. Ben was an old guy who had been retired even when Jase had been in high school. He didn't even know what Ben had done for a living before that. He was just a fixture in Bad. A part of the landscape here. Jase nodded. "Okay. Get me their numbers. You can text them to me."

She frowned. "Why? What are you going to do?"

"I'm taking care of my business, Cilla," he told her. "Your mom is the tiebreaker then, right? If it's three to three?"

Cilla nodded. "Yes."

"Is the best way to reach her just calling City Hall?"

Her eyes went wide. "You're going to call my mother?"

"I am."

"Jase—"

"Cilla, you handled it your way. Now I'm going to handle it mine."

"I'll text you those numbers," Aaron said. He held out his hand.

Jase put his phone in Aaron's outstretched palm and the older man entered his number, then handed it back. Jase texted that number so Aaron would have his.

"Thanks," he said.

Aaron nodded.

"I'm going to get to work," he told Cilla.

"But… I'll drive you."

"I'd prefer to walk." He had a lot to think about. Plans to make. And, frankly, he was a little pissed at her.

She needed to own her shit.

But before he could really tell her that, he needed to own his.

He headed out into the sunny afternoon to do just that.

CHAPTER
NINETEEN

THE PORK and Peach really was the stupidest name for a strip club ever.

Priscilla was so glad that damned sign was down.

She sat in her car, staring at the front of the building, much as she had seven weeks ago. Her heart was pounding as it had been then. She was eager and excited and dreading seeing Jase Hawkins, just like she had been then.

But everything was different now.

The building was completely different. She'd seen the transformation happening piece by piece as she'd come to see Jase every day, but she was still amazed by how different it looked.

The building was symbolic of her and her life.

The outside looked the same. Physically, she looked the same. The things she did—work, hanging out with her friends, interacting with her family—all looked the same. But inside, *she* was different. The things she did felt different. Her work felt different because Jase had validated her. He'd helped her truly acknowledge that what she did mattered and that it was okay that she didn't want to be the mayor or lead the town or be in charge, that what she was doing, the stuff she *loved* doing, was important.

Being with her friends felt different too. Because now Jase was a part of that group. He was one of her friends. Maybe her best one. He knew her in ways that no one else did. He saw things about her that no one else did. But he also fit in with those people so well that it felt strange to think he *hadn't* been there for the past ten years.

And being with her family felt different. Yes, she'd been keeping her relationship with Jase from them. At first, it had been because she hadn't wanted to deal with them and what they might say or feel or think about it. But as the last couple of weeks had gone on, she truly had realized that she didn't care what they thought. She didn't care if they didn't like it, if they weren't going to give Jase a chance, or if they didn't want her bringing him over. That was all fine. She wanted to be with him and, if that wasn't important to them, then she would choose him. Every time.

Of course, her grandfather had surprised her by *not* having a problem with Jase and being actually hurt that she hadn't told him about the relationship.

She was actually here now, in the parking lot of what had once been the bane of her grandfather's existence—or so she'd thought—because her grandfather had told her to come after Jase.

He didn't have to tell her that. She was going to follow Jase no matter where he went. But she was glad her grandfather realized that she didn't need to stick around and hash everything out with him. They would have time for that. Or maybe they wouldn't need it.

It was crazy to think about how huge the rift between Aaron and Jarvis had seemed. It had certainly been big enough. But of course the town preacher would denounce a strip club, and of course the strip club owner would think the preacher was condescending. Because her grandfather really could be.

And back in high school, before she had proven to him that she could handle herself and make good decisions and do the right thing, maybe her grandfather would have had a problem with her hanging out with Jase. Or hanging out with Jarvis when she was hanging out with Jase. That probably would have been a problem, come to think of it.

But Priscilla had to appreciate the fact that Aaron seemed to respect her enough now to make this decision.

That was great. That would make her life easier, for sure. But all she *really* needed to know was that *Jase* knew she was in love with him, and she was going to be with him.

Well, she was going to be with him eventually.

Whenever she freaking *found him.*

He wasn't here.

His RV was still here, thankfully. And he wasn't here packing up to leave. But his truck wasn't here, and he wasn't answering his cell or returning texts.

She thought about waiting for him here, but she had another meeting in about twenty minutes. No, twenty minutes wasn't *really* enough time to apologize and tell him how much she loved him and beg him to stay and forgive her for the blackmail thing and try to explain. But she had to try.

She could skip the meeting. She *wanted* to skip the meeting. In fairness, it was a meeting of the women's group at church, so she always wanted to skip it, but she especially did today.

However, her mother would be there. And Marie. Who she had blackmailed into voting for Jase remodeling The Pork and Peach into the new community center.

Priscilla needed to apologize to her for that. And see how angry her mother was.

Crap. This was the thing about her "job" and position in this community—there was always somewhere she had to be, and sometimes there was more than one at the same time.

She drove to Main Street. The guys had finished lunch and were back to work, but she pulled up at the curb outside of Luke's garage and rushed in.

"Do you know where Jase is?" she asked him as he straightened from the car he was working on.

He nodded. "City Hall."

"Thanks." She started for her car, but then stopped and swung back. *"Where?"*

Luke pointed with the wrench he was holding. In the direction of City Hall. "Said he was going to talk to the mayor."

The mayor.

Her mother.

Oh… God.

"Don't know what it was about though," Luke added.

"I do!" she called as she turned up the sidewalk and started running toward City Hall.

It was only a block so running was faster than getting in her car, driving, and parking. Plus, burning off some of the "oh, shit" adrenaline that was coursing through her seemed like a good idea.

She burst through the doors to the mansion and ran down the hallway to her mother's office.

Kelsey looked up as she rounded the corner. She didn't look all that surprised to see her.

"You can't go in," she said.

"I have to." Priscilla was panting slightly. Dang, she was a little out of shape. "I have to…" She wasn't sure what she had to do because she wasn't entirely sure what Jase and her mother were talking about, actually. It just seemed like a bad idea to have them meeting privately.

"I was told that you might stop by and that you're supposed to wait out here," Kelsey said, pointing to one of the chairs.

She started for her mother's door. "But my mom doesn't know—"

"Jase is the one who said to keep you out."

Those words took a second to sink in. Priscilla's hand was on the doorknob when they really hit her. She frowned. Her heart stuttered. Her stomach dropped.

She lifted her hand. "Oh."

Kelsey looked sympathetic when Priscilla turned back to face her.

"I'm sorry," she said. "I don't know what they're talking about exactly, but he said you might stop by and that he doesn't want you in there."

Ouch. Priscilla blew out a breath.

Kelsey lowered her voice. "I *can* tell you that your mom asked me to let the church ladies know she won't be making the meeting. And they called Bill. They have him on speaker phone now."

Bill was the city's attorney. Priscilla frowned. What the hell was that about?

"How long have they been talking?" She'd left the senior center within minutes of Jase. But she'd driven out to The Pork and Peach first. Maybe he'd come straight here?

"About twenty minutes. It could be a while yet."

Priscilla let out a breath. Crap. She looked at the clock on the wall. The meeting at church was starting in five minutes. She looked back at her mom's door. She *really* needed to talk to him. But as soon as he looked at his phone, he'd see the missed calls and the texts from her asking to talk and saying she was sorry.

He wouldn't leave without talking to her.

She was ninety percent sure.

Then her stomach dropped again. Maybe he was in there selling the building to the town right now and he was getting out of here. Maybe he was taking a loss. Maybe he wanted out so bad he was giving it to her mom for whatever she asked. The guys he'd hired could maybe finish it up. Her mother would go for it if the price was low enough.

Priscilla felt tears pricking the backs of her eyes.

"I'll tell him you were here," Kelsey said. She looked worried.

Probably afraid Priscilla was going to break down sobbing.

Or that she was going to puke on Kelsey's desk. Her face probably looked like either of those things were possible.

"Okay." Her voice sounded funny. Like she was trying very hard not to cry or puke. "Tell him I'll be at..." She took a deep breath. "The church," she finished.

How ironic.

"I will," Kelsey promised.

Priscilla turned and walked back out. Much slower than she'd come in.

She'd messed it all up.

The blackmail had been a mistake, of course. Her grandfather and Jase were both right—she hadn't even given anyone a *chance* to be supportive or see the good in the plan. Or in Jase. Or in her.

But more, she'd hurt Jase. He'd thought getting that building project meant he'd have more work in town when it was over. He'd thought it meant that people didn't hold his family's reputation against him and that he could come back and fit in and make a life here.

And he could. But she'd just made it harder for him to believe that.

Dammit. Fuck. Son of a bitch.

She got the swearing—even though it was only in her head— out of the way before she walked through the doors of Bad Faith Community Church.

Everything about the building was as familiar as her childhood home. She'd spent so many hours in the church, it really was her second childhood home. It did comfort her, in spite of the confusion and conflicts it also represented, and she took a deep breath as she walked toward the meeting room where the women's group would be gathered.

Everyone greeted her, including Marie Butler and Priscilla gave her a smile. Taking a deep breath, she chose the seat next to Marie.

The rest of the group continued their conversations as they

found chairs and got ready to start, and she took the opportunity to say quietly, "I need to apologize to you."

Marie gave Priscilla her full attention. She didn't say "For what?" or "Oh, no that's not necessary."

Priscilla took another deep breath. "I'm very sorry for threatening to expose your secret. That was completely inappropriate and wrong of me to do, and I want you to know that I would *never* do that."

"Well, I already voted in favor of the remodel," Marie said. A little huffily.

But she had a right to be huffy.

Priscilla nodded. "I know, and I feel terrible for putting you in that position and even worse for manipulating you that way. I really am very, very sorry."

Marie looked at her for a long moment. "It must have mattered a lot to you for you to do something like that. That was very out of character for you, Priscilla."

She nodded. "It really was. And yes, it mattered a lot to me. The man who's doing the remodel, Jase Hawkins, is... very special to me. I was trying to help him, and I made a mistake."

She was glad Marie thought it was out of character. It *was*, of course. But she was grateful the people here knew that.

Finally, Marie nodded. "I forgive you."

Priscilla couldn't believe the rush of relief she felt. Her eyes prickled with tears. "Thank you." She kind of wanted to hug her. And she'd never hugged Marie Butler in her life.

"Okay, let's get this meeting started," Erika Finley said from the head of the table.

"And I'm not sorry I voted for it, by the way," Marie added in a whisper.

Priscilla nodded. She wanted Marie to feel good about her vote, even if Priscilla wasn't proud of forcing it to go her way. "It's less expensive, and it will be done sooner this way," she whispered back.

"Well, that," Marie said. "And if it's your boyfriend who's doing it, then I know it will be good."

Priscilla stared at Marie even as the older woman pivoted to face Erika.

Priscilla realized she was an idiot. Of course, she could have made a good case for the building. *Of course,* she could have. There were solid, common-sense reasons for people to support it. And, even more, people in this town *did* trust her. They liked her. They'd known her all their lives and, up until she black-mailed two wonderful people, she'd been a good, decent, upstanding part of the community.

She was so embarrassed.

"Excuse me, ladies."

Priscilla whirled around so fast at the sound of the deep, masculine voice that she nearly tipped her chair over into Marie.

Jase was standing in the doorway. He looked so, so good. Big and confident, not at all intimidated about striding into Bad Faith Community Church and interrupting a meeting of the women's group.

He was wearing those faded blue jeans that molded to his strong thighs and tight ass, his work boots, and a faded, green t-shirt that stretched over his wide shoulders, hard chest, and flat abs. He looked like he could build a woman a house, then hunt, kill, and cook her some dinner, and then take her to bed and make her praise the good Lord that got so much attention in this very building. All in one day. With his bare hands. Without straining a single one of those gorgeous muscles.

Or maybe that was just her.

He also looked serious. And completely focused on her.

"I need to speak with Priscilla, if you don't mind," he said to the room at large, his gaze on hers.

She swallowed.

Well, she'd wanted to talk to him. But there was something about his demeanor, the way he was looking at her, or maybe it was just everything that had happened in the past hour and now him standing here, in the church, coming for her that had her heart pounding and her mind spinning in a million directions.

"Oh, well, of course." Erika looked at her. "Priscilla?"

As in, *Why are you sitting there just staring at him like an idiot?*

"Is that him?" Marie asked, her eyes wide.

Priscilla nodded.

"Wow," she said. "Yeah, I'd probably blackmail somebody for him too."

And that was exactly what Priscilla needed. She snorted, grinned at Marie, put an arm around her shoulder and gave her a little side hug, and said, "Exactly."

Then she got to her feet and crossed the room to Jase.

"I came to find you," she said.

"I heard." He turned and stepped out of the doorway, clearly intending for her to follow.

She did, pulling the door to the meeting room shut behind her.

"Jase, I—"

"Not here. Come on." He started down the hallway. But not toward the front of the church.

He was heading toward the addition off the back of the building. Where the Sunday school classrooms were.

Her traitorous body reacted with heat and tingles and *oh goodies* even as her brain said that he was probably only trying to find some privacy.

But then he stopped outside of the third-grade classroom. *The* third-grade classroom. The same one where he'd first gotten her naked.

They faced one another, his hand on the doorknob, her heart in her throat.

"I'm sorry," she choked out before he could turn the knob. If he was going to break up with her, taking her into that room to do it was downright mean. He could just do it right here and now. "I shouldn't have manipulated them. I know that. But I've apologized to Marie and I will to Chuck too. I will never do something like that again. And it wasn't about you or the building or if they could or would trust you or if you'd do a good job. It was all about me. I know that I can trust the people in this town, and I'm going to…" She wasn't really sure how to end that rant. She'd kind of expected him to cut her off before this. "I'm going to… be good," she finally said.

One corner of his mouth quirked at that. "Well, I certainly hope you're not going to be *too* good." Then he twisted the knob and pushed the door open. "Let's go inside, Pris," he said.

Pris. Okay, that was good. That was affectionate. That was one of the names that told her he cared about her.

She stepped into the classroom, her stomach still jumping, but feeling a little bubble of hope in her chest.

He moved in behind her and shut the door.

She turned to face him.

"Please don't leave," she blurted.

"I'm not going anywhere."

Relief so strong swept through her, it made her knees actually feel weak. "Oh, thank God."

"This is my home," he said. "My roots are here. My history is here. My friends are here. My job is here now. And the woman I love is here."

Tears welled up in her eyes so fast that her nose stung. She blinked and sniffed. "She is?"

He shook his head, a small smile playing on his lips. "Of course, she is. You know I love you."

"But you're mad at me."

"I'm disappointed in you. And surprised," he said. "And yeah, maybe a little mad. But this won't be the last time. If we're going to be together, I expect we're gonna piss each other off once in a while."

She took a shaky breath. "Are we going to be together?"

"I sure as fuck hope so."

Her heart swelled in her chest. *Thank you, Lord.* And she

meant it more than she'd ever meant those three words. And she'd said them a lot inside this building.

"Good," she said. "I want that. I want you. I want to be together."

"Okay then."

Could it really be that easy?

"What did you talk to my mom about?"

"I told her all the reasons why her remodeling The Pork and Peach made the most sense for Bad and why she should agree to it."

"What did she say?"

"She agreed."

Her eyes widened. "Wow."

"But then I told her that I was changing the deal."

Priscilla froze. Then frowned. "What?"

He nodded. "I was thinking about everything and the fact that we're asking the council, the town really, to take a chance on me. And that's great that they're willing." He narrowed his eyes at her. "Assuming that there were only two that *weren't* willing?"

"Only two," she nodded quickly. "And Marie said she would have voted for you anyway if she'd known you were my boyfriend."

One of his eyebrows went up. "Well, see, that's really nice too —that they trust you and would back this just because you want them to."

She nodded. That was more than nice. That was... everything.

"But," he went on. "I realized that while I was pushing you to show everyone who you really are, *I* hadn't done that myself. I'd showed up at The Pork and Peach and started working, living in my RV, intending to avoid interactions as much as possible, and then get the hell out of here." He moved in closer to her. "Even after you showed up and turned everything upside down—"

Her heart flipped at the look in his eyes. That was love. He did love her. She'd turned his life upside down, but he'd done the same to hers.

"—I still was clear out there. I started going out more with the guys and everything, but I never reached out to the council, never got involved in anything in town."

"You've only been here for seven weeks," she pointed out.

"It's Bad," he retorted. "You can be ass-deep involved in this town in two days if you want to be."

That was true. She nodded and waited for him to go on.

"So, I realized that I might have to prove myself a little bit and that's okay. I needed to get the chip off my shoulder and accept that what people know about my family is just the surface… and it's our fault. That's all we let them know. My granddad had a huge wall up. He didn't let people close. He let them just think whatever they wanted to think. But I don't want that. I want them to know me. So, I have to let them in."

She nodded. She'd always known him because he let her. He let her see another side of him. Not the wild, tough, party side, but the sweet, patient, funny side. Just like she'd let him see the more vulnerable side of Priscilla Williams.

"They're going to love you," she said, her voice thick.

He smiled at that. "I hope so. I think I know a way to start finding out. I'm going to throw a party. At the new building. Next weekend. Invite the town so they can see what we've done, fill them in on the rest of the plans. Even though it's not finished, I think people should come out and see the progress."

Priscilla gasped. "I think that's a great idea." Open it up. Let people in. Make it clear this was now a place for everyone to come. "I really like that," she told him with a big smile.

"All our friends will come. And that will encourage others to come take a peek," he said.

"Absolutely. Having Carter and Jackson and Luke and Mark and Randi and Regan telling people they should stop out will be huge."

He grinned. "I feel good about it. I know they all have my back." His expression softened. "I know *you* have my back."

"I do. Absolutely. We all do," she said. "But you changed the deal on my mom?" she asked, going back to that huge reveal.

He nodded. "I'm going to finish the building and then the city is going to lease it from me for the next two years. If, after that time, they want to go ahead and build their own building from the ground up, they still can. They're not out a lot of money and haven't committed to anything. But if, by then, they love how things are going out there and agree that building is just what they want and need, then the money they've paid will go toward the purchase and they'll buy it from me."

She felt her eyes widen. That was… wow. "You're willing to do that? What if they don't buy it in two years? Then you're stuck with the building."

He shrugged. "Then I'm back where I started when I came to town, I guess." He grinned. "But I don't think that's going to happen. I'll definitely have won them over by then."

She felt her own grin stretch her lips. He would. She had no doubt about that.

"And you're going to keep doing building projects in the area?" she asked. "Work here? Start a business?"

"I am," he said. "I think, ironically, that The Pork and Peach will be the perfect advertisement for what I can do and that it will bring me business."

That sounded perfect.

"But," he said, "the first thing I'm going to build is a house."

A house. Yes. That was solid and permanent and meant he was planning to stay for a while. "I think that's a great idea," she told him.

"I just need to know if you want me to put our master suite on the first floor or second," he said.

She realized then that he was walking her backward.

"*Our* master suite?" she asked.

Her back bumped into the wall. The wall where he'd put her ten years ago.

"Yes. *Our* master suite in *our* house where we're going to live together," he said. He got down on one knee. Also a lot like he'd done ten years ago.

Her body responded to that memory *happily*.

"Um…"

"Focus, Peach," he said, putting his hands on her hips and grinning up at her.

"It's hard with you down there, like that, in here."

He nodded. "I know. But I had to do this here."

"I'm very okay with you doing this here," she told him.

The door didn't lock but she thought the chances of any of the ladies coming down here looking for them were slim. As long as she could stay quiet. She'd have to work on that.

"Not *that*," he said. He took one of her hands. "Priscilla, the last time I brought you into this room and got on my knees, I gave you my heart. I didn't even realize it, but I handed it right over. And I never got it back."

Oh. My. God. Suddenly, the tears were back in her eyes, and her heart was pounding so hard she could hear it in her ears.

"Jase…"

"And so it's only right that I bring you in here and tell you that you still have it. And I never want it back. I want it to be yours forever."

She pressed her lips together. She couldn't believe that this man, this Bad boy, was on his knees in front of her, saying the most amazingly sweet and *good* words she'd ever heard.

"And I want your heart too. Forever," he said. "Cilla, will you marry me?"

A sob escaped as she threw herself into his arms, nearly knocking him over. Thankfully, he was a lot stronger than she was and he just clasped her tightly to his body and let her squeeze him.

"Oh, Jase! Yes! I… yes! Of course!"

He was laughing when she pulled back and took his face in her hands. "I love you so much."

"I love you too. I always have."

She nodded. "Me too."

She kissed him. He cupped the back of her head, and the kiss deepened, sweet and hot and full of promise.

When he lifted his head, she smiled up at him. "Admit it," she said. "The blackmail thing, me being a bad girl that way, was *kind of* hot, right?"

He shook his head. "No. No more of that."

"But… I thought you liked my naughty side."

"Yep. When it's just about you and me. And all the naughty things I can get you to do with my cock."

He practically growled those last two words, and her whole body lit up.

"Got it," she said, sounding breathless already. "Bad girl in the bedroom. Good girl everywhere else."

"Well," he said, stretching to his feet and taking her with him. "Maybe you could be bad girl a few other places." He pressed her up against the wall again. "Like… in church."

"We're not *really* in the church," she teased. "This is the addition."

"Choir loft it is then," he said, bending as if to throw her over his shoulder.

She giggled and squirmed away. "No, no, this is close enough! This would be very bad."

He gave her a wink. "Thank God."

Then he started kissing her again while his big, confident hands undressed her. He touched and stroked and murmured dirty, sweet words. Pleasure and happiness and love all washed over her in one full, crazy, amazing wave.

She could *not* have sex—oral or otherwise—in the choir loft. She couldn't be *that* bad of a girl.

But as Jase Hawkins got down on his knees one more time in

that Sunday school classroom, she had to be honest and add a... *probably.*

Thank you so much for reading Jase and Priscilla's story! There's a lot more sexy, fun from Bad!

These books are all standalones and don't need to be read in any particular order!

The Best Bad Boy: (Jase and Priscilla)
A bad boy-good girl, small town romance

Bad Medicine: (Brooke and Nick)
A hot doctor, workplace, small town romance

Bad Influence: (Marc and Sabrina)
An enemies to lovers, road trip/stuck together, small town romance

Bad Taste in Men: (Luke and Bailey)
A friends to lovers, gettin'-her-groove back, small town romance

Not Such a Bad Guy: (Regan and Christopher)
A one-night-stand, instalove, small town romance

Return of the Bad Boy: (Jackson and Annabelle)
An enemies to lovers, bad boy-good girl, pretend relationship, small town romance

Bad Behavior: (Carter and Lacey)
A hot cop, second chance, small town romance

Got It Bad: (Nolan and Randi)
A nerd hero, tomboy, opposites attract, small town romance

Find all of my books at
ErinNicholas.com

ဢ
And join in on all the FAN FUN!

Join my **email list!**
bit.ly/Keep-In-Touch-Erin
(be sure you get those dashes and capital letters in there!)

And be the first to hear about my news, sales, freebies, behind-the-scenes, and more!

Or for even more fun, join my **Super Fan page** on Facebook and chat with me and other super fans every day! Just search Facebook for Erin Nicholas Super Fans!

WANT MORE FROM THE BAYOU?

There's so much more from Erin's Louisiana bayou world!

Head down the road to Autre next and dive into the Boys of the Bayou series (where you'll first meet the Landry family)!

All available now!

My Best Friend's Mardi Gras Wedding

Sweet Home Louisiana

Beauty and the Bayou

Crazy Rich Cajuns

Must Love Alligators

Four Weddings and a Swamp Boat Tour

———

And be sure to check out **the connected rom com series, Boys of the Bayou-Gone Wild**

Otterly Irresistible

Heavy Petting

Flipping Love You

Sealed With A Kiss

Say It Like You Mane It

Head Over Hooves

Kiss My Giraffe

———

And the **Badges of the Bayou** (where you get to know Michael LeClaire and JD Evans!)

Gotta Be Bayou, book one

Bayou With Benefits, book two

Rocked Bayou, book three

————

And MUCH more—

including my printable booklist— at

ErinNicholas.com

ABOUT ERIN

Erin Nicholas is the New York Times and USA Today bestselling author of over forty sexy contemporary romances. Her stories have been described as toe-curling, enchanting, steamy and fun. She loves to write about reluctant heroes, imperfect heroines and happily ever afters. She lives in the Midwest with her husband who only wants to read the sex scenes in her books, her kids who will never read the sex scenes in her books, and family and friends who say they're shocked by the sex scenes in her books (yeah, right!).

Find her and all her books at
www.ErinNicholas.com

And find her on Facebook, Goodreads, BookBub, and Instagram!